Serious As a Heart Attack

Also by Louisa Luna

Crooked
Brave New Girl

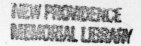

Serious As a Heart Attack

A Novel

Louisa Luna

ATRIA BOOKS
New York   London   Toronto   Sydney

MYS
Lun

ATRIA BOOKS
1230 Avenue of the Americas
New York, NY 10020

ISBN: 0-7434-6660-8

B*T 23.00 9/04
First Atria Books hardcover edition May 2004

10 9 8 7 6 5 4 3 2 1

ATRIA BOOKS is a trademark of Simon & Schuster, Inc.

Interior design by Davina Mock

Manufactured in the United States of America

for Nonno

Acknowledgments

Thanks to: Greer, Suzanne, Annelise, Mayhill, Clement, Mom & Dad, Zach, and very most of all, Josh.

Serious As a Heart Attack

Monday

It was June, the middle of June, and it was a Monday, and Queenie woke up with her face stuck to the pillow with drool. How exactly did last night end? she thought. And how did there get to be so much drool—foamy waterfalls on Meade's red futon couch, all around her as she lifted her head and looked at the clock on the VCR, which read: 8:20. Have to get up, she thought, gotta get up, maybe a few more minutes, maybe you can be an hour late today, she thought. No, no, wait, you can't. You have to get fired today.

She rolled off the futon and stood up, head full of mush, and walked to the kitchen and foraged for food for a minute, opening and closing cupboards. Spices and a can of beans. All the bastard had in the refrigerator were raw turkey burger patties separated by thin paper sheets in a styrofoam tray.

She stared at the kitchen table and tried to focus, and she held her head with both hands. It felt like it was wobbling from side to side on its own.

She picked up the cigarette boxes on the table and shook them, but they were empty. Not that anyone around here smokes, thought Queenie. Who knows how these got here. She sure didn't buy them, because she didn't smoke anymore. She used to carry around a folded-up Post-it in her wallet with three rules. A message from sober Queenie to drunk Queenie. It said,

1) Don't smoke.
2) Don't stay up all night.
3) Don't fuck anyone.

After she'd broken all three she'd made an amended list that read,

1) DON'T SMOKE.
2) Don't stay up all night unless you are forced to.
3) Don't fuck anyone unless you really really want to.

The first was definitely broken, but she'd been pretty good about the second two. The second two were softer than the first, the first really was a nutcracker, but two out of three wasn't bad. And she really hadn't had much of a chance to break the third, to be honest.

There was one cigarette left in the American Spirits box. She shook it out and lit it and started coughing immediately. She went to the bathroom and spit up some phlegm. Yellow and red. Great, she thought. Now I'm coughing up blood. That's just super.

She looked at her face in the mirror, at her doll hair in spiky little strands everywhere, snaky curves and dry ends. Her eyes were squinty, almost sealed shut with piecrust. Cut on her upper lip. How did I get that? she thought. She leaned in to the mirror and peeled the skin on her lip like an envelope flap, and her fingers shook and trembled, and she stared at the cut that looked like a small red blade of glass leading to the inside of her mouth. She touched it with her fingertip, and it burned.

She took Meade's toothbrush from the sink and opened the cupboard, grabbed the toothpaste, flipped the cap, and squeezed too hard. Green gel spurted out in a lurid way. I must've excited it, she thought, toothpaste dripping all over her hand.

It really wasn't until right then, when she was standing with toothpaste sliding down her fingers and on the T-shirt she'd borrowed from Meade, that she realized she honestly did not have a clue as to what to do next—it could have been that she was supposed to wipe her hands and brush her teeth and clean herself up and get dressed and go to work, but it just as easily could have been that she was supposed to rub the toothpaste in football-player strips under her eyes and cut all her hair off and do a handstand. It wasn't really until right then that Queenie realized she wasn't hungover. She was still drunk.

She started sweating like nobody's business on the E train. She wasn't wearing any socks because she couldn't find them at Meade's house, and that made things all the worse because she had three-dollar shoes and a serious sweating problem. Even though it wasn't very hot yet, every time she wore shoes with no socks in the summer her feet smelled like pure meat and cheese.

She looked up at the advertisement for Dr. Zizmor. Come to me, he seemed to say, let me take away your scars, your blemishes. Come to my luxury Third Avenue office, and I will lay you down and zap that thing right off your forehead. No thank you, thought Queenie; she preferred her personal skin care method, which included scraping pimples off her face with her nails or tweezers or a safety pin or whatever was around.

She did that at work a lot. She'd go to the bathroom and stretch her skin and examine it and soon she'd be finding pimples that weren't pimples yet, and she'd squeeze them until something came out (blood, ooze—it really didn't matter what), then go back to her cube with a wet tissue pressed against her forehead or her chin. Her bosses, Roy Cohn and Joan Crawford, had definitely noticed and looked at her strangely but never asked when she'd come to meetings with two tissues in each hand, pressed against parts of her face. And, Queenie thought, if they're not going to ask, I'm not going to tell them. They can just imagine what I've got behind these tissues. It could be shafts of healing white light that they will never know because they are too afraid.

But boy, she knew they'd have their way with her today. Roy Cohn might even be compelled to use the phrase, "talk turkey." "Eugene, send Queenie in here right now and tell her we have to talk turkey," he'd probably say. He liked to used the intercom even though their whole office was about nine hundred square feet, and you could hear everyone's intercom from everywhere else.

You really screwed up this time, she was thinking when she saw a figure out of the corner of her eye rise and approach her. She didn't look up at him until he said, "Queenie? Queenie Sells?"

She knew exactly that it was Hummer Fish from high school. He still had gray eyes that looked a little stoned, but he looked bigger and broader than she remembered. He wore khakis and a green button-down shirt. Professional, she thought. Ten bucks says he's in publishing, or marketing, or consulting.

"Oh, God, Hummer, how are you?" she said, and they hugged.

"I'm good, you know this is so weird, the other day I was saying, 'The only person I don't see in this town is Queenie Sells, and I know she's here,' " he said.

"Right. Here I am," she said.

She looked at the lines in his face and remembered his parents. She remembered that Mother Fish would always slip in little spikes about "the great unclean," meaning anyone who lived outside of appropriate places to live in Boston, and certainly anyone who lived in Lowell, where Queenie lived with Uncle Si. Father Fish had money so old it practically played bingo. The few times Queenie was at their house both Fish parents looked at her like she would steal the china if she were left alone.

"So where do you live?" Hummer said.

"The Burning Grounds. In Brooklyn."

"Oh man," said Hummer. "How long does it take you to get here in the morning?"

"Three, three and a half hours," Queenie said. "I drink a lot of coffee."

Hummer covered his mouth. "Are you kidding?"

"Yes, I am," she said, gripping the slippery metal pole that separated them. "It takes fifteen minutes. It's one stop on the L train."

"Oh," Hummer said, nodding.

"What about you?" she said, to be nice.

"I'm on Mercer and Waverly, near NYU."

"Cool," said Queenie, and she racked her brain trying to think about something interesting to say about Mercer and Waverly, but nothing was coming up. Goddamn it, what is an interesting thing to say about Mercer and Waverly?

"I'm sorry," Queenie said, putting her hand to her head. "I'm a little out of it."

"It's early," he said, and he looked over both shoulders quickly.

"Yeah," Queenie said. "So hey, though, I get off at Forty-second Street, where do you get off?"

Ha-ha, she thought. You hear that, Dr. Zizmor, I asked Hummer Fish from high school where he gets off.

The train eased into Thirty-fourth Street. Many people got out. Not as many people got on.

"Me too. Forty-second," said Hummer.

"Oh good," said Queenie.

Can conversation last that long, she thought.

"How's your grandfather?" Hummer asked.

"Okay, I guess. Dead about thirty years," she said.

"Shit, that's right," said Hummer, and he shut his eyes hard. "Who was the older guy, the fellow you lived with. . . . " he said, trailing off.

Queenie let him hang on for a second, and then she dropped it, making it sound like she'd just remembered it herself.

"My uncle," she said.

"Uncle, right," Hummer said.

Then it was Forty-second Street. People rushed passed them and came between them. Queenie lost her grip on the pole and almost tipped over. She and Hummer edged out onto the platform, and it was hot. Queenie heard the black woman who stood above the wheelchair ramp singing the *Titanic* theme. It was always either the *Titanic* theme or "Killing Me Softly."

"Which way are you going?" said Queenie loudly.

"Just over to Broadway," said Hummer.

They walked up a crowded stairwell, and Queenie lost her breath and felt her legs go numb a second. They weren't at street level yet, walking through the wide space under Port Authority with all the poster shops and clothing stores, where simply everything was ten dollars.

Queenie was hoping the conversation would still not be focused on her uncle, but she was shit out of luck.

"So how's your uncle?" Hummer asked.

"Not very well," said Queenie. "He's eighty-seven."

"Wow," said Hummer. "That's old."

Wow, thought Queenie. You're a fucking jarhead.

"Yes, it is. He's fairly ill. Sometimes he's there, and sometimes he's not."

"Jesus, I'm sorry," said Hummer.

"It's all right," said Queenie, not looking at him. "That's what you get for hanging out with old people."

Hummer laughed, and Queenie guessed that was because he thought she was being funny, that she had said that thing about old people to be funny. She smiled so that he wouldn't feel uncomfortable. She didn't know why she wanted him to feel comfortable.

They finally made it to the street and began walking east. Many people were walking quickly, looking busy. There were a lot of cups of coffee and newspapers.

Queenie couldn't help looking at the big theater signs, the life-size photos of dancers on the doors of the closed lobbies. God, look at those legs, thought Queenie. You could snap someone's neck with those thighs.

"What do you do up here?" said Hummer.

"I work for a calendar company," said Queenie. "But I'm getting fired today."

"Oh. Why?"

"Because I fucked up daylight savings. I'm the proofreader. It was the wrong Sunday."

Hummer appeared confused.

"In October," she added.

"Oh," Hummer said again.

"So what do you do?" she asked.

He perked up. "I'm working for this magazine—I helped start it, actually. I don't know if you've heard of it, it's called, *Set It Up*—it's a cultural magazine exploring the current climate of young people living and working in urban areas," he said quickly.

"That sounds really interesting," said Queenie.

"Yeah," Hummer said, cocking his head to one side. "It's a groove."

And what the hell does that mean? thought Queenie.

They came to Broadway, large TVs and strips of light and billboards. Queenie stared at a huge sign of someone's feet. She knew it was an advertisement for shoes, but that didn't make it any less disturbing, seeing such big feet hovering, pasted against the side of a building.

"So do you need money?" said Hummer.

"You know, at some point," she said.

Why, you need a new housekeeper? she almost added. They turned north, and Hummer became very quiet. He looked down.

"I've got to go this way," he said, when they reached Forty-fourth. "But look, if you need a couple hundred bucks, you should call me."

Queenie stared at him.

"No, I don't mean it like that," he said, and laughed nervously. Queenie did not know what he didn't mean it like. Sex, maybe. Ha-ha, he made a joke about paying me for sex. Hi-larious, she thought.

People milled around them, and Hummer looked at his watch, and said, "You might be able to do me a favor is all—not a big deal. It's just something I can't really do myself."

Queenie continued to stare at him.

"Look, I can't really explain now, but let me give you my cell number," he said, reaching into his pocket.

He produced a pen. "Do you have paper?" he said.

"No," said Queenie.

Hummer took her hand.

"No, don't write on my hand," she said. "I sweat too much."

She didn't mean for it to be an excuse. It was really true.

"Write here," she said, and she pointed to a patch on her forearm.

Hummer scribbled his number, pressed down the blond hairs on her arm, and the ink bled and got fuzzy.

"What's yours?" Hummer said.

Fake number, she thought. Switch eight to six; it'll be a victimless crime. But then again, she did only have thirty-seven dollars in the bank not counting her final paycheck, which would only be about a week's worth. It was in her best interest to give Hummer Fish from high school her number. If he was for real. If he really did have a job for her.

"Look, are you for real? Do you really have a job for me?" she said.

Hummer laughed, then stopped bluntly like a television track cut off.

"I can't talk now . . . you don't have to give me your number, but it just might be easier. . . ." he said, trailing off again.

Queenie took his palm and flipped it up, and for some reason thought about how that would be the last thing she'd see if he were to hit her. She wrote her name and number down, and as soon as she was finished, Hummer grabbed the pen and slid it into his breast pocket. He began to laugh again, and Queenie tried to smile but was unnerved. It was creepy how he was laughing so much when no one was saying anything.

"So look, you should come out with us—Nuggie McPhee and Trevor One live here too. And Cela Canth just got married, and she and her husband, they met in law school, they have parties all the time. You should come out," he said.

That sounds like fun, but I think I'd prefer to eat a bunch of hair, thought Queenie.

"Yeah, sure," she said.

"All right, well, take care, Queenie," he said, leaning forward awkwardly to kiss her on the cheek. "We'll talk later," he whispered.

"Okay," she said.

She had his hands in hers, somehow they'd gotten all tangled up, both of her hands in both of his hands. She pulled them away.

"So, bye," he said quietly, and then he turned quickly and left, down Forty-fourth, not looking back.

Queenie stood there for a second, then kept moving. What the hell was that about, she thought. And why does he laugh all the time. Did he always do that? She passed the Lazer Tag-arium where Meade had his twenty-seventh birthday party last year. She really wanted to go in and strap on the helmet and the vest, run around in that hot maze and play the giant five-dollar arcade games. We never had that shit as kids, she thought. Chuck-e-fucking Cheese for us, and these kids get to shoot each other with LASERS.

She arrived at the building where she worked, went through the revolving doors, and nodded to the black security guard reading a French newspaper. Senegal, thought Queenie. Maybe he's from Senegal. Or the Ivory Coast, right—African countries where people speak French. There were islands, too, she thought. The Lesser Antilles. Martinique. She read about them in French class in high school. She saw pictures. The pictures were always of outdoor markets, and two people were always having a discussion over a papaya or Other Exotic Fruit.

Queenie stepped into the elevator with a young woman who worked on her floor in one of the design companies. The woman gave Queenie a tight smile and looked her up and down. Queenie noticed the woman had one very hard nipple. It wasn't something Queenie would normally notice, but that thing was at attention. A goddamn pushpin, she thought. And why just one?

They got off on the eighth floor and went their separate ways, and Queenie walked down to the very end of the hall to her office door. Before she opened it she leaned her head against it, against the CALENDARIA logo and smelled the whiskey on her breath.

She opened the door and walked in and saw Eugene leaning against the front desk. Her leg was in a cast.

"What happened to you?" asked Queenie.

The cast looked huge and made Eugene look ultrasmall, smaller than usual, even made her coffee can glasses look tiny.

"I broke it playing basketball," said Eugene, and she made a face, stretched her lips out like she had just drunk something really hot.

"Whoa," said Queenie. "Did a really fat person fall on you?"

"Oh God, no," Eugene said. "I just fell on my own. I'm really a dork."

"No you're not, Eugene," said Queenie. "These things happen. How long do you have to wear that?"

"Six weeks."

"Fucking hell," Queenie said, and she saw Eugene react, little eyes get big behind the thick lenses. Watch your mouth, thought Queenie. "Can I sign it, or what?" she said.

Eugene smiled.

"Oh yeah, no one's even asked yet, totally, yeah."

Queenie was glad it seemed to make her so happy. Nice kid, thought Queenie.

"I gotta find a Sharpie," Queenie said. "You know, a, uh . . ." She rubbed her nose. She could see the pen in her head but forgot what it said on the side. "You know, one of the skinny ones."

"Ultra," said Eugene.

"Right. Ultra. There's got to be one on my desk," Queenie said. She glanced down the hall, and whispered, "Joan Crawford in yet?"

"No, not yet," Eugene whispered back. "Roy Cohn is, though."

Piss, thought Queenie.

"I'm supposed to call him and let him know you're here," said Eugene in the hot-liquid way.

Queenie wiped her mouth. She held up two fingers in a V.

"Two minutes," she said. "Gimme two minutes."

"I'll try," said Eugene, looking worried.

Queenie left and padded along to her cube, looking straight ahead.

"Morning, Queenie," someone said loudly from another cube.

Queenie winced but was relieved to see it was Jin, the efficient Korean. Queenie looked over the cube wall and smiled.

"Hiya, Jin," Queenie said back. "Gen sha now?"

"Nay gen sha now," said Jin.

Jesus Christ, she looks gorgeous, thought Queenie. Dressed to kill and done up like a superstar on Monday morning—leather pants and a silk ruffled shirt. Kind of a riverboat gambler vibe, and so clean and dynamite blade thin. What do they eat in Korea? thought Queenie.

She sat in her cube and dropped her bag to the floor. She put her head in her hands. Jin's face appeared over the left wall.

"I heard about the October thing," Jin whispered.

"Oh yeah?" said Queenie, not lifting her head. "Yeah, I guess everyone has. Roy Cohn's been talking, huh?"

Jin nodded and looked sorry. "Let me know if I can help."

"Thanks, girl. I don't think anything can be done now."

Jin's head sank back down, and Queenie leaned back in her chair and looked at all the calendar month sheets pushpinned to the walls of her cube. No photos, just the white sheets and black lines and numbers inside that were the days. They weren't days yet; they were just numbers inside of boxes, but next year they'd make it. April was in front of her, above her computer. Queenie reached out her hand and brushed her fingers against the sheet. You'll make it, she said to the April numbers in her head. You'll be real days next year, full and lovely, twenty-four hours apiece.

Then a very small shadow came over her. Queenie looked up and saw Roy Cohn, short and stocky, wearing a tight white T-shirt, almost sheer. Those are the second and third nipples I've seen today that haven't belonged to me, she thought.

"Queenie," he said quietly. "Can I see you in my office?"

"Sure thing, boss," said Queenie, and she stood up.

Eugene hobbled up behind Roy Cohn, and he turned to her, and said, "Eugene, we're going to have to work something out," he said, looking at her leg in the cast. "I told you five minutes ago I needed to see Queenie."

"Maybe you can get her a wheelchair," said Queenie.

"That's very funny," he said. Then he held his arm out so she could go ahead of him.

Queenie tilted her head back and sighed, then rolled it on her shoulders a little bit and started to walk. Jin looked at her with concerned puppy eyes, and Eugene stood back and bit her bottom lip. Nice kids, thought Queenie. They honestly felt bad that she was getting fired because of the October thing. Anyone who wasn't Queenie's boss liked her quite a bit.

Queenie walked in front of Roy Cohn into his office and sat down. She looked at the framed picture of him and his "girlfriend." Like he's not queer as five red hats, she thought.

Roy Cohn smelled strongly of man-cologne; Queenie could feel it burning her eyes when he passed her to sit down. Not actually sit down, actually stand behind his desk menacingly. Actually it would maybe be menacing were he not five-foot-five.

Roy Cohn had a stack of calendars on his desk, the top being Greek Isles. Shit, thought Queenie. She forgot about Greek Isles.

Roy Cohn flipped open Greek Isles to a sheet marked by Post-it tape. October. The Greek isle looked like a small rock in a bright blue pond.

He pointed to the third Sunday. It read, Daylight Savings Time Ends.

"Do you have anything to say?" he said.

Queenie leaned forward and squinted at the sheet.

"I forgot about Greek Isles," she said.

"Oh yes?" said Roy Cohn. "You thought it was only Majestic Creatures?" he asked, incredulous. "Well, it's Creatures and Greek Isles and Ice Figures *and* Southwest Scenes."

Queenie closed her eyes. He'd really punched "Southwest Scenes." He really wanted her to feel that one.

"I didn't realize," she said.

"What?" said Roy Cohn, gripping the back of his chair.

"I didn't realize they were all on my proof."

"Well," he said, blustery, pretending to be speechless. "What did you think you were doing?"

"I really don't know, Roy Cohn."

Roy Cohn nodded, and said, "You know we're going to have to let you go."

"Yeah."

"I want you to know I had to talk Joan Crawford into giving you even last week's pay. Frankly," he said, rubbing his chin where he was still hoping to grow hair, "we can get almost anyone here to do your basic layout and"—he lifted his hands in bunny ear quote marks—"proofreading."

"Yeah," said Queenie.

She stared at a memo she had signed last week, sitting on the top of Roy Cohn's In pile. She couldn't for the life of her remember what it was about. Now she just squinted hard at the "Q" she left as her signature, and then she let her head roll back. She wasn't forcing it; it just seemed to fall back on its own, everything in her head—eyes, brain, skull, all heavy, all feeling like dead skin.

"Queenie," said Roy Cohn.

"Yeah?" said Queenie, her head wobbling forward. Her eyes went blurry. Roy Cohn was fuzzy.

He covered his mouth and appeared surprised.

"Have you," he said, then stopped and started again. "Have you been drinking this morning?" he said slowly.

"No way," said Queenie, putting her fist down on her knee definitively. "Not for a good two, three hours."

By eleven Queenie was back at her apartment in the Burning Grounds section of Brooklyn. She dropped her keys and wallet and her small box of office things on the floor and fell on her bed facedown. It felt wet for some reason. Call Meade, she said to herself. He'd say, You're not supposed to make personal calls at work. She'd say, I'm not at work. Aw shit, he'd say, those cow-fuckers shitcanned you?

"Yes," said Queenie aloud, into the sheets. "Those cow-fuckers shitcanned me."

She rolled over and stared at the ceiling, then looked at the phone, and when it didn't do anything provocative, she rolled off the bed and onto the grubby floor. Hands first, then feet, and she pushed herself up, her arms shaking. You have no upper body strength, she said to herself.

She got to her feet and eventually the phone and picked up the receiver and dialed Meade's first three numbers when she stopped and looked at the calendar above her phone table. It was one of the company's extras: Elegant Elks. Apparently Elks weren't a big seller last year; nobody seemed to care if they were elegant or not. Twelve different candids of elks in their natural habitats. Elks eating, elks drinking from streams, elks running, two elks nuzzling each other.

Queenie stared at the calendar and found today's date. Monday in June. Call Si, it said inside the box. And it said the same in Wednesday's box and in Friday's.

"One elk, two elk," Queenie said, hanging up the phone.

She picked it back up.

"One elk, two elk," she said, dialing the number with her thumb. "Three elk. Many elk. Look at all the many elk." There was a ring on the other line. "Are those your elk?" she said to herself. "Those are fine-looking elk."

Then someone picked up, and it didn't sound like Nancy.

"Clear Skies," she said.

"Hi," Queenie said. "Nancy?"

"No, Nancy's out today. What is it that you need?"

"I need to speak with Silas Sells. He's in room 2E as in Edward."

"Who's calling please?"

"It's Queenie."

"And what's your relation?"

"Pardon?" said Queenie, staring at the elk.

"Friend, family?" she said.

"Oh, I'm his niece," said Queenie.

"His niece?" the woman said, sounding doubtful.

Queenie made a fist and punched the elk lightly. "His great-niece, grandniece, but look, don't tell him that, he won't know who it is. Just say it's Queenie."

The woman paused. "I'll put you through, one moment."

The phone clicked on hold.

"Jesus," muttered Queenie.

The phone rang three more times, and he finally picked up.

"Ha-llo," said Si.

"Uncle Si, it's me, Queenie."

"What's doing, Queenie?" he said, sounding happy.

"How are you today?" Queenie said loudly.

"Can't complain," he said, and Queenie felt relieved for a second. Then he started to speak lower: "I lost forty dollars, though."

Queenie shut her eyes.

"You think you could bring me forty dollars, Queenie?"

"Come on now, what do you need forty dollars for, Uncle Si?" she said softly.

"I gotta get home," he said sadly. "I don't got any clothes either. I gotta get my clothes clean."

"C'mon, what are you wearing now? Whatcha got on?" she said.

"I don't know what the hell this thing is," he said. "It's like somebody made an outfit outta towels."

"Well that's all okay," Queenie said optimistically. "You got your sweat suit on, that sounds okay to me."

"Yeah," he said. "Sweat suit."

They were quiet. Say something, thought Queenie. Say some goddamn thing.

"What d'you say, Queenie, why don't you come over here?" he said suddenly.

"I'm still in New York, Uncle Si."

She said it like she'd just been there for the weekend and not for nine years.

"New York, huh?" he said. Then he yawned. "When you comin' back up?"

"You know, soon."

"Yeah, you comin' to stay?"

"No," Queenie said, her voice dry. "No, I'm staying down here a little more."

"Oh," he said.

More quiet. Queenie heard him breathing and pictured him in the plaid room he shared with his roommate. He kept getting new roommates. No one stayed very long. They either died or wanted to be moved because Si screamed at night. Sometimes it was for his old best friend, Jasper; sometimes it was for his brother, sometimes for Queenie.

"How the Sox doing?" Queenie said. That's it. Sports.

"They don't got a prayer," Si said, animated suddenly.

Queenie laughed.

"They don't got a damn prayer. This kid, Rice, he's supposed to be a big superstar—He's just a hot dog, you know. Wastes all his time trying to be tough for the papers. He's a good hitter but that don't do much good for Tiant. Orioles took them to school, eleven–three. They're all a buncha clowns."

Queenie laughed. She didn't really mind that he was talking about a game that happened in 1975. Rice was always a hot dog, and the problem was always with the scouts picking hitters. And the Orioles always took them to school, eleven–three.

"Where do they get these guys?" she said.

"I tell you where they get them—the scouts are lookin' for the wrong thing, they look for hitters, just hitters, so they got a team full of hitters and garbage for pitching. No outfield talent neither."

"Maybe next season," said Queenie.

"Yeah," said Si. "Uh," he said.

"You feeling tired, Uncle Si?"

"Yeah. I'm pretty tired."

He paused. Queenie felt worried.

"Forty," he said, sighing. "I gotta get forty dollars. Goddamn, I had forty dollars in my pocket. I think somebody took it all."

"Hey, Uncle Si," Queenie said gently. "You don't need forty dollars. You shouldn't worry about it."

"Hell I don't," he said, getting louder. "Everybody around here's a crook. They're watching me like a hawk," he said. "And where the hell are you?"

"I'm coming soon."

He laughed roughly. "A lot of good that does me—you're leaving me with a bunch of crooks."

"Bye, Uncle Si, I love you," Queenie said.

"You hang up on me, Queenie, you can forget taking my car on the weekend—"

She hung up. He would keep talking for a few minutes, and when he wouldn't hear anything back, he'd forget who he'd been talking to and why he was on the phone. Then he would either harass the nurses for forty dollars or fall asleep.

Queenie fell on her bed again. All she could think about was macaroni and cheese and Jimmy Dean sausage, Si frying it up in a pan, mashing it to pieces with a wooden spoon. It was Queenie's job to unwrap four slices of American cheese. "Here's the secret," he said quietly, as if they were being spied on. "Extra cheese—that powder ain't enough."

She ate macaroni and cheese and Jimmy Dean sausage three times a week her entire childhood, with tall, weird-smelling glasses of orange juice on the side. Si used to give her soda pop until the mother of the boy next door said you can't feed the girl soda all the time, it'll rot her teeth. What should I give her? he asked. Juice, said the mother, almost disgusted. Fruit drinks, milk. Oh, said Si, good-natured. Laughed and scratched the back of his head. I don't have kids of my own, he said, trying to explain.

Call Meade, Queenie thought. No, I don't want to call Meade, she thought. Get drunk. Call Meade, and then get drunk. No, don't wait for Meade. Get drunk right now. Smoke ten cigarettes. Have a Popsicle. Listen to the radio. Rip the skin off your face very slowly.

She did none of these things. She stayed just where she was and let spit pool in the back of her throat, and she remained very still until she fell asleep.

* * *

She had one of her two recurring dreams: This was the one where she was trying to catch the subway. She would run through the station, dream-run—have an unlimited amount of energy but be wearing no shirt, sometimes just stockings. No panting, but still running, heart pounding, getting thirsty, her feet heavy. She could see the train winding around a cul-de-sac track, black tunnels laid bare, and the platforms stretched all the way through to the next station so you could run alongside the train and jump for it like folks did in movies, grip the handle at the door and sail through the tunnels, lights flashing past.

But Queenie never made it. It would always happen so she would run and run, seeing the train turn the loop and drag to the stop, but it would always, always pull away too soon, and she'd miss it every goddamn time.

She'd forgotten to turn the ringer off on her phone. She woke up with a trail of drool from her mouth to the collar of her shirt. You are one sexy sexy girl, she said to herself, wiping her mouth. Her phone sounded like a laser gun, and it hurt some very tender solid part deep inside her ear. Eardrum, she thought, standing up.

She lunged for the phone and slapped it out of the base, and it hit the floor just as she slammed her toe into the metal leg of the phone table.

"FUCK!" she yelled.

She crumpled hard to the floor and squeezed her toe with one hand, picked up the phone with the other.

"Hello," she said through her teeth, sounding constipated.

"Queenie?" a man-voice said, not Meade.

"Yeah?"

"It's Hummer."

"Oh," she said, sounding disappointed. "Hi, Hummer."

"How are you doing?" he said, not waiting for an answer. "Did you end up getting fired?"

"Yeah," she said, holding her foot. "I just stubbed the shit out of my toe."

"Oh, ha-ha," he laughed, like she was making a joke. "Look, Queenie," he said, serious suddenly, "I'm beginning to think it was fate I ran into you."

"I don't believe in fate, Hummer," Queenie said, massaging the toe like bread dough. "Or God. Or Santa."

"Right," he said. "Not fate, then, just, like, luck. I don't know what your job prospects are right now," he began.

"Unemployment."

He laughed. "Is that like welfare?"

Queenie rolled her eyes, and said, "Never mind, it doesn't matter. Why Hummer? What are you getting at?"

Hummer coughed, and said, getting quiet, "Are you doing anything tonight?"

Queenie dropped her foot and was confused. Fuck's sake, she thought, is this cupcake asking me out?

"Um, no, not really," she said, and thought, I might be ripping the skin off my face, but that's not set in stone.

"If you were free tonight, and wanted to make, I don't know, a couple hundred bucks, I might have something for you," he said.

"What is it? Drugs?" she said hopefully.

This might be easy, she thought. Maybe he's too scared to pick his coke up. Then again, she thought, that never stopped him in high school.

"No, no drugs," he said. "It's more like a personal favor to me. It's a sensitive situation."

He stopped.

"Hummer? You there?" said Queenie.

"Yeah, I'm here. Sorry, I'm at work, I never know when someone's listening," he said. "I'm looking for this girl," he started. "She works at the Paper Doll Lounge three nights a week. Do you know it?"

Queenie knew it. She'd been there with Meade. He had two words to say about the women who danced there, with respect to their labia: roast beef.

"Yeah," said Queenie. "She a friend of yours?"

"Yes and no," he said, and coughed again. "I've sort of been dating her."

"Okay," Queenie said, and her eyes started to comb the floor for loose change.

"She was supposed to meet me on Saturday night and never showed up," he said.

Queenie found a thumbtack and a cough drop wrapper.

"Uh-huh," she said.

"Apparently she hadn't come to work beforehand either. And I haven't heard from her since Friday, and that's when she worked last. So I would just need you to go down there, to the Paper Doll, and ask around, see if anyone knows where she is."

"Don't you, like, have her phone number?"

"Actually, no, she has mine—my cell, but I don't have hers," he said.

"Why's that exactly?" asked Queenie.

"That's just what she preferred."

"So okay, Hummer, why can't you go down there and ask around," she asked, fingering the thumbtack.

Hummer sighed. "Because, actually, I'm engaged."

"You have something more important to do?"

"No, no, engaged—engaged to be married."

Queenie smiled. "Not to the dancer, I guess, huh?"

"No, not to her. To someone else. Her name is Charlotte."

"You're a very popular guy."

Hummer sighed again. "I have to be as discreet as I can."

"That must be difficult."

"You know, Queenie, I can do without the attitude."

Queenie laughed. "Oh yeah? I'm real sorry." She stopped laughing, and said, "You called me, remember?"

"Yes, I know. I'm sorry," he said. "This is something I really can't do myself, not because I don't want to but . . ." he paused. "Like I said, I have to be very discreet. And on top of that, nobody seems to like me very much down there—they don't tell me much when I call, and they aren't so friendly when I show up, so I thought, if you could go down there, maybe someone would tell you something, just if she got fired, or left town, or something."

"Why would they tell me this?" Queenie said.

"I don't know," Hummer said. "Maybe you would ask the right questions."

"Why's that?"

"Come on, Queenie, you know, you might be able to talk to the people down there."

"Down there, huh?" Queenie said.

"Yeah, you know, because you could always fit right in with any crowd," he said, laughing nervously.

"Yes, like a chameleon," said Queenie. "I've been told that before, that I'm very chameleon-like."

Queenie had never once been told that she was like a chameleon or chameleon-like.

"It's true," said Hummer, enthusiastic. "So will you do it?"

Will I do it, Queenie thought. She stood up and looked out the window at the overgrown lot across the street and the four mysterious piles of asphalt that had been there since she moved in.

"Yeah, sure, I'll do it," she said.

"Thanks, Queenie, I don't know what to say."

"Say you'll pay me up front."

"Right, no problem. I'll messenger the money to you right now. What's your address?"

"You know, don't send it here. Send it to 605 Lorimer, Basement. That's where I'm going to be."

"Burning Grounds?"

"Yeah, Burning Grounds. Hey, Hummer, what's this chick's name?"

"Trigger Happy."

Queenie smiled. "That's a good name."

"Right," said Hummer, not listening. "Look, can we meet tomorrow and go over what you found out?"

"Fine. When—nine?"

"Let's make it eight. I've got work, you know?"

"Well, no, personally I don't know, but I can understand. Where, though?"

"Um, I don't know," Hummer said. "How about Starbucks?"

"You're going to have to be more specific."

"Oh, right, Starbucks on Eighth Avenue and Fortieth, or Thirty-ninth, one of those."

"Okay," said Queenie, grabbing a pencil off the phone table. "Hey, Hummer?"

"Yeah?"

She tapped her thumb against the phone. "Is this for real?"

He paused. "Yes, Queenie, it's for real."

Queenie got to Meade's place around two-thirty. The sun hit that particular block in a bright and hot and almost punishing way, and it was always like that, never a break. There were hardly any trees either.

The old ladies weren't on their stoops yet. One of the old men was, though. He had thick glasses and dark eyes. Queenie smiled at him. He didn't smile back. None of the old neighbors liked Queenie since she had vomited in the street at noon on Easter Sunday earlier that year. Queenie remembered children standing there too—a lot of pink dresses.

"Hiya," she said.

The old man nodded. She opened the creaky gate and skipped the steps to the basement entrance. The drain by Meade's front door made a gurgling noise, and a stench came up, like dirty diapers being boiled for flavor.

The door was ajar. Queenie pushed it open and thought what she'd say to Meade. Your door was ajar, your door was ajar, she thought. Your door was a jar. I just turned the lid and dropped right in, scraped the glass walls with my crunchy insect feet.

Queenie walked in and closed it behind her and locked it. The living room still smelled like smoke, and the red futon was still unfolded as she left it. The TV was on with no sound—music videos with a lot of cars.

"Meade?" she said quietly.

There was no answer. She walked into the kitchen. There was a plate on the kitchen table with a half-eaten turkey burger with no bun, and barbecue sauce in a gushy swirl on top. Also a cup of dark coffee, half-full.

She listened for noise upstairs—footsteps, voices, but there wasn't anything, and to be honest, she got a little nervous. Why was the front door unlocked? Meade never really had anyone over for lunch. She went to his utensil drawer and rifled through. There were your basic forks and knives and three wine openers but not one really good sharp knife. There was a skewer, though, with two prongs at the end, long and thin and rusty, and she pricked it on her fingertip, and it didn't exactly hurt but she thought it would do in a pinch.

She approached the staircase and started up. The steps creaked. The whole stairway was built crooked, slightly to the left, but so was Meade's whole apartment. When it rained heavily, water trickled in under the back door and settled in the middle of the kitchen, where the center of the floor dipped.

Queenie got to the landing and stopped. The door to the upstairs bathroom was open, the shower curtain pushed back, the window exposing a corner of the backyard. She could see out to the brown wooden fence next door.

Queenie looked briefly into Tommy Roses's room and saw his unmade bed, his sheets tacked up over the windows for curtains, his inflatable Mets chair.

Meade's door was closed. Queenie put her ear against it and heard quiet rustling.

It was possible that someone had broken in while Meade was eating lunch and was now holding Meade at gunpoint. Queenie pictured him with a gag in his mouth and naked for some reason. What did the intruder want, though, she thought. If he wanted porn or a framed photo of chipped beef on toast, he had come to the right place.

Queenie knocked firmly twice. She heard low voices and started to get scared, thinking maybe she was right. How could she be right?

"Meade!" she shouted, trying to twist the knob, banging the door hard with her other fist.

Then the door opened, and Meade stood there, naked, his hair smashed to one side.

"What, Queenie, Jesus," he said.

"The front door was open," Queenie said, catching her breath.

"What? So what?"

Meade turned around and bent over, looking for clothes. Queenie looked to the bed and saw Anti lying on top of the sheets in jeans and a bra.

"Hey, Queenie," she said.

"What's doing, Anti?" said Queenie, letting her arms drop to her sides.

"I'm taking a long lunch," said Anti, eyeing the skewer.

"You guys should really make sure the front door's not open," said Queenie.

Meade stood up and shook out a pair of pale blue boxer shorts.

"It's always open," he said.

"No, it's always unlocked—it was open, actually open," she said, glancing back and forth between the two of them, and when neither responded, she added quietly, "Ajar."

"Ajar?" said Meade. He pulled his shorts on and rubbed his eyes.

"Yes, ajar," Queenie said.

Anti buttoned her blouse and shrugged.

"I didn't close it all the way?" she said, looking down at the buttons.

Meade shook his head and sighed.

"Who knows, who cares," he said. "Queenie closed it, yes yes?"

"Yes," said Queenie.

"Great. Crisis averted."

Meade picked up cigarettes from his bedside table and pulled one out.

"I have to go," Anti announced.

"See you later," said Meade.

"Bye, Anti."

"Bye, Queenie."

Anti left. Queenie heard her skip down the stairs and slam the front door. Meade lit his cigarette and held it out to Queenie like it was a joint. Queenie took a drag and coughed. She bent over and held on to her knees.

"What the hell's this?" Meade said, taking the skewer from her.

Queenie stood up. "I thought someone had a gun to your head."

"Okay," Meade said slowly. "And you were planning to dip them in cheese?"

Queenie looked at the skewer.

"That's for fondue?" she said.

"This is for fondue."

"Do you have a fondue pot?"

"In fact I do."

"I've never seen it."

"That doesn't mean it doesn't exist."

"No, but why don't you use it?"

"I used it once, and I got sick," Meade said, picking up brown pants from the floor. "Have you ever vomited cheese?"

"No," said Queenie.

"It's something," Meade said, and he pulled his pants on, jumping twice quickly into them. "This was a Swiss-cheddar mix—I followed the recipe to the letter, but two hours later it came up like a goddamn oil slick."

Queenie closed her eyes and tried not to think about cheese vomit.

"Here's the bitch—it was *connected*, one long strand, and it got caught coming up. I had to literally pull it out like a rope."

Queenie swallowed spit and opened her eyes. Meade was smiling.

"You know, back when I ate cheese," he said.

Then he lifted he shirt and slapped his stomach.

"I gotta get new pants," he said.

Queenie sighed. She knew she was supposed to say, Why, Meade,

why do you need to get new pants? Didn't you just buy those pants? Are you too skinny to fit into your thirty-ones?

"Yeah, just went down another size," he said.

He tucked his shirt under his chin and looked at his stomach.

"Great," said Queenie.

"I'm just fucking sick of punching holes in my belt."

"Right," said Queenie. Then she added, "So I got fired."

"No," he said.

Queenie nodded.

"Those pig-fuckers shitcanned you?" he said.

Queenie nodded. Pigs, not cows, she thought.

"The daylight savings thing?" he said.

Queenie nodded.

"So what're you gonna do?"

She leaned against Meade's door. "It's funny you should ask," she said.

Then she told Meade all about running into Hummer Fish on the E train and how he was smarmy but still rich enough to pay Queenie two hundred dollars to ask questions about his stripper girlfriend, because Queenie understands the people "down there."

"Is this girl one of the two-ton Tinas?" asked Meade.

"I don't think so."

"Svelte junkie?"

"More like a svelte junkie."

"Two hundred dollars?" Meade said again. Queenie nodded. "To talk to the denizens?"

Queenie nodded.

"Bullshit," Meade decided, and he walked past her, out of his room, toward the stairs.

"It's not bullshit," said Queenie, following him.

"He's bullshitting you," Meade said when they reached the kitchen. "Probably gets him off."

Then the doorbell rang.

"Who the piss is this?" said Meade.

"That's my money," said Queenie.

Meade raised his eyebrows.

Queenie went to the front door and opened it. There was a messenger there. Queenie could tell he was a messenger because he wore fingerless gloves and a helmet. He held out a manila envelope with "Queenie Sells, 605 Lorimer, Burning Grounds, BROOKLYN," written on the front. Queenie signed for it and said thank you and came back inside. Meade stared at her.

She tore the envelope open. Four fiftys. No note. She held the money up for Meade to see, and Meade rubbed his chin and smiled.

He said, "So does that cover drinks, too?"

The Paper Doll Lounge was quiet. There were two dancers on the small stage, which was really more a long counter with a mirror behind it. One was about 250 pounds and white and in a red G-string. The other was thin and burnt-out-looking, and had darker skin and fanned-out hair and a green G-string. Both were swaying gently, looking a little out of it. There were five men in the audience, at the tables in front of the stage, and no one was sitting at the bar on the side.

Queenie walked over to the bar and sat down. The bartender was a rockabilly with slick hair and a tight black T-shirt and tight jeans, and he was a little chubby. He nodded at Queenie, and she ordered a Bud Light.

She swiveled around on her stool and looked at the five patrons, making notes about them in her head—what is also known as "mental notes:"

Patron 1) Black, thin, smoking Marlboro reds, probably early forties.

Patron 2) White, stringy hair, mouth open. Drinking beer in a glass with ice. Late twenties, early thirties.

Patron 3) Black/Hispanic mix, dark blue suit, drinking something with a slice of lime so withered it looked like a piece of tissue paper. Little spriggly hairs on his cheeks and chin. Midthirties.

Patron 4) Sitting with Patron 3, Hispanic, sport jacket and
tweed pants. Drinking a clear drink without accou-
trements. Also thirties.

Patron 5) White, older, possibly sixties, thin and pale, drinking a bottle of Miller High Life. The champagne of
beers, thought Queenie. He kept chewing something, but Queenie didn't think offhand it was
gum, even though he was kneading it around in his
teeth, keeping his mouth closed. It looked like he
was gnawing on the inside of his lips. Where they
met in the middle was a tight little line, looked like
a closed window.

Queenie left the bar and went to sit at a table next to the man with the
window lips. She looked up at the dancers. The fat woman wasn't
dancing so much as vibrating. Or she'd just take a step or raise her
arm, and the rest of her skin would roll. It looked like cake frosting.

The burnt dancer was really thin. Her hipbones jutted out and
were so sharp they looked like they could snap the G-string and cut
it right in half. She was beginning to squat and push her crotch in
Patron 3's face. Patron 3 seemed reserved but pleased. He nodded
rhythmically. "What is love, baby don't hurt me" played quietly in
the background.

Patron 3 gave the thin dancer two wrinkly dollar bills. She nodded and tucked them into the side of her G. Then she pulled the strip
of underwear away from her crotch so her business was in Patron 3's
face. It was shaven along the sides. Queenie thought she could see
small red razor burn spots, but then thought she might have been
imagining it. Then again, maybe not—Uncle Si always told her she
could've been a sharpshooter with her eyesight.

Then Patron 5, the old man, laughed, and said, "She's got a great
bush."

Queenie turned to him, and he nodded and kept chewing.
Queenie glanced back at the thin dancer, then back at Patron 5.

"Why?" she asked him.

Patron 5 laughed again. His lips flapped out like blinds. He didn't have many teeth.

"What? You don't like it?" he said.

Queenie looked at the thin dancer again, but she had snapped the G-string back over her business. Patrons 3 and 4 laughed conspiratorially. Queenie turned to Patron 5 again.

"No," she said. "I like it fine. I just don't get what makes it a great bush. I think I can imagine what would make it a bad bush—you know, not exactly, but I think I have a ballpark idea."

"Ballpark?" said Patron 5, and he got a blank look on his face. It reminded Queenie of Si. Then his eyes wandered, swiveled like wheels on a TV cart back to the thin dancer.

"Great bush," he said again. He looked at Queenie. "Great bush," he said, bossier, like it was an order, and she better agree with it.

"What's so great about it?" Queenie said, and she took a sip of beer.

"What are you, joking?" Patron 5 said.

"No."

"That kinda bush," he said, shaking his finger at the dancer, "you wanna climb right inside."

"That so?" said Queenie.

He sipped the foam off his beer and nodded, licked his lips. Queenie saw a tooth that was almost all brown.

"I only seen two, three bushes looked that good," he said.

"Yeah?" said Queenie. "When?"

Patron 5 looked surprised for a second. Queenie thought it was kind of funny that he should look surprised seeing he started talking about people's bushes in the first place.

"Hell, the first when I'm all of thirteen thick—my birthday," he began, and then he stopped to chew again. Queenie now knew for certain there was nothing else in his mouth but his pale gums and brown teeth. "Daddy takes me to Miss Susie's house, and it ain't so much to look at. There was two gals sitting in the living room, the radio was on the news program. Men, too, reading the paper, the gals reading *Look* magazine. I think, this is what the hubbub's about—

people sitting around like they in a goddamn library. Nobody talkin', nobody doing anything—it's like the same business at home, except my ma and my sisters don't look like the girls sitting there.

"Daddy tells me to sit on the chesterfield, he goes over to one of the ladies, she was blond, and Daddy leans down and whispers something in her ear, and she nods and goes upstairs.

"Then it feels like we sit there for hours before the blond come back down, she come back down with a cigarette and she nods to my daddy again—she's not looking at me. And Daddy grabs the back of my neck like he do, and says, 'You wash your hands after and you say thank you when you're done, you got that, boy?' I says, 'Yeah, Daddy.'

"So the blond look down at me and we're all staying put right there and then she says, 'Well, come on,' all impatient, like she's my ma, and I stand up and I put my head down and she walks up the stairs real slow. Her dress ends right at her knees, and I can't get my eyes off those two stitched lines on her stockings. Each time she steps her skirt raises right up a little so I can see more and more of the back of her knees and her legs, and we get to the upstairs and she walks up to a door and knocks on it, and there's a gal inside that says, 'Yeah?' and the blond, she still don't look at me, she opens the door and then she turn around and goes back downstairs.

"Then I hear, 'Are you coming in or aren't you?' 'Yes, ma'am,' I says, and I go on in, and there's a brunette sitting at a dressing table, she's looking in the mirror at herself. She's touching her cheek with her fingers—she's not putting any makeup on herself, just touching her cheek.

"She don't look at me neither. She says, 'Close the door' so I close it, and she turn around and puts her hands around her hair, patting her hair clips. She's wearing a white dress, a little bit like what my ma wore for a bathrobe except Miss Susie's is real thin, look like paper to me. She got it open at her chest, too, real low-cut, and she's not wearing a brassiere or nothing. She got a red belt—it's holding her dress closed just a tiny bit at the waist. She's wearing it with a big slit up the front, and she got red heels on and no stockings. She says,

'C'mere,' and I do it and I get up close to her face—she look so smooth, everything on her look smooth.

"She says to me, 'Lemme see your hands,' and I show her, knuckles up like you did at school. She don't touch them, she just nods. And then she goes around and sits on the edge of the bed and crosses her legs, pats the space next to her. I sit down where she says to and look down at my shoes, and it's like I'm looking at them from real high up, they look so small. She says, 'So you're Jack's boy.' I says, 'Yeah.'

"She scoots the robe off her legs, opens it up even more so I can see everything—not everything, but I can see she got no underwear on, I can see this little patch of fur there, and I really start sweating like a bastard. She says, 'Why don't you put your hand there?' I says, 'Where, ma'am?' and she says, 'You know where.' And I can't move, I'm frozen like an iceman, and she says, 'You're not much like your daddy at all.' Then she goes and undoes the red belt, and it snaps, and she opens the robe so I can see everything now, and she says, 'Put your hand here,' and I'm so scared to look where she means but I do anyway, and she touches her stomach. I don't look nowhere else. 'Well go on,' she says, and she says it like she's real angry.

"I reach out and I touch her there, where she said to on her stomach, and there's a strange thing about it I can't put my finger on. It's smooth, the skin there but also it's pudding soft, and she got these scars like she been scratched up—I must of looked confused 'cause she says, 'What? What're you making a face for?' I take my hand away and look at her stomach again, it's like these tiny ribbons she got, and I says, 'How'd you get those scars?' And she starts laughing and laughing like it was the funniest thing. She look pretty, too, when she laugh , it's the first time I really think she look pretty—her face is all stars and smiles. Then she says, 'Everybody's mama's got them scars. Ain't you ever seen your mama's belly?' I says, 'No way I ever see no skin on my ma except for her face and her arms and her legs.' And Miss Susie says, 'Hell, I got three boys, one of them older than you, I bet. How old are you?' she says. I says, 'Thirteen.' 'Yep,' she says, 'Joey's fourteen last month.'

"Then she goes and puts her hand on my hand and she starts to move it down south, and I touch it on top and it's warm, the warmest thing, and she says, 'Dip your fingers in now,' so I do. I put two fingers in and I can't look at her, can't look at nothing, and my head's all red, feels like the top's coming right off. And she starts moving— she starts swinging her hips a little, shaking them down, and I, I do it right there, mess myself up all over my pants just on account of her moving her hips like that.

"She says, 'Aw, lookit what you did. Now you're gonna have to wait.' And she pulls my hand out and stands up and walks over to her powder table and sits down and lights a cigarette. I ain't moving, I'm stuck there. She says, 'Well go on, go tell your Daddy to come up.' I says, 'Can I wash my hands first, ma'am?' She says, 'Yes you can.' So I go on back to the bathroom and wash my hands three or four times, and I look at my pants, and they don't look so bad 'cause they're dark pants. When I get back into Miss Susie's room, I says, 'Thank you, ma'am,' and she laughs, and says, 'What for? You didn't even make it out of the gate.'

"Then I run downstairs and sit on the couch, and my daddy gives me his hat to hold, which I'm glad for so I can put it over my pants. And Daddy says, 'How was it,' but he don't let me answer, he just pushes my head down, and says, 'Hell, you don't know how it was, you never had any before.' "

Patron 5 paused.

"I'm just glad he don't see my pants," he said.

He licked his lips and stared straight ahead. By this time, the burnt girl with the great bush was swaying slowly again; she seemed to have lost some energy. The fat woman had turned around and was making her ass jiggle. Queenie thought it was really something, almost hypnotic, the ripples.

"Say," said Queenie to Patron 5. "Do you know somebody who works here named Trigger Happy?"

"No. Nope. No," said Patron 5.

"Well. Bye, then," said Queenie, standing up.

"Bye, then," said Patron 5.

Queenie went back to the bar. The chubby rockabilly nodded at her, and she ordered another beer.

"Hey, friend," said Queenie. "Loosie?" she said, nodding to his Lucky Strikes.

The rockabilly looked quickly at the pack and grabbed it and shook out a smoke. Queenie fished for a quarter.

"Nah, forget it, sister. Just three-fifty for the beer."

Queenie put five on the bar and thought about how useless change was. Even quarters, which are sometimes fun and of course good for phone calls and gum and loosies, even they quickly become a burden. And nickels, dimes, and pennies are just silly and should be eliminated altogether, thought Queenie.

Then she remembered why she had come.

"Got a light?" she said.

The rockabilly lifted a small Bic, and Queenie puffed. There was no filter. It's not goddamn 1955, she felt like saying. There is no need to smoke this. You know, she thought, filters are pretty popular now and make smoking easy and enjoyable. Even for children!

"Is there a girl here named Trigger Happy?" Queenie said.

"Yeah," said the rockabilly. "She hasn't been in for a few days."

"She sick, or what?" Queenie said, trying to sound casual.

"You a fan?" the rockabilly said.

"Not really," said Queenie. "I've never seen her perform actually. She's my cousin."

The rockabilly nodded, suspicious.

"Why don't you try her at home?" he said.

Queenie tapped her smoke lightly on the edge of the plastic tray and watched the ash tumble off.

"I thought she was working tonight," she said.

"She doesn't work Mondays," the rockabilly said. Then he was quiet and tried to stare Queenie down.

Queenie sipped her beer.

"I *thought* she was working tonight," she said again.

The rockabilly shrugged and seemed to give up being a tough guy. Queenie thought it was fairly obvious she was not a stalker.

"Nah, she works weekends usually, but I don't think she showed on Saturday," he said.

"She sick?" Queenie tried again.

"Couldn't say," said the rockabilly. "Baby filled in for her," he said, looking at the skinny girl who was still swaying gently.

Queenie nodded, dropped another five on the bar for luck, and said, "Excuse me." The rockabilly nodded.

Queenie sat at a different table than before, as close as she could get to the stage and to the burnt girl, next to Patrons 3 and 4, who were talking to each other quietly. The burnt girl, Baby, had her eyes closed. The music was fast with a lot of bass, but Baby moved a lot slower, twisting her hips around and around in lazy circles. She played with the dollar bills in her G-string, ruffled them with her fingers.

Queenie pulled two twenties from her pocket and set them on the table. The next time Baby opened her eyes she'd see them, figure bigger fish to fry than Patrons 3 and 4, maybe step down from her perch.

Queenie glanced over at Patron 5 for a second. He wasn't looking at anyone's bush anymore, lips folded over the rim of the glass for good, it seemed.

Burnt Baby opened her eyes to tiny paper-cut cracks and saw Queenie's twenties. She half walked, half swayed to the end of the stage. Queenie thought she was trying to be graceful, but she really looked more like a drunk deer than anything else.

Baby stood above Queenie, wiggling with as little energy as possible.

"That for me, honey?" she said to Queenie.

"Could be," said Queenie.

Baby tried to squat but couldn't seem to balance. She came down on her knees a little hard, hitting the stage.

"What do you want?" said Baby, trying to be seductive.

"I just wanna talk," said Queenie.

"You want me to do something to you while you talk?"

"No," said Queenie. "I want you to talk, too. Both of us. So it will be like a conversation."

Baby sat back a little and shook her hair out.

"You a cop?" she said.

"Why would you think that?" said Queenie.

"Only cops pay to talk."

"Is that right?" said Queenie.

Baby rolled her head to one side.

"Not really. Usually they make you pay them, turns out," she said.

Queenie nodded.

"I'm not a cop," she said. "Look at me."

Baby slid her tired eyes up and down Queenie's clothes, ratty old corduroys and a light blue T-shirt with coffee and sweat stains, which read, SOMEONE SHOULD GET THE PHONE. Baby turned her head and glanced at the other dancer. Then she stood up, unsteady.

"Hey, hey," called Patron 3, waving a dollar.

Baby held up one finger. One minute, sugar. She nodded to the other dancer, who nodded back and moved to the center of the stage, in front of Patrons 3 and 4. They were not as pleased with the larger model.

Baby left the stage and was gone for a minute, and then came out from behind a dark red curtain next to the stage. She'd pulled a sweatshirt over her shoulders but was still topless underneath, still wearing heels and her G-string. She clacked up to Queenie's table and stood uneasily with her hands on the back of a chair. Her eyes were heavy.

"Please sit down," said Queenie, pointing to the chair.

Baby sat down and crossed her legs. Her breasts were thin and long and pendulous. Queenie could see the reedy bones of her sternum.

Baby looked down at the money again and pulled out a pack of cigarettes.

"You sure you're not a cop?" she said.

Queenie nodded. "I'm just looking for a friend."

Baby leaned back and ran her tongue, thick and snaky, across her teeth. She laughed, and her breasts shook.

"Aren't we all?" she said.

"My name's Queenie," said Queenie. "Can I have one of your cigarettes?"

"I'm Baby Watson," Baby said. "They're menthols."

"That's cool," said Queenie. She took one.

Baby Watson blinked heavy, heavy lids, heavy eyes, everything drooping and pulling to the floor. Queenie lit her cigarette and Baby's.

"What you think of Charlie?" Baby said.

"Who?"

"Charlie." Baby nodded at Patron 5.

Queenie thought for a second about Charlie-Patron 5 with his father's hat in his lap after he came on himself. She really wasn't that surprised that he'd told her all that. Sometimes people told Queenie things. She noticed it when she was in high school, even after she started going to Boston for day school with the rich kids; the kids in her neighborhood, the mill kids, would still find her, not ask for anything, and just talk themselves hoarse, tell her all their secrets. Abby Malone described how her brother tried to give her an abortion in their basement. Mickey Hill told her how he shoplifted small jars of mayonnaise from every store he was in and had no idea why. Jim Schaw told her how he watched the family doberman give birth to six puppies, how he was the only one home, and then, for reasons he couldn't explain, how he killed them, smothered and strangled every one of those puppies while he kept the mother tied up with a rope. And when he let her loose, she didn't jump him, she just sprawled her body out over her dead pups and licked their paws. Then he'd gone and told everyone they were born still.

"He's a nice guy," said Queenie.

"So are those really for me?" Baby said, glancing at the twenties.

"If you want them," Queenie said, blowing smoke above her head. "You don't have to tell me anything if you don't want to. You can tell me a lot of horseshit if you want to. I won't know the difference. I'm looking for a friend."

"Who?" said Baby.

"Trigger Happy."

Baby nodded. "She hasn't been here."

"I know. The gentleman at the bar said you covered for her."

"Yeah?"

"Do you know where she was, or where she might be?" Queenie said.

Baby laughed and started to say something, but her lips seemed to get stuck on her teeth, smearing, slurring words.

"Shit, I don't know. Sometimes she doesn't come to work," she said, then paused. "Sometimes I don't come to work."

"Did she call in sick?"

Baby shrugged. "I don't think so. But it really isn't a big thing she didn't show, just weird 'cause it was Saturday and it's a big money night. Why you looking so hard?"

"I'm an old friend."

Baby leaned her head back and blew smoke up in a cone. She laughed and rubbed her eye with her thumb.

"Trigger didn't have any friends," she said.

"Aren't you her friend?" said Queenie.

Baby looked serious suddenly and tilted her head back up. "Look, I don't know shit. I knew her as much as anyone. She had some money boyfriend, and she had a punk boyfriend . . . she liked to wear purple on stage." Baby closed her eyes, like she had a headache. "I don't know anything else about her. Me and her weren't buddies, we didn't have fucking slumber parties.

"All her hairspray and shit's still in back. She's got a real Kate Spade bag, too," Baby said, standing up, uneasy. Smoke framed her. "She doesn't come back soon, I'm gonna take that shit."

"More power to you," said Queenie.

Baby smiled. "Goddamn right."

Then she left, disappeared behind the dark curtain. Patrons 3 and 4 stood up to leave. Queenie turned around and saw the rockabilly on the phone at the other end of the bar.

Queenie stamped out her menthol and followed Baby, behind the curtain.

Behind the curtain was a black door. Queenie tapped it lightly, and there was no answer so she opened it. There was a counter with two or three square mirrors and chairs and bare lightbulbs above. At the end of the counter was a urinal. Next to the urinal, crouched, leaning against the porcelain, was Baby. She rubbed her knees slowly and looked to Queenie, her eyes dim.

"Hey, girlie, you can't be back here. It's for us performers," she said slowly.

"I'll only be a second," said Queenie.

Baby did not visibly seem bothered by this. She closed her eyes and continued to rub her knees.

Queenie stepped up to the counter. There were makeup bottles and powders, cigarette boxes, razors. She saw a clipping, looked to Queenie like it was from the *Voice*, couldn't have been much bigger than one and a half by two. "Weekends at Paper Doll: Thin Skins and Hefty Hotties."

Queenie walked the length of the counter, not very long at all, and saw an opened douche box, a blue dildo, a box of oyster crackers, a half-finished Rolling Rock. She saw a picture of two little black kids, smiling, sitting on a stone wall. Queenie didn't want to touch it and fuck it up.

She saw a Frederick's of Hollywood catalogue and started flipping through. A lot of pushed-up boobs. Queenie looked at her own boobs. They were average size, maybe a little bigger, but she'd never felt compelled to push them anywhere. The models looked strange to her; some of their heads were too big for their bodies, some had extra long arms. Did they just paste the girls together? thought Queenie.

She examined a picture of a purple garter belt with fake pearls sewn into the straps. The ad was circled three or four times over in silver. Queenie tapped the page with her finger and glanced at the counter and saw a thin silver eyeliner pencil. She turned the catalogue over; it was addressed to the Paper Doll Lounge, attention: Tara Rote.

Queenie dropped the catalogue on the counter and grabbed the silver eyeliner and walked back over to Baby. Queenie squatted down and said, "Baby? Baby?" Baby didn't stir, but blew air through her lips, and they flapped.

"Huh," she said.

"Is Tara Rote Trigger Happy's really name?" said Queenie quietly.

Baby sniffed and still didn't open her eyes. "Yeah, yuh, Tara— after *Gone With the Wind,*" she said, trailing off.

"No shit," Queenie said.

Baby started twitching a little in her fingers and eyelids, and Queenie stood up and stepped out backward, slowly, through the black door and the red curtain. Then she turned around and walked out quickly, past the rockabilly who was chewing a toothpick, who didn't say anything but stared her down all the same.

It was a little after ten, and Queenie made a professional decision that if she was going to do any more research for the night, she would have to be drunk. She bought a pint of Bushmill's and walked up to Canal to a phone box. She cracked the Bushmill's and started sipping, found a quarter in her pocket, then dialed information and heard Darth Vader say, "Welcome to Verizon local and national four one one." Then a perky female robot said, "What listing?"

"Tara Rote. R-O-T-E. In Manhattan," said Queenie.

The phone was sticky. *Always wipe first, always wipe first,* said Meade.

"Thank you. Please wait while an operator looks for that number," said the lady robot.

Queenie sipped the whiskey and kept an eye peeled for cops. It was a cool night, a nice breeze, people wearing shorts and T-shirts but not sweating their balls off just yet.

Then a real voice: "That's a residence?"

"Sure," said Queenie.

"I have a T. Rote on East 104th."

"Great. I'll take it. Anything else?"

"There is a T. Rotte, with two t's . . ."

"Could I get both of those? Whatever you have."

Queenie held the whiskey between her arm and her chest, the way she saw suits hold the newspaper on the subway. She searched her pockets for a pen and could only find the silver eyeliner.

"Four twenty-five East Twenty-sixth Street for T. R-O-T-T-E, phone number's 212-686-3638. Address for T. Rote, with one "t," listed as 336 East 104th Street, hold for the number."

Queenie wrote in long strokes on her forearm, near Hummer Fish's number. The silver pencil tip was gummy and starting to bend. Queenie lightened up her grip and thought, Two for two, not bad.

The lady robot returned, and said, "The number is 212-850-9051. That number again—"

Queenie hung up and swung her arm a little so the liner would dry.

She found change in her pockets, dimes and nickels, goddamn dimes and nickels, and rested them on top of the phone. She picked up the receiver again and put in two dimes and a nickel and dialed the first number, where there was a busy signal. Then she put in one dime and three nickels and dialed the second number, where she got a ring. It rang three times, and then a female voice said, "Hi, please leave a message."

Queenie hung up again.

Then she started walking north and looked up at the sky. Where does the six stop on the east side after Union Square? she thought. Twenty-third probably. In the end, though, she decided to walk it, and she saw various people along the way. She saw the neighborhood change from Chinatown to Chine-Italy to Little Italy to SoHo to Great Jones, but then she turned east and walked up Second Avenue, through the East Village, and saw all the rich people and college kids and arty girls from Connecticut with really big shoes. Queenie laughed at most of them, drinking her whiskey and thinking about the Indian. The Indian used to walk around the East Village and Alphabet City, huge body made of brick, drunk and high as a kite, holding his arms out, and shouting, "This is MY island. . . . This is MY FUCKING ISLAND."

"God bless you, you crazy bastard," Queenie said loudly to the sky. Some people looked.

She turned east again on Twelfth Street and started up First Avenue. She passed a bar called, Hog, where apparently you used to be able to get a decent handjob in the back room for ten bucks. There was a neon hog in the window.

She walked up First and kept her eyes on the street signs, which seemed to go by fast. There were all kinds of pizza shops and greasy chopsticks on the way. All the Chinese food places had bright square pictures of the dishes they served there, all lit from behind. She remembered Meade saying, *I like any restaurant where you can see a photo of what you're going to eat.* She stared at Shrimp in Lobster Sauce. That always seemed like overkill to Queenie. Either shrimp or lobster, you know? No need to get crazy.

Then she came to Twenty-sixth Street, which wasn't a nice-looking street in any way. Most of the apartment buildings had entrances below street level. Queenie tripped a little on the curb and wondered if she was on the right side of the street.

It turned out she was, and then she found 425. It had a sunken entrance and was made of bricks that looked gray. There was a Plexiglas sign by the door with a sheet of labels—last names and first initials. Queenie staggered down the stairs and ran her finger down the list.

"Rotte, Rotte, Rotte," she said.

She found it. T. Rotte. Apartment 3F. As in Fantastic.

Queenie buzzed. There was a pause, and a scratchy male voice said, "Yes?"

"Hi," Queenie said. It sounded like she was talking into a bucket. "Is Tara home please?"

"Uh, I think you have the wrong apartment."

Queenie leaned back and squinted at the list.

"Is this the, uh, T. Rotte apartment?" she said.

"Yes, but there's no one here by that name," the voice said again, very politely.

"That's a real pisser," said Queenie. Then she realized she probably woke him up. "Sorry, sorry about that," she stammered, but he was already gone.

Queenie turned around and walked back up the stairs very carefully and pulled the Bushmill's out of the bag. She had a good inch left. Enough to last her the walk from Twenty-sixth to Fourteenth, and if she was lucky, enough to last from the First Avenue stop to Bedford on the L train.

Tuesday

At eight-thirty the next morning, Queenie was on the E train again. She was sweating even more than usual because she didn't have any clean shirts left, no shirts that she hadn't worn at least three times, so she wore her blue zip-up hoodie with just a bra underneath. It was still breezy outside, but it was hot and moist in the subway.

Queenie got off at Forty-second and laughed privately to herself about how she wasn't going to work at the Calendaria today, and never would again. Ha-ha, she thought. They won't have me to kick around anymore. Ha-ha, unemployment. Joke's on you, Queenie, old girl.

She made it to street level and sifted through the businesspeople and tried not to look up at the large colorful signs around the Port Authority because they made her head hurt.

Then she got to the Starbucks on the corner of Thirty-ninth and Eighth Avenue, and it was swamped with assholes. Queenie felt sorry for the people who worked there, even though they had health

benefits. Meade had worked at a Starbucks for about forty-five minutes. They fired him because he drank skim milk from the pitcher
that was for the customers, in front of the customers. That kind of
thing was frowned upon by management, despite their progressive
ideals.

Queenie walked in and saw Hummer immediately at a table in the
corner. He held his hands up and looked angry. Queenie said,
"Excuse me," quietly and made her way to the corner, cutting
through some of the assholes in line. Some of them sighed at her
because it is a real inconvenience to be in line somewhere and then
have someone cut in front of you perpendicularly. Can't she just
walk around? they think. Wouldn't that be better for all of us?

She knocked her knee into a tabletop and winced because it hurt,
coughed a bit, and sat down across from Hummer. There were
three large Starbucks cups in front of him. He looked annoyed and
tired.

"You're almost an hour late," he said.

"Oh yeah?"

He looked at his watch purely for effect, all exaggerated, and
said, "I'm supposed to be at work in five minutes."

"Then I'll make this quick," said Queenie. "May I?" she said,
pointing to the cups. She picked one up, and it was empty.

"Here, have this, I've already had two, I'm not going to drink
anymore," he said dramatically, pushing one of the cups to her.

"Thanks. So here's what I found out," Queenie began. "Another
dancer named Baby Watson filled in for Trigger Happy on Saturday
night. Apparently Trigger only works Fridays and Saturdays, and
nobody really cares too much that she didn't show because everyone
needs the money on the weekends."

"I know that," said Hummer, snotty. "I already knew all that."

Queenie squinted at him. "Okay. Well," she said. "Anyhoo, her
real name is Tara Rote."

Hummer sat back, looking surprised.

"What?" said Queenie. "Why are you making that face?"

"I just," he began. "I didn't know that."

"Did you ever ask her?"

He stared off wistfully. "Once. She said everyone called her Trigger."

Queenie nodded and pretended to look interested for five or six seconds.

"And I also found out that she does not live on East Twenty-sixth street, though there is someone who lives there named T. Rotte, with two t's," Queenie said, and she took a sip of coffee. It made her mouth water it was so sweet, and it took a long time getting down her throat. "What *is* this shit?" she said.

Hummer leaned forward and crossed his arms. "It's a White Chocolate Mocha."

"There is, however," Queenie continued, "another T. Rote who lives in Spanish Harlem, and there's a female voice on the answering machine. That's all for T. Rotes in Manhattan. I didn't have time to check other boroughs."

"Spanish Harlem?" Hummer said, like he just learned the words.

"Yes. East 104th Street."

Hummer stared at her, confused. "You didn't go up there?"

"No, I didn't go up there," Queenie said, getting pissed. "I already'd hauled ass to Twenty-sixth Street from the Paper Doll."

Then she relaxed a second. What do you care? she thought. You were drunk the whole time anyway.

"Well, look," she said. "Do you have a pen?"

Hummer gave her a uni-ball. Queenie pulled up her sleeve and looked at the silver eyeliner, faded, but still there. She took a napkin, and wrote, "T(ara) Rote, 212-850-9191, 336 E. 104." She slid the napkin to Hummer.

"So this is probably her. Now you can call herself. Or show up on her doorstep," Queenie said.

Hummer stared down at the napkin and back up to Queenie, expectant.

Queenie didn't know what else to say. "Oh, and this," she said, "This may or may not be her eyeliner." She rolled the eyeliner across the table to him.

Hummer picked up the eyeliner and looked at it like he was waiting for it to say something.

"I can't go," he said quietly. "I already told you. I can't go looking for her." Then he whispered, "I'm getting married."

"That didn't stop you from fucking her," Queenie said at full volume, shrugging.

People around them stared. Hummer closed his eyes and breathed deeply through his nose.

"No, it didn't," he said. "But I can't go up to 104th street," he said, almost disgusted.

"Of course not," Queenie said, laughing. "You wouldn't want to get your shoes dirty."

"I didn't mean it like that," he said. "I just mean I can't go up there now, and I can't go up there after work because of—" he said, and he stopped to take a pregnant pause.

"Because of Carmen," said Queenie.

"Charlotte."

"Right. Charlotte."

"I can't take the chance that she'd find out."

"Well, what does she think when you and Trigger have dates?" said Queenie.

Hummer looked away. "We usually meet on Saturday nights, and Charlotte is busy on Saturdays."

"Oh yeah? Is that when she meets *her* stripper?" Queenie said, grinning.

Hummer was not at all amused. "No, that's GNO," he said, pouty.

"What—she goes to the gynecologist?" whispered Queenie, confused.

Hummer pursed his lips and shut his eyes hard for a second.

"No. GNO—Girls' Night Out," he said dramatically.

He continued to stare at Queenie and sighed.

"She's taking this wedding preparation class, and one of the assignments is to set aside a night for yourself every week without your fiancé," he rattled off. He put his hand to his head, like it ached. "You know, to assert freedom within the relationship."

"I guess you would have aced that one, huh?" said Queenie, laughing.

Hummer leaned across the table, aggressive. Queenie could feel his breath. He reached into his pocket and pulled out a smooth black wallet. He opened it and took out a fifty without looking and pushed it across to Queenie with his thumb and didn't say anything.

"What's this?" she asked.

"What do you think?"

Queenie tilted her head and pretended to look at the fifty sideways.

"Look," she said. "I appreciate the work—it was a nice little gig, but you really don't need me." She was about to add, You really didn't need me, but she didn't want to risk him asking for his money back.

"You found out her real name," he said.

"It really wasn't that hard," said Queenie.

Hummer gritted his teeth, and said, "It'll take you a half hour to get up there."

They were both quiet for a minute, both of them staring at the other and not the money.

Then Queenie said, "You're late for work."

"Yes, I know," he said. "You're not late for anything."

Queenie smirked. You smug fuck, she thought.

She placed her hand gently on the bill.

"And what do I do if she's there?" she asked.

Hummer looked hurt all of a sudden, but then something switched. Furrowed brow, tense lips. Angry fish, thought Queenie. He stood up and pulled another fifty roughly from his wallet and dropped it on the table.

"Give her this and tell her to call me," he said, not looking at her, and then he left.

Queenie took the S Shuttle from Times Square to Grand Central and transferred to the six. There were various kinds of people on the train at nine-forty-five in the morning on a weekday, and most of them were sketchy or looked like they had something to hide. It was a strange mix after rush hour. Queenie watched a guy in the corner wiping his nose and knocking his knees together. He had dirty sweatpants. Then she looked down at her hoodie, and it had grease spots and small red crusty flakes that she couldn't identify.

It was one of those new six trains that was bright as hell inside and had many different robot voices announcing the stops. Queenie tucked her head low and stuck her fists in her pockets. Her stomach growled.

She rode to 103rd and got off, and when she came up above ground the sun blared right in her eyes, and she winced and lifted her hand to her forehead. She looked around and figured out where east was and started walking. She noticed a lot of garbage on the street, bags and bags stacked unusually high. When are they supposed to pick it up? Queenie thought. Why don't they clean the fucking street? she thought, getting indignant. It looks like a goddamn state fair up here.

She saw a man, probably around her age, sitting on a crate in front of a bodega, drinking a beer in a paper bag. She slipped past him into the store and looked up at the yellow awning with red letters so he wouldn't think she was staring at him.

A metal fan spun in the back and hummed. Queenie walked down an aisle and found a pack of Hostess crumb cakes. Then she walked to the refrigerators and looked at the soda. They had mango soda in a pull-top can. Queenie didn't trust anything in a pull-top can, except peaches or pineapples. And only in their own juices, none of that heavy syrup bullshit.

She slid a door open and felt ice on her face and neck, and she took a Country Time Lemonade. Then she glanced at the cooler to her left and saw beer. There was really no good reason why she shouldn't have a Bud Light. It was almost ten, and the guy outside had already started. What made him so special, she thought.

She paid for her beer and crumb cakes and walked back out into the sun, tucked the beer into her pocket, ripped open the crumb cakes, and shoved one in her mouth. It was very moist. The plastic bag was moist; the cardboard the cakes sat on was moist. The cake itself tasted like a sugar sponge. Which isn't so bad, thought Queenie. Nothing to sneeze at, Uncle Si would say.

When she hit Third Avenue, she opened her beer. An old overweight Hispanic woman sat on her stoop, fanning herself.

"Morning," Queenie said, tipping her beer.

The woman smiled uneasily. Queenie looked down again at her ratty clothes and the sweat circles growing in her armpits. Greasy hair and drinking beer out of a bag at ten in the morning. You don't look like a nice girl, thought Queenie.

A group of men stood on the corner of 104th and Second, four or five of them standing around with coffee and cigarettes, laughing, speaking Spanish. Queenie walked past them, and they became silent, staring at her. Not lecherously, just suspicious. Then Queenie felt a rare thing: She was embarrassed by her beer. How dare you be embarrassed of beer, she thought. Just think of all beer has done for you.

She saw a little girl in a pink dress sitting on the curb. Where's her folks, Queenie thought. Queenie smiled at her. The little girl frowned and looked away.

Queenie found Number 336, and it was an old brownstone with intricate moldings, and it obviously had been beautiful when it was first built, whenever that was. Now it looked pretty worn down on the whole, though; all the edges of the windows looked cracked, bits of stone and plaster crumbling off every ledge.

Queenie walked up the stairs and fixed her eyes on the list of occupants and buzzers. Her eyes ran down and stopped at ROTE. Apartment 7. She drank the rest of her beer and set it gently on the ground. Her fingers felt cramped for some reason; she shook them out and pressed her thumb against the buzzer. There was no answer. She backed up a few steps and looked up. Which floor? she wondered.

I could leave a note, she thought, and she patted her pockets down. She had no paper. I could get some paper, she thought, and then leave a note, saying to call Hummer Fish. There's no way she was leaving fifty dollars lying around though.

Which made her think about this: What was *she* doing anyway, coming up here for fifty dollars? Fifty clams. A finsky. Was a finsky five or fifty? she thought. Was that a translation of a language or just a phrase people used. And the clams—was there ever a place where people used clams as currency? Atlantis maybe.

Suddenly, two boys, either nine, ten, eleven, or twelve years old (Queenie wasn't good at telling children's ages) burst through the glass front door. They were hooting and laughing. One of them was chubby, and his pants were practically falling off his butt.

Queenie slid against the wall and caught the door with two fingers.

The chubby boy turned around, and yelled, "You're a chickenhead!" to Queenie.

"You're fat," said Queenie.

The boy appeared surprised at first, his friend running off behind him, then he said, laughing, "You *still* a chickenhead!"

Then he ran off. As Queenie pulled the glass door open, she thought, He's right, you know. You *are* a chickenhead, coming up here because Hummer Fish gave you fifty dollars, running all over town to find his hooker. You do things for no reason, she thought. No you don't. You do things for money. So you are also a hooker. But who isn't? she asked herself.

She opened the second glass door on the other side of entrance vestibule, which she was glad to find unlocked. The hallway on the ground floor was dark and stuffy, and there was a stairway on the left. She assumed that Apartment 7 was not on the ground floor, because it was a fairly narrow building, three or four apartments to a floor at most, so she walked up.

She heard various apartment-type sounds as she went. A dog was barking; there was music playing; a television commercial was on somewhere. The second floor was long and thin, and she walked the length of it and counted off—four, five, six. She made her way to the third floor.

It was dim and cool in the hallway. A window was open at the end of it. She approached Number 7 and put her ear to it and didn't hear anything. Then she knocked.

There was no answer, so she knocked again, and there was no answer again. She realized she'd forgotten to get paper. The whole "chickenhead" thing had thrown her off. She knocked one more time and decided to rattle the doorknob. She turned it, and the door opened a few inches.

Queenie looked over both shoulders because she felt that was the appropriate thing to do. She touched the knob gently with two fingers and pushed the door open a bit farther and stuck her head in.

The first thing she noticed was that the walls were purple, mostly purple—the paint didn't reach the top. It was uneven, like whoever painted it wasn't quite tall enough and didn't have a ladder so they gave up. The room was a small rectangle with two windows, both open, the blinds blowing in a little. Queenie assumed it was a studio.

"Hello?" said Queenie. "Miss Rote?"

No answer.

"Tara?" she said, louder.

Queenie closed the door quietly behind her. Breaking and entering, breaking and entering, she thought. Not breaking, just entering.

There was a folded-out sofa bed that looked rumpled on one side, the sheet and bedspread turned over. There was a tiny TV on a child's school chair, and a small white bedside table with a framed picture and some mail.

Queenie picked up the mail. Con Ed and Exciting News from Citibank for T. Rote. She set the envelopes down on the table and picked up the framed picture. There was a young woman with straight dark hair in a ponytail, thin, wearing a sweatshirt that said, NEW YORK, and a younger blond boy, no more than fourteen. The brunette was smiling big and confident, her teeth looking huge in her thin face.

"Well look at you," Queenie said to the picture.

She put it back and started thinking about how she should probably find some paper to leave a note and get out of there before someone, somewhere, heard her or saw her.

But instead Queenie walked to the window and looked through the blinds for a second, onto a brick building. Then she turned away from the window and stared at a small child's school desk a couple of feet from its matching chair, where there was a cordless phone and a spiral notebook. There was also a small purple book with slips of paper and Post-its sticking out of the sides.

Queenie opened the cover of the purple book. "Dave at work," was scribbled in pencil—a 212 number. She closed it and tapped the spine on her hand and kept looking around.

She stood in front of the tiny kitchen alcove. There was nothing on the range. She opened a cupboard and saw two plates. There was an ashtray in the sink, facedown. Queenie brushed the address book along the edge of the stove top.

Then she heard a creaking noise, like a footstep. She turned around fast, paranoid, but there was no one, nothing, the front door still closed. Probably a cockroach, she thought. One of those Godzilla motherfuckers with wings that hijack all the way from Miami. Now really, she thought, as far as bugs go, a roach pretty much has everything going for it, being huge in general and able to slip through tiny spaces and climb up drains and eat sandwiches— the things practically have their own clothes, do they really need wings, too?

Then Queenie remembered her first homework assignment as a freshman in high school; some hippy-dippy English teacher who wore wooden beads and had white-people-dreadlocked hair handed out a sheet of paper that said: "Answer the following questions and write a paragraph each in explanation. 1) Would you step on a cock-roach for a million dollars? 2) Would you pull the wings off a but-terfly for a million dollars?" Queenie answered, "Yes," to the first, and asked Si what he thought about the second. She remembered he shook his head, and said, "So this is why we jumped through hoops to get you into private school?"

"Yup," said Queenie.

"Jeez, Beauty Queen, I dunno," he said, rubbing his head. "Yeah, my answer's yeah," he finally said. "But I'd feel bad about it. Is this an offer? Are they making offers like this?"

"No, Si, it's just homework. It's supposed to make think what you would and wouldn't do. You know, in your heart. I think it's kind of dumb though. It doesn't *mean* anything."

"You can't say that, now, Queenie, that's not right to say that to a teacher. You just go on and do it like they say. Maybe you can ask a question about it afterward."

She ended up writing this:

Q: Would you step on a cockroach for a million dollars?
A: Yes, I would step on a cockroach for a million dollars because they are disgusting and everywhere. They also carry disease. I would step on a cockroach for five dollars.
Q: Would you pull the wings off a butterfly for a million dollars?
A: Yes, I would pull the wings off a butterfly for a million dollars because then my uncle would not have to make house payments. In addition, everyone thinks that butterflies are harmless, but do we really know for sure?

Queenie remembered thinking that the last bit was especially provocative.

Then she heard the creak again, and it was too loud to be a roach—it had to be a footstep. She whirled around, 180, like a ballerina on a music box. Nothing, no one.

Her stomach growled loudly again, louder than the creak. She reached into her pocket and pulled out the other crumb cake and shoved it into her mouth.

Maybe it was a mouse, she thought. It was very possible. It even smelled kind of mousey around by the kitchen—wooden and dusty. She held the crumb cake on her tongue and thought she'd peek in the bathroom on her way out and check the medicine cabinet, which was her favorite thing to do in strangers' houses.

The door to the bathroom was open slightly, and she reached out to push it when she stepped in something. What the fuck's this now? she thought.

She lifted her shoe up and saw some kind of viscous yellow goo.

She touched it and sniffed her finger, and it smelled like lotion, like flowers. But when she pushed the door open all the way, the mousey smell took over and became rotten, and Queenie thought about how there must be a dead mouse somewhere close.

It wasn't a dead mouse. It was a dead girl. At least she looked like a girl, wrapped three or four times over in a hazy shower curtain. She lay next to the bathtub, parallel, straight up and down like a mummy. There were bottles of shampoo and conditioner and lotion tipped over at her feet. The lotion had leaked and spurted out in a line toward the door.

Queenie swallowed the crumb cake dryly and knelt down and covered her nose. It wasn't a horrible smell, but it wasn't pleasant. She stared at the girl's face. It was the girl in the picture, in the sweatshirt. Trigger Happy. Tara Rote. She liked purple. She was naked under there. Her mouth was open slightly. There was no blood that Queenie could see.

Queenie had seen her share of dead bodies in her life, the first one having been her father's when she was six years old. He'd fallen off the top of the house while roofing, and no one quite knew if it was an accident. He'd landed facedown on a small wire fence that surrounded a bed of flowers below, and the fence had ripped his mouth open and impacted deep in his jaw.

Not only did Queenie see all that, and also his limbs crunched up above him, his eyes still open, but her awful grandmother insisted that there be an open casket. Si always said he never understood his sister as far as he could throw her, which turned out not to be that far. Queenie's awful grandmother also arranged to have Queenie's father's face repaired as best as it could be, which turned out to be not very well. His mouth was stiff, lips stretched out so wide you could fit a watermelon rind inside. His cheeks looked plastic.

She had also seen two dead bodies on the ground near a car accident, after they had been removed from the car—a man and a woman, peaceful, not particularly bloody, side by side. She was probably ten.

Jim Schaw, in addition to strangling puppies, also rounded up a group one time, Queenie included, to come see the dead body of a person who was so fat that it took two sets of paramedics and some firemen to lift him. He was one of those fat people that never left the house and lay around in a sheet. By the time word had gotten around that his heart had stopped, Jim Schaw had already made phone calls and knocked on doors, and Queenie and half of her seventh-grade class watched them haul the huge body out through the window because the front door wasn't wide enough. There wasn't a gurney big enough to hold it either. Just this huge mass, a giant mushroom bulb, being carried by nine or ten red-faced sweating men. "Mmm, mmm, love that barbecue," said Jim Schaw.

Then there was Si's best friend, Jasper, who died when Queenie was a junior in high school. He had been sick from stomach cancer, the worst kind, the kind that ate you from inside out. Si stayed with Jasper's wife and children the last week of his life, in the extra bedroom of Jasper's house. Queenie took Si's car a lot those days, and Si usually got a ride with Jasper's son, but then there was the night Si called her from Jasper's room. He seemed composed at first, saying, "Yep, looks like Jasper's gone," but then his voice came down, and Queenie got the feeling Jasper's family had left the room, because Si started whispering and quietly weeping. "Queenie, you gotta come get me," he said, breathing fast. "I can't be here no more."

Queenie went to pick up her uncle Si, and when she arrived, she shook the hands of Jasper's wife and children and hugged them and said she was sorry, and then she went into the room where the body was, and Jasper looked the same, more or less, just looked like he was sleeping, his mouth open a bit. Si sat at the bedside, his head down, running his fingers through his hair. Queenie put her hand on his shoulder, and Si looked up at her, and said, "You gotta take me home, Queenie." So Queenie took him home and held his hand while he cried and cried.

Queenie thought she was glad Trigger Rote Tara Happy was wrapped in the shower curtain as opposed to just lying out bare, but frankly, Queenie wasn't really thinking anything too clearly.

She stood up and slowly backed away and kept staring, noticing

T. Rote's toes were pointing up, and her hands were at her sides. Queenie wasn't thinking anything just then, just fixating on the girl in the shower curtain so hard that she didn't turn around when she heard the creak again behind her.

All she felt was something really hard, frozen steak, she thought for some reason, on the side of her head above her right ear, and then it felt like warm water was pouring all over her head and her hair, and all her bones went to applesauce, and she was knocked clean out before she hit the tile.

Then Queenie was in the house where she lived with Si; she was hovering above, floating gently through the attic and down to the second floor and down again to the ground floor and through the small hallways to the living room, and then she saw herself sitting next to Si on the couch, which didn't seem odd to her. She was the age she was now instead of being eighteen, which was the last time she'd sat with Si on the couch watching *Kojak*.

Si wore his heavy green work shirt.

"It's cold in here," he said.

"How can you be cold?" Queenie on the couch said, and she looked down at her blue zip-up hoodie with huge pit circles and strange red flakes, and she felt drops of sweat slide down her face and inside her bra.

"I'm burning up," she said, and she shut her eyes.

When she opened them, her head was pressed against something cool. There was a splitting pain on the right side of her head, above her ear. Then she noticed she was on top of a dead person.

She was lying across Trigger Happy's midsection, her forehead pressed against the bathtub, her abdomen flush against Trigger's small solid breasts.

Queenie scrambled to her feet and felt nauseous and dizzy immediately. She stumbled backward toward the doorway of the bathroom and caught a glimpse of herself in the mirror; she was pale and pasty and looked fairly insane, eyes wide and panicked, her hand over her mouth.

She turned toward the living room and stepped in the tiny pool of lotion.

"Fuck," she said.

She stepped out of the bathroom and wiped her shoe on the edge of the rug and hurried to the middle of the living room and turned around frantically, looking for someone, something. No one seemed to be there. She placed her hand gently on her head where it ached and pressed gently. It almost felt as if there were tiny indentations in her scalp, like she'd been hit with a really heavy Lego. Her mind began to race. She stared at her hands, still shaking. You've been hit, you've been hit, she heard in her head, like she was in a plane, like it was *Top Gun*.

She shuffled with little steps, as if she had just learned to walk, over to the purple phone. She picked it up and pressed 9-1-1 and watched the phone shake in her hands.

"What borough is your emergency in?" a woman said on the other line; she sounded very calm.

They must teach these kinds of things in 911 school, thought Queenie. Even if someone tells you their hair is on fire or that they've just run over a bunch of babies, you have to be cool as ice, ask them what borough they're in.

"Manhattan," Queenie squeaked out.

"What is your emergency?"

"There's a dead person," Queenie said. As she heard the words, she scolded herself. Give them more information; they need more information. "There's a dead girl in the bathroom," she said. Good girl, very specific.

"Are paramedics needed?" the 911 lady asked.

Then Queenie felt silly, nothing being much of an emergency anymore.

"Um, I don't think so . . . she's you know, dead. But someone did hit me on the head," Queenie said hopefully, like she was happy she didn't waste the 911 lady's time.

"Are paramedics needed?" the lady asked again, in the same tone.

"Oh, no," Queenie said, looking around. "I don't think so."

There was no immediate response.

"But it would be great if some cops could come over," Queenie added.

"What's the address?" the lady asked.

Queenie looked at her arm.

"Three thirty-six East 104th, Apartment 7."

"Phone number?"

"Eight nine oh—wait." The eyeliner had smudged. "Eight *five* oh, nine oh five one."

"What's your name, please?"

"Queenie Sells."

"Sells with two l's?"

"Yes, like the word," Queenie said. As if one was selling something, she thought. He, she, or it sells.

"Please stay where you are, Miss Sells, until the police arrive, and don't touch the victim."

"Okay," said Queenie. No worries, she thought. Wasn't planning on giving old Trig a foot massage.

"Thank you," said the 911 lady.

Queenie didn't know how to respond.

"Um, you're welcome."

Then they both hung up.

Queenie pressed her head again, and it continued to ache. "Ow," she said aloud, quietly.

She glanced around the room, not even sure of what she was looking for, and then she walked to the refrigerator and opened the freezer. There were only two items inside: a dainty little ice tray that looked like it was made for Barbie's dream house, which was empty, and there was also some sorbet on the door. It was raspberry. Queenie picked it up and examined it. There was frost around the plastic top, and it made her fingertips hurt.

She pressed it to the bump on her head and thought, I am forced to admit that helps. Then she started to laugh. Forced to admit to who? she thought. There was also a gummy trail of sorbet frozen to the side, and it was sticking in Queenie's hair.

Queenie pulled the carton away and turned it around so she could press a nongummy side to her head, but the whole lid seemed to be gummy. She examined the carton for a second and saw that it was a pint. Queenie simply could not believe that the little carton had as much stuff as a pint glass of beer. Was it a difference between solid matter and liquid? she thought. No way, that's crazy talk. If you froze the beer, it would be like a sorbet, and if you froze it in a pint glass, a plastic one, there'd be much more than in this little carton. Wouldn't there? And what a nice summer snack that would make.

What are you talking about, Queenie? she thought, her hands still shaking, the carton of sorbet chilling her palm, vibrating against her head.

Without making a conscious decision to do so, Queenie went to stand in the doorway of the bathroom and stepped in the lotion trail again.

"Piss," she said, wiping her feet on the rug in the living room. Again.

She walked softly into the bathroom, around the lotion, and stood at Trigger's feet. She suddenly felt very embarrassed. Well, this certainly is awkward, she thought. Not only dead but in her altogether. Queenie stepped over her and tiptoed to where Trigger's head was, and she knelt down and examined her cloudy face. What was the last thing she saw? Some crazy bastard about to kill her.

Queenie thought about how shitty that was. She thought about how probably a lot of folks, maybe not a lot but quite a few had something nice to look at right before they died, like their loved ones or a bunch of flowers. Queenie had never thought about how nice hospital room flowers were until Uncle Si had the first stroke and was laid up in the old people ward at Lowell General, and Queenie thought that was really it for Uncle Si, that he was ready to throw in the towel, the way he kept waking up every couple of hours and didn't seem to recognize her, lolling his head around like a baby. Three or four people sent flowers, and they were really nice and colorful, and Si would wake up and just stare at them sometimes, like he was able to see them in a way he couldn't see Queenie. And Queenie had thought, That's not a bad thing to see right before you go, all those flowers. Even little stuffed bears or elephants, or balloons or whatever they sell in the gift shop.

Then Queenie started to get pissed off. Pissed off that someone made this little girl look at something horrible right before she died. Queenie thought about how Trigger didn't get to look at her purple walls, or the backstage counter at the Paper Doll. She didn't even get to see her old pal Baby Watson or stupid Hummer Fish.

"Son of a bitch," Queenie said.

Her fingers were almost totally numb, as was the bump on her head, which was a nice break from the pain but still not what she would've preferred. She closed her eyes and began to lose her balance so she opened them back up and stood up straight. She spoke aloud because she thought she might pass out if she didn't.

"You got any ibuprofen, Trig?" she said, holding on to the doorjamb with one hand to steady herself. Her voice sounded strange—gravelly and rough. "Sure you do, you've got to. Hard-living girl like you," Queenie rambled.

She stepped over Trigger's feet to the sink, and opened the flimsy mirror door of the medicine cabinet.

"What d'you got here?" she whispered, running her fingers over the tubes and bottles.

There was antibiotic cream, and a container of Tums, and three bottles of nail polish, and Q-tips, and some prescription bottles with faded labels. On the bottom shelf there was generic Motrin, and Queenie grabbed it.

"Attagirl," she said, picking it up.

She stepped over Trigger's legs, dodged the lotion this time and stepped into the living room and over to the kitchen counter.

"Water, water, water," she said like a mantra, and she opened the cupboards above the kitchen sink and found some mugs.

She set the sorbet down and filled a mug with water and gulped it fast, and it spilled in little streaks out of the corners of her mouth. She filled it again and set it next to the sorbet, and she picked up the tiny bottle of Motrin. "Barn-Trin" was actually the name, because it came from the Drug Barn. Queenie kind of liked it when companies made up new words. It made your everyday trip to the drugstore more unpredictable. Barn-Trin and Barn-Profen for pain, and Barn-Eve and Barn-Pons for your feminine hygiene needs.

Queenie examined the lid. Line up the little arrows and pop the top. Easy squeezy. She lined up the plastic arrows—they weren't really arrows, actually just little triangles, little marshmallow pizza slices, and she tried to push the lid off with her thumb but it didn't give. She tried again, scraped her thumb tip against the lid, and still couldn't get the sucker open, and then her fingers began to get sore.

"Come on, " she said, and she leaned against the counter and hiked her knee up and set the bottle on it so she could push with both thumbs. She rubbed them against the razor-sharp triangle until it almost broke the skin, then she felt it coming loose, and all at once, the top flew down to the floor and the bottle slipped out of her hands and dropped into the blue plastic garbage can in front of the sink.

"Jesus Harold Christ," Queenie said, feeling exhausted, leaning over.

Now I'm going through garbage, she thought. Great. This is exactly what I want to be doing. There wasn't much garbage in the garbage can, and it didn't seem like particularly sticky or leaky garbage either, but that didn't make going through it any more fun. There were a lot of paper towels, and some scraps of thin tissue.

Queenie held up a flimsy square and widened her eyes, staring at a brown smudge. This could be her blood, she thought. She turned it sideways and saw that it was a lipstick blot and felt stupid.

Queenie dropped the tissue back in the garbage can and kept sifting for the Barn-Trin. It had sunk to the bottom, and she reached her hand down and grabbed it and brought it up with some stray pieces of paper.

She stood up and set everything down on the counter and held the bottle firmly and shook out two pills. She popped them in her mouth and uncrumpled the papers.

There was a receipt for a train card for fifteen dollars, and a Post-it with a phone number written on it, and a receipt from the Drug Barn. Queenie scanned the Drug Barn receipt, and it read,

1 TY FLU NIGHTT 24CT
1 IVORY SOAP BAR 3PK
1 PT 5MIN 1T
1 INSTKW 1T.

Then the buzzer rang six or seven times in a row, and Queenie jumped and scrunched the receipt up in her hand. She grabbed the sorbet and pressed it against her head again and walked tentatively over to the door and opened it. No one was there.

She shut the door and stared at the black intercom square. It had three buttons, and none of them had labels, everything scratched off, so she started pressing all of them with her thumb.

She heard static and snatches of words: "Po . . . Ope . . . Let . . . Police, police."

When she pressed the middle button for a few seconds, she heard, "NYPD, open the door."

"I'm trying," Queenie shouted, just about at the end of her rope.

Then the voices stopped, and Queenie stepped back and began to hear rumbling—heavy footsteps getting closer and closer. She thought it sounded fairly ominous.

She opened the door and stood there, as she heard the slaps of their shoes on the old tile stairs becoming louder. They sounded like a herd of buffalo, she thought. Then they began to come into view.

There were four cops in blue, short sleeves, their fetching summer look, thought Queenie, and a guy in plainclothes, a suit, Irish-looking, red cheeks and blond hair, probably midthirties. He hustled past the blues and took big strides to the doorway and stood there and flashed his badge.

"Are you Queenie Sells?" he said.

"Yeah," Queenie said, looking over his shoulder.

The blues swarmed in from behind him and pushed past her. They hurried into the room and took turns standing at the bathroom door.

"I'm Detective Olds. This is Detective Miner," he said, as Detective Miner came up the stairs, a large black man.

"Hi," said Queenie meekly.

Detective Miner nodded to Queenie and slid past her to join the rest of the cops in the bathroom.

"I'm going to have to ask you some questions, Miss S—" he began, then closed his eyes and tensed his face up like he had the hiccups, "Miss Sells."

"Don't you want to see the body?" Queenie said.

"Right now I'd like to talk to you. Let's go into the hallway," he said.

Queenie followed him into the hallway, to the window at the end. Queenie's palm stung.

Olds pulled a small pad and a pen from his breast pocket.

"Your name is Queenie Sells," he said.

"Right."

Queenie heard a loud deep voice from within the apartment shout, "Goddammit, will you move?" Then, laughter.

Queenie turned to look, and said, "What are they doing in there?"

"Don't worry about that, Miss Sells, just try to answer my questions."

"You haven't asked me anything yet," said Queenie.

Olds looked up from his pad. Now he was annoyed, and that made Queenie happy for some reason.

"First, do you need medical assistance?" he said calmly.

"I don't think so," she said. "I just took some Barn-Trin."

"Some what?"

"Barn-Trin. It's Motrin," said Queenie, and Olds looked at her blankly. "From the Drug Barn."

"So you do or you don't need medical assistance?" he asked again.

"No. Not right now."

Olds nodded.

"What's your address?"

"Two two two North Eleventh, Brooklyn."

"Apartment?"

"Three R."

"Ph—," he said, and then he closed his eyes again and crunched up his lips. "Ph-one?" he said, drawing the word out.

"Seven one eight—seven nine two—five eight four seven," said Queenie.

"Queenie Sells your real name?"

"Yes," she said. "But I wasn't born with it."

"Then it's not your real name," said Olds, a bit combative.

Queenie sighed. "It's just not on my birth certificate, but it's on every other legal thing I've ever signed."

"Could I see your identification?"

"Why, sure," said Queenie. She pulled out her wallet and handed the whole thing to him.

He opened it and examined her ID.

Queenie peered at it, upside down. "You see how it says Queenie Sells, there?"

Olds nodded slowly. "This doesn't exactly look like you," he said.

"I'd been waiting in line for a while," said Queenie.

"And," he said, matter-of-factly, "it's expired."

She smiled. "Yeah, I don't really need it to ride the subway."

Then there was more pounding, more footsteps, and Queenie whipped around quickly and saw more Irish guys in suits coming up the stairs, and two paramedics, and a guy with a camera.

"What—Is he going to take pictures of her?" Queenie said.

"It's a crime scene, Miss Sells," he said, handing her wallet back to her. "He's going to take pictures of everything." Olds glanced back at his pad. "So when did you arrive here?"

"Probably around ten-thirty, eleven."

"You placed the 911 call at two eighteen. What have you been doing for three hours?"

Queenie pulled the sorbet away from her head and pointed. "I've been unconscious. Someone hit me when I got here," she said. Olds stared at her. "On the head. You can touch it if you want to."

"No, that's all right," Olds said. "How do you know the victim?"

"I don't, really."

"You don't?"

"No, I never met her. I'm a friend of a friend."

"Who's the friend in the middle?" said Olds.

"His name's Hummer Fish. That's his phone number," Queenie said, pulling her sleeve up.

Olds squinted. "Which one?"

Queenie looked at her forearm sideways, like a kindergarten teacher opening a book for the class.

"This one," she said, tapping Hummer's number, the one in black.

Olds scribbled it down. "So why were you here?"

"Trigger was missing."

"Trig—" he said, closed his eyes, paused, bit his lip. "Trigger?"

"Trigger Happy. That's her, that's the girl. Her real name's Tara Rote, and Hummer asked me to come up here and check on her, to make sure she wasn't sick or something."

Queenie paused, and Olds kept scribbling and didn't say anything, so she continued.

"So I got here around eleven and came up here and the door was open, and I let myself in. I found her in the bathroom."

"And then what?" said Olds.

"And then someone hit me."

"Who hit you?"

"I don't know who hit me—they were behind me."

"You didn't hear them behind you?"

"No. Well, yes, I heard a creak and thought it was a cockroach," said Queenie.

"There was a person behind you and you thought it was a cockroach?"

"Yes," Queenie said, then she was silent.

"Did the person behind you hit you with their fist, or with an object?" said Olds.

"With an object."

"Do you have any idea what it was?"

"No, I don't," Queenie said, thinking about it. Olds looked at her expectantly, so she started talking. "If I had to guess, I'd say a frozen steak, but I think I've just seen that *Hitchcock Presents* too many times, where the woman kills her husband with a frozen leg of lamb."

Olds stared at her.

"And she, you know, she cooks it and feeds it to the cops who come to investigate the murder," Queenie rambled.

Olds continued to stare.

"It's downright creepy," Queenie added.

"Then what happened?" said Olds.

"Nothing. I woke up, and I called 911."

"Uh-huh," Olds said, squinting. "Why exactly were you here, again?" he said.

Queenie sighed. The gummy line of sorbet was beginning to liquefy and drip down her temple.

"This guy, a mutual friend, Hummer Fish, you know," Queenie said, and she held her forearm up again. "He hadn't seen Trigger . . . Tara in a while, and he asked me to come up here and check on her."

"Why couldn't he do it?"

"He's working. Look, can't you call him and ask him all this?"

"I'll ask him everything I'm asking you. What do you do for a li—," Olds said, eyes closed, head cocked forward. "What do you do for a living?" he said.

"I'm unemployed as of yesterday," Queenie said. Sorbet trickled down her cheek.

"You lost your job?"

"Yes. Yesterday."

"Where was that?"

"A calendar company. The Calendaria. It's on West Forty-fourth Street," she said, feeling compelled to give him more information.

"Why were you fired?" he said.

"I screwed up Daylight Savings," she said.

Olds squinted at her again.

"You know?" she said. "You know Daylight Savings, right?"

He nodded.

"You know how it's always on a Sunday?"

He nodded.

"I fucked it up. I put it on the wrong Sunday. Is this really relevant, though?"

"Maybe," he said thoughtfully, gazing back at his pad, tapping his pen on it.

Queenie heard something ripping. She turned around and saw one of the blues stretching yellow caution tape across the front door.

"Dan," Detective Miner called from inside the apartment.

Olds looked up.

"Excuse me," he said to Queenie, and he walked past her, into the apartment.

Queenie followed him. She wiped the side of her face but it was too late—the sorbet stream had dried down her cheek and now felt like a thin bandage, breaking whenever she moved her mouth.

She stood right outside the front door. The man with the camera was taking pictures of the bathroom, and two of the blues and one of the suits had on latex gloves.

Detective Miner stood at the door of the bathroom, and Olds walked up to him.

"See here," Detective Miner said. "He slipped in the lotion."

"Wait, no," called Queenie from the doorway, and she lifted the tape up and slid under it. "No, that was me, I slipped in the lotion."

Miner nodded and glanced up at Olds.

"There's another print here—another slip on the way out," he said.

"No," Queenie said. "That was me, too."

Olds scratched his forehead and held his hand up to Miner, telling him to stop.

"Tell you what," said Olds, stepping back over to Queenie.

"Why don't you tell me everything you saw when you came here, everything you saw and did since coming into the building, up until you were knocked out."

So that's just what Queenie did. She told Olds about the kid who called her a chickenhead, and how she said he was fat, and how she walked up the stairs and heard a dog barking and how she knocked on the door but there was no answer, but the door was open so she came in and looked around a little bit and looked at the picture of Trigger and the blond boy on the table, and said, "Well look at you," and how she flipped open the address book (Queenie stretched the truth a little here; she said she opened the address book looking for stray paper to leave a note; she didn't want to say how she liked going through people's personal things), and she how ate her other crumb cake and thought she smelled a mouse and she went into the bathroom and saw Trigger dead and was standing there, fairly shocked, when she heard a creak and honestly did think it was a cockroach, and how she was then hit with what might or might not have been a frozen steak and was in a great deal of pain when she first woke up but was now only in a fair amount of pain.

Olds looked over at the bored paramedic standing next to the window, who glanced at Queenie blandly.

"Are you requesting medical assistance?" he said. He was chewing gum.

"No, forget it. The sorbet's really doing the trick," she said, smiling fakely.

"Did you touch anything else?" Olds asked.

"No," said Queenie. "Wait, yes, the Barn-Trin. The Motrin. Over there," she said, pointing to the open bottle on the counter. "Hey," she said, turning back to Olds. "Am I free to go?"

Olds turned around to glance at Detective Miner. Then he turned back to Queenie.

"Sure, Miss Sells, you're free to go."

"Thank you," Queenie said, sounding relieved.

"But I want to let you know," he said quietly, almost under his breath. "It wouldn't be a smart thing to leave town right now."

Queenie was confused. I'm not leaving town, she thought. Were other people leaving town? Was it a three-day weekend coming up?

"Is it a three-day weekend coming up?" she said.

"No," said Olds. "All I'm saying is you seem like a smart young l—," he started, then stopped but he didn't close his eyes or flinch. This one didn't seem to be as painful. "Smart young l—" Almost but not quite. "Young lady," he said.

Queenie combed his face for signs. What is he getting at? she thought. He better not ask me out. That would just be the whipped cream on the rocky road at this point, she thought.

"Thanks?" Queenie said tentatively.

"You're welcome," he said slowly, a little bit annoyed. Then he handed her his card which read, "Detective Daniel Olds, 37th Precinct, 256 E. 98th Street, 212-850-7273." And then, quieter, he said, "Stay close to your phone, Miss Sells. I'm going to be in touch with you within the next thirty-six hours."

"Sure. Right on," said Queenie.

"You'll remember what I said about not leaving town?"

"Yes," said Queenie, exasperated.

He nodded and looked incredibly serious just then. Queenie smiled wide like an idiot and stared at his face. Then she got it.

"Wait," she said, turning her head slightly. "Am I a *suspect* for crying out loud?"

"No, Miss Sells, not as of yet. We'll be in touch with you shortly," he said quickly, all business.

"Look, I didn't do this—I didn't even know this girl," Queenie said.

"A friend of a friend. You told me," said Olds.

"Yes, but something tells me you weren't listening so good."

Olds held his hands up, almost in defense.

"It would be best for all of us if you left right now," he said, somewhat gently.

Queenie stared at him. Then she looked to Detective Miner, who had his hands on his hips, skirting his blazer up. He turned away.

"Good-bye, Miss Sells," said Olds.

"Bye," said Queenie, and she left.

By the time she hit the street, the sorbet felt like a lukewarm bean bag in her hand. She knocked the pint gently against her temple and shook her head, unable to believe her shitty, shitty luck.

An hour later Queenie was back in her apartment with ice in a paper towel pressed to her head, trying not to fall asleep. The TV was on; she was watching cartoon robots. It seemed like they would be very heavy and slow-moving, being made of metal like they were, but they didn't have any trouble flying and jumping and generally being pretty nimble.

Then the robots began to make her nauseous—leaping around with their big clunky bodies. Her head throbbed every time their feet left the ground. She turned the TV off.

Her eyes hurt from being open; the lids felt like plastic wrap. Don't fall asleep, don't fall asleep, she thought—what if you have a concussion. Just close them for a second. Close your eyes for two minutes. Set your alarm, she thought. She pictured herself standing up and twisting the knobs on her clock radio, watching the numbers flip to four-something, and it was all so real, the way the sun was coming through the window, and how the ridges of the clock dial felt on her fingertips; she could've sworn she was actually doing it, actually setting the alarm for herself so she didn't go into a deep Sleeping-Beauty-Queen-style sleep and not wake up for days and days.

She was long gone. The sleep was hard and deep and black. When she opened her eyes, Trigger Happy was lying on the floor of her apartment, at Queenie's feet. Queenie thought, You see? Just a dream. You fell and hit your head and dreamed you saw a dead person.

Then a chorus of people she couldn't see shouted, "Poor Queenie!"

"I guess you hit your head," said a voice that sounded like it came from an invisible game show host, happy and smarmy.

She'd had a few hallucinations on a semiregular basis, but they consisted mostly of black inkblots swimming around out of the corner of her eye, and as soon as she'd turn her head to get a better look, they'd disappear.

"So that's what must have happened," the game show host said again, really so happy to be sharing all of this.

"Yes," Queenie tried to answer, but her mouth was full of marbles.

Then Trigger Happy's body rose and started to float in front of Queenie, naked and stiff as a diving board, nothing moving, her small hard breasts and tiny shaved bush, her collarbone and pelvis protruding because she was so damn skinny, like Baby Watson but sexier somehow. Even then, even dead, floating in front of Queenie she was somehow sexier.

"See what can happen when you don't eat from the four major food groups?" the game show host said.

Queenie tried to say, They don't have the food groups anymore—it's a pyramid now, but again her mouth was stopped up.

She stretched her hand out to touch Trigger's body. Then her arm started to shake violently, out of control, like a tight guitar string.

Then Trigger, still looking fairly dead, grabbed Queenie by the wrist, opened her eyes, and screamed, "BITCH!"

And then she heard, "Maggots! Maggots! Maggots are falling like rain!" Who is screaming that? she thought, her eyes fluttering open. It was her answering machine—it was Gwar. You know—the band, a voice said in Queenie's head. You saw them play on Halloween a few years ago. They threw blood on you. It was very festive.

Queenie was still sitting up on the couch; her head had just fallen back. Her ass and legs were wet from where she had dropped the paper towel and the ice had melted. She was sweaty and weak and hungry and hot, almost like she had a fever. Her fingers and toes were freezing cold.

She couldn't understand why Gwar was on her answering machine. She couldn't believe she'd put it on her outgoing message and just forgot.

Then the voices got quieter; the receiver was pulled away from the speaker, and a voice said, "Wake up, bitch!"

It was Meade.

Queenie reached out to grab the phone but saw three of them floating in front of her. She shut her eyes hard and reached for the handset, batting it with her knuckles.

"Meade? Meade?" she said when she finally lifted it to her mouth.

"Jesus, what the hell are you sleeping off? I called three times," he said.

Queenie looked at the clock radio, and it said 5:12.

"Oh God," she said, holding her head. "Where are you?"

"I'm at Wintertown. Where the hell are you?"

Queenie wiggled her fingers in front of her face. Fifteen shrank to ten, ten not quite down to the regulation five; a couple still had twins, but it was better than before.

"I was asleep," she said slowly.

"No kidding."

"No, Meade, I have, like, a concussion."

Meade was outraged. "So what the hell are you doing sleeping? Isn't that the worst thing for it? Couldn't you die from that, or go into a comatose state? Isn't that, like, Rule Number One on concussion pamphlets?"

"Yeah, probably."

"What you need is BEER," said Meade proudly.

"I don't think I can drink anything right now," she said meekly.

"If you're not here in a half hour, we're no longer friends, and you're out of the will," he said, and then he hung up.

Queenie stood up and went into the bathroom and took four Phar-Profen, then left to go meet Meade.

On the way to the subway, she stopped at Zia Maria's for a slice of pizza because she hadn't eaten since the crumb cake and was starving. She approached the counter and put her hand on the warm glass, looking at all the different kinds, wanting to buy them all, like they were puppies in a pet store. Except she didn't want to eat the puppies, per se, but at that moment she was so hungry she probably could've nibbled on a soft little hind leg if she had to, listen to their soft black noses sizzle in a pan.

There were a pair of idiots standing next to her.

The girl was saying, "I told them I wasn't drinking anymore, and everywhere I go, if I like, see someone in a bar, they always say, Hey, sit down, have a beer, and I tell them I'm not drinking anymore. And they say why, and I say, Because I have a medical condition."

The guy said, "Yeah."

"And they're like, Oh well, okay, and then they don't call me anymore, and it's like, If you guys were only my friends when I was drunk, then you're not my fucking friends."

" 'Cause you have . . ."

"Right, 'cause I have a *medical condition*, " she said.

No kidding you have a medical condition, thought Queenie. You're boring as shit.

Then the tiny Puerto Rican guy came to the counter and smiled at Queenie, and everything was okay because soon she would be fed. Everyone who worked at Zia Maria's was so tiny, so compactly built. Fun size, thought Queenie, like those little Snickers bars.

Queenie tapped the glass.

"Tomatoes?" the Puerto Rican guy said.

"Tomatoes," said Queenie.

Queenie figured she didn't have to skimp just yet, and she might as well get one of the fancy three-fifty slices since she had so much money left over from Hummer, and she'd had such a bitch of a day.

The fancy pizza had thick wheels of mozzarella and tomatoes and basil leaves, and Queenie thought it was probably the best thing she had ever eaten. Her appetite had been all screwy since the weekend between hangovers and concussions. If it's not one thing, it's another, thought Queenie. She swallowed her pizza in the six or seven yards between the pizza shop and the subway.

The station was full of people getting off the L from the other direction, the Manhattan direction. Queenie was pleased to see that the train itself was not crowded. She sat next to a man reading a

Polish newspaper. She stared at the letters and thought how she couldn't guess how to pronounce those words correctly in a million years, not if someone had a gun to her head.

She was pleased, however, to see that the letter, Q, existed in Polish. Maybe it didn't sound the same, but she couldn't afford to be picky when it came to other languages. She liked seeing a capital "Q" printed in a newspaper headline, big and black and strong. It was better in a way than seeing her full name.

She had used only the "Q" for years, until her first-grade teacher made her write the whole thing, the intricate and tiresome "Queenie." She never remembered learning the Q—she knew that Uncle Si had taught her, but no matter how far she could think back, she just always seemed to know it.

The first time she remembered actually writing it, though, was not long after her father's funeral, when she sat on Uncle Si's lap in the government lady's office. Queenie's awful grandmother was there, and the government lady told Queenie's grandmother and Uncle Si where to sign, and they did, and then Queenie tugged at the sleeve of Uncle Si's sweater.

"She wants to sign it, too," said Uncle Si.

"There's no place for her to sign. She's a minor," said the government lady.

"Right, I know, miss, but maybe you could pretend there was a little space at the bottom where she could sign," Si said to her, winking.

The government lady shrugged, and said, "I guess she could sign over here," tapping the left margin.

"We sure do appreciate it," said Uncle Si. "Say thank you to the lady," he said to Queenie.

"Thank you," said Little Queenie.

Queenie's awful grandmother rolled her eyes.

Queenie gripped the pen and bit her bottom lip, and in the left margin, she made a long oval Q.

The train chugged to a stop at First Avenue, and Queenie got off and walked through the East Village, which was somewhat busy, and finally crossed Houston into the Lower East Side. Houston was jammed with cars and cabs and horns. There was a crowd of people milling up from the F train stop, but not many on the street.

She walked to Orchard Street, to the doors underneath the red neon BAR sign and went inside.

Meade was behind the bar at the other end, talking to a girl with a bike chain around her waist and to Felix, who was drinking a martini.

"Hey, Queenie," said Stanley, the large black guy with dreads who worked the door. He was standing at the pinball machine.

"Hiya, Stanley," said Queenie. "How's tricks?"

"Very good," said Stanley.

Queenie walked up to the bar.

"Queenie, helloooo," called Felix, wiggling his fingers.

"Hi, Felix," said Queenie.

"Well, well, well," said Meade, flipping his head from side to side in a sister-daughter way. "Look who thought kindly enough to join us."

Queenie sat down, leaving a barstool between her and Felix. Meade continued talking to the girl with the bike chain as he opened the cooler and pulled out a bottle of Bud Light.

"The only way I can describe it," he was saying, "is that I had to pull it out like a rope."

"So, Queenie," Felix said, touching his hair gently. "Have you heard the one about the one-legged jockey?"

"I think you told me last week," she said. "But you can tell me again if it'll make you feel good."

Felix laughed. "Oh, fuck it."

Meade set the Bud Light down in front of Queenie and grabbed her chin. He turned her head to the right, then left.

"So where's the concussion?" he said. "I don't see a goddamn thing."

Queenie shook her head free, and it hurt a little.

"It's right here," Queenie said, pointing to her temple. "You can touch it if you want to."

"No, no, I believe you. Ours is a friendship based on trust," he said, shrugging. "So what happened? You fall?" he said, and he took a swig of his beer. "Little Queenie-queen fell and broke her crown."

Queenie shook her head quickly and rolled her eyes over at Felix, and he noticed.

"That's okay, ladies," said Felix. "I've got to powder my powder anyway."

"Felix, you're a special guy," said Queenie.

"You're a honeybee," he said, standing. He took his martini by the stem and walked gracefully to the bathroom.

"He takes his martini to the bathroom?" said Queenie.

"He takes his martini to church," said Meade. "So what the hell happened to you? Spill it."

Queenie spilled it. She told Meade all about the dead girl and getting hit on the head and stepping in the lotion and the cops. She also told him he may have saved her life by waking her up from a concussion sleep, but he shouldn't let this go to his head.

Meade listened attentively. "Wow," he said. "That's something. Have you called the Fish?"

Then the front door swung open and three loud girlies tripped in, all after-work crowd. They sat at the other end of the bar and tittered.

"Who feels it on a Tuesday night?" Meade hollered, holding his arms up, as if in victory.

No one responded. The girls at the end of the bar looked at him like he was a squid.

"I feel it, baby," Felix said, back from the bathroom.

"Thanks, Felix," said Meade. Then he walked down to the newcomers, and said, "Now what can I get you people who don't feel it on a Tuesday?"

She drank her beer and listened to Felix tell the one about the one-legged jockey to the girl with the bike chain around her waist. Meade repeated orders: "Two T and Ts, one Absolut Cape Cod, one Amstel."

Queenie sipped her beer and couldn't help but think of Trigger. I guess this is just one of those weird things, she thought. One of those things you just happen to see, then you remember it forever. Uncle Si used to tell a story about being on a ship in the war, making runs from New York to Bombay, very mild, very antiseptic, no real threats. The first time they made the passage, when they pulled into the port at Bombay, coasting into a narrower and narrower canal, there were dozens and dozens of bodies floating in the water, rotting—old people, young people, children, dogs. Si said the stench was unbearable. He said, *"I don't know they been killed or if those folks just didn't bury their dead."* But the weirdest thing was, he said, was that his shipmates, some of whom had made the passage ten or fifteen times, never warned him about the bodies and didn't ever acknowledge them. Si said the sailors would lower dinghies into the water now and again when they were docked, and they'd push on through the bodies, arms and legs knocking against the paddles and the sides of the boat, and the sailors who'd been there a while just ignored them. "Thought I was damn near going nuts," said Si. "Thought maybe they wasn't there at all."

He'd told Queenie he thought about those floating bodies almost every day of his whole life.

"Hey, Felix," said Queenie. "Can you spare a quarter?"

Felix opened his man-purse and fished around. He pulled out a quarter and waved it at her. Queenie took it from his fingers. It was wet.

"Sorry," he said, licking his fingertips. "Olive juice."

"Don't worry about it," she said. "Thanks."

Queenie stood and walked to the pay phone near the bathroom and called Hummer's cell number, and the phone told her to deposit seventy-five more cents.

Queenie groaned. Cell phones are a real pain in the dick, she thought.

She hustled back to the bar and hiked herself up, balanced the balls of her feet on the gold bar that ran across the floor. She tapped the quarter loudly on the edge.

"Meade, Meade," she called.

Meade was still at the other end, making eyes at Cape Cod.

"Hey!" Queenie shouted, and she pounded her fist like she was tenderizing meat.

Meade walked over with a shot glass in his hand.

"Wait your turn. Jesus," he said, opening the cooler.

"No, I need change for a dollar," she said.

"Oh," he said, turning around. "So you don't need another beer?"

Queenie rolled her eyes. "Yes, I need another beer."

Meade raised his eyebrows. "Aren't you forgetting something?"

Queenie sighed. "Yes, *of course* I need another beer."

"That's better," he said.

He reached into the cooler and pulled another Bud Light, popped the top, and set it in front of her, along with four quarters.

Queenie went back to the phone and deposited seventy-five big fat cents, and dialed Hummer's number and thought about what else she could spend seventy-five cents on. A flashy sticker of the Virgin Mary or a shamrock on a key chain from the quarter toy machines at Key Foods, at least.

"Heyyyy," Hummer's voice mail said, sounding stoned. "It's Hummer Fish here. I can't take your call right now, but please leave a message of up to thirty seconds. Thanks. Bye."

Shit, thought Queenie. This isn't really a thirty-second message. This message needs at least a full minute. Not that she knew what she was going to say, but she was hoping it would come to her.

"Hiya, Hummer, it's Queenie. Um, you've probably already heard from this guy, Olds—he's a cop, you can't miss him, he's got a mean-ass stutter. But if you haven't," she said, and she paused and contemplated just saying, Gimme a call, big guy, but that would mean she'd have to talk to him in real time. Best to just tell him now, she thought. "So if you haven't heard, from this guy Olds—Trigger, you know—Tara's dead. I went to her apartment, and she was dead there. Somebody, I think somebody killed her." Queenie thought about saying, They kinda think it's me and thanks for the capital Tee-rouble, but she didn't. "So, look, I'm sorry. They hit me on the head, too," she said, feeling defensive. Then she felt like she should say something comforting. At least you have your fiancée, she thought. "Anyway, I don't really know much else, because they sent me home, but she looked . . . she looked real peaceful though." What the fuck are you talking about, Queenie? "And I gave the cops your number, this guy named Olds so he might call you. And you can call me when you get—" and then the phone beeped at her.

"Fuck," Queenie said. Who the fuck is making money by cutting voice mail message time short, she thought.

She hung up the phone and shuffled back to the bar. Meade was still talking to Cape Cod but glanced at Queenie and came back over. Cape Cod looked confused. She had red hair and a face like a melted candle—all droops.

"You talk to him?" Meade said.

"I left a message."

"You left a message? Saying 'your girlfriend's dead'?" Meade said, incredulous.

"Pretty much."

"Jesus, Queenie, that's not a thing to do. You can't do that," he said, taking a bottle of tequila from the rack.

"What'm I supposed to do? I gotta tell him, right? I can't let him think she's alive. I'm supposed to tell him everything's jake?"

"You say, 'Call me back, chief.' "

" 'Big guy.' "

"Right—chief, big guy, princess, what have you. You don't leave that shit on voice mail."

"I'm not home, Meade," Queenie said, getting pissed. "Who knows when he's gonna call—and the cops probably got to him anyway."

"Probably," sniffed Meade. "But you never know."

Queenie shook her head. "I refuse to feel bad about this. I didn't do anything," she said quietly.

"Oh shit," Meade said, covering his mouth.

"What?"

"I don't think I should say."

"What?"

"I don't think I should say."

"Goddammit, am I going to have to go outside for five minutes?" she said.

"It's just that," Meade began slowly and dramatically, narrowing his eyes. "What if you killed her and you blacked out and thought it was someone else? Like *Angel Heart.*"

Queenie stared at him. "Possessed by Satan?"

"You can take or leave the Satan part."

"Then it would be more like *Primary Colors.*"

"I don't think you mean *Primary Colors.*"

"What's *Primary Colors?*"

"It's a roman-a-clef about Bill Clinton. John Travolta's in it."

"Then what do I mean?" Queenie said.

"Primal Fear."

"Right. *Primal Fear.* Sure. It was a split personality. They're gonna track me down and throw me in the clink and lethally inject me with whatever that shit is—Jim Jones Special Kool-Aid."

Meade looked sad, but only briefly.

"I could be your spiritual advisor," he said.

He poured a shot of clear tequila and passed it to Queenie. Queenie drank it. It stung.

"Sure you can," she said. "You're a real asshole. I'm never speaking to you again," she said, standing.

"All right then, good-bye forever," said Meade.

Queenie looked at her beer. "Can I have a cup please?" she said.

Meade gave her a glossy blue plastic cup, and Queenie poured the rest of her beer into it. Meade looked over at Cape Cod.

"Are you gonna hit on that girl?" Queenie said.

"I don't know," said Meade. "There's something weird about her."

"I'll tell you what's weird about her—she looks like a damn candle."

Meade's eyes widened. "You know, that's not what came to mind at first, but I guess you might be right."

They watched her suck down the Cape Cod through the skinny red straw.

Queenie shook her head. "You'd have droopy Richard Nixon babies."

Meade threw his hands up. "It's always going to be something."

Then a crowd of assholes poured in from the street, already drunk. They were mostly girls, cropped tops and smeared makeup.

"Oh Christ," Meade said. "Start mixing the Seabreezes."

"I gotta go," said Queenie.

"Where the hell are you going?"

"The Sisters."

"Have fun."

"Uh-huh."

Queenie stood and picked her cup up, waved to Felix. He waved his straw at her. She walked past the giggling girls as Meade announced, "I'm sorry, you just missed last call." He always said that to drunk people, no matter what time it was. The girls gasped and clucked. Queenie smiled and left.

It was a beautiful day out on the street. The sun wasn't down yet; it hung low like an ornament and was turning orange. Queenie drank from her cup of beer and walked down Orchard, then took a right on Stanton.

She dropped the empty cup into a garbage can and looked at a young black woman, maybe sixteen years old, wearing a bandanna and reading *Chicken Soup for the Teenage Soul*. The girl looked up at Queenie and scowled. They should rename it, thought Queenie. *Chicken Soup for Girls Who Look Like They Can Kick Your Ass Right into Next Tuesday*.

Queenie looked up at the sign flashing LAS HERMANAS. It was twisted neon bulbs, all green, two Spanish dancer ladies with their skirts kicked up. They didn't have faces, though. Queenie just figured faces were too hard, had too much detail to curl into those neon strips.

Queenie pushed the door open. The restaurant was full. People talked loudly and appeared to be very involved in their conversations. Queenie wondered how many of them were actually bored to tears and just faking.

The thing about The Sisters was that the food was subpar but the margaritas were amazing, and you could get them to go, which was right up there with the electric car in terms of ingenious ideas, to Queenie's mind. It didn't rightly matter how good or bad the food was anyway; it smelled good just then and even though Queenie had had that fancy slice of pizza, she started thinking about a tamale, and her stomach growled like a bull-pup.

Dogs will eat pretty much anything, thought Queenie, as she made her way to the tiny bar. They won't care if it's a tamale or not. Meade had a friend named Davenport who had a really old cat named Silky, and the poor thing's body had seriously started to break down. It must have been twenty years old, thought Queenie— had a face like a hubcap. Davenport also had a really young big stupid dog named Sweet Mary, and one time apparently, Silky had rejected her lunch and barfed in a neat little pile in front of the TV, which Davenport was watching. And Davenport was building up impetus to wipe the barf up when Sweet Mary rolled in and licked it all up like it was ice cream.

At least they were kind of self-sufficient, thought Queenie; Davenport could go on vacation anytime he liked and not worry about the pets because Silky was always producing waste and Sweet Mary was always eating it.

Queenie didn't really want to think about tamales anymore.

She walked up to the bar, and the old Mexican guy nodded at her.

"Can I get one to go?" said Queenie.

"Mixing right now," he said, pointing to the machine. "Ten minutes?"

"Sure," said Queenie, sitting down.

There was a Spanish newspaper on the counter; Queenie pulled it closer. There was a photo of an older lady drinking a cup of coffee, her head leaned back, laughing. The headline next to the picture read, "Murio Silvia Cortez." Queenie looked at the first sentence. Queenie did not speak Spanish but put together that Silvia Cortez was an actress who had died: *"La actriz Silvia Cortez fallecio esta madrugada en su domicilio a las 01:30 horas."*

That's too bad, thought Queenie. Silvia Cortez looked like a nice lady, but maybe the photo was from a movie. Maybe she was just *playing* a nice lady. But even so, thought Queenie, it's a testament to her talent. The next sentence in the article read, *"Silvia Cortez participo en 38 cintas, como* El Rey de Tijuana *y* Belleza."

Wow, thought Queenie. Thirty-eight cintas is nothing to sneeze at. Most people would be lucky to be in one cinta.

Then Queenie began to think about if Trigger Happy would get an obituary. How did it work in New York? Did the family have to call up the *Times?* Queenie began to write one in her head: Tara Rote, age twenty-five or twenty-six, died yesterday, or maybe the day before, anytime, really between Saturday and today. She was a stripper and liked purple.

Would there even be a funeral? Maybe the young blond boy in the picture would come. Maybe her estranged father, thought Queenie—yes that was it, her estranged father, with white hair and a v-neck sweater, old and blustery, hasn't seen his only child Trigger in ten years, no Trig's too young—seven years. But if he's coming and is a virtual stranger, then who sets up the funeral. Maybe the crew at the Paper Doll. Forget that part, thought Queenie. Trig's father would come reluctantly, only because he heard about it through the blond boy who is also a relation, a cousin maybe. And he gets on the train from Connecticut, or somewhere in Westchester and he rides and doesn't read anything and looks at all the commuters and thinks, Thank God I'm retired.

And then when he finally gets there, to the funeral parlor, somewhere uptown, near where Trigger lived, he walks in and the place is full, not bursting at the seams but all the seats are taken, and he walks up the aisle and everyone turns around, and whispers, That's her estranged father. He all but disowned her when she moved to the city seven years ago. There's Baby Watson in the front row, and the rockabilly bartender, and Hummer and his fiancée, curiously enough, and they all watch, and Trigger's father approaches the coffin and looks down.

Then it's like something gets unleashed or unlocked, and he turns, panicked, and runs back down the aisle, out the door, knocking into Queenie on the way out.

"Hi, Queenie!" And now Queenie turned and saw that it was Meggy Bunny, who once dated Tommy Roses for a solid three weeks.

"Oh, hey, Bunny," said Queenie, thinking, please no hug, no hug.

But Bunny hugged her anyway and was wearing some kind of shampoo or perfume that smelled faintly of urine.

"How have you been?" said Bunny.

"Fine," said Queenie. "How about you?"

Bunny smiled. "Great! Did you see the review of my show in the *Press?*"

"Show?" said Queenie. God, what did Bunny do? she thought. Does she have a band, is she an actor? Queenie couldn't remember.

"Yeah, my play," she said, her eyes wide.

She kind of looked like a japanimation superhero—big head, big dark eyes, stick-bundle body.

"No, I haven't seen it. Did you get a good write-up?"

"Oh God yes, they *never* like *anything*, and they said it was a postmodern masterpiece—that's exactly what they called it—a postmodern masterpiece."

"Wow," said Queenie.

"Yeah, it was really great because I got an agent and a manager out of it, and my manager has an office in L.A. so I can, like, move there and get totally hooked up."

"Wow," said Queenie.

"Everyone who sees it can't believe it's the first show I've ever had professionally produced. I mean, they're all like, where have you been, and I say I've been putting stuff on in black boxes since college, so now my agent wants to put up the one I wrote a couple of years ago, *Sawmill*—did you ever see that one?"

"No," said Queenie.

"That's the one about Hiroshima bomb survivors. I did a lot of research on that one. I read eleven books."

"Wow," said Queenie.

"But the one that got the review in the *Press*—that's the one everyone knows about. Maybe you've heard of it—it's called *Five U.S. Gallons*. It's about what would happen if there was a drought, if all the water, all the oceans and everything dried up. Did you ever see *Waterworld?*"

"No," said Queenie. She was lying. Of course she'd seen *Waterworld*, but Bunny didn't need to know that.

"Well, it's like a reverse *Waterworld*. That's exactly what the *Press* said—a reverse *Waterworld*."

"Wow," said Queenie.

She glanced at the old Mexican man, who grabbed a wax to-go cup and pulled the lever on the margarita machine. White icy margarita crawled out. Queenie licked her lips.

Bunny was still squawking.

"Anyway, it's still going on, and you should come—I might be able to comp you. Oh wait, no, now that I think about it I probably won't be able to. But I can give you a flyer . . ."

Queenie looked at the old man. He held up seven fingers. Oh well, thought Queenie. Pricey, but worth it. Queenie couldn't think of many things that were over in ten minutes and worth seven dollars, but a margarita from The Sisters was definitely one of them.

She counted out eight ones and laid them down. Bunny was still running off at her bony little mouth.

"It'll be up for three more weekends, and then it might extend through next month. You can buy tickets on-line if you want."

"Actually, Bunny, I'm leaving town pretty soon," said Queenie.

"Oh," said Bunny, deflated. "Where are you going?"

"Niagara Falls," said Queenie, and she took a sip of margarita.

Man, that's GOOD, thought Queenie. It was impossible for her to express how good it was without doing or saying something obscene, something that might gotten her arrested had she lived in Montana or Missouri or one of the more sensitive states.

"Oh, cool, for how long? Because the show's probably going to run through July," Bunny said hopefully.

"I'm actually moving there," said Queenie. "Indefinitely."

"Oh, wow. Why Niagara Falls?"

"That's where my fiancé's from," said Queenie.

"Oh my God! You're getting married? Congratulations, I had no idea!" Bunny said.

No shit, thought Queenie. If you'd shut your skeleton mouth for a fucking second and let someone else talk, maybe you would've found out about my fucking engagement.

"Who is he? Do I know him?" Bunny said.

"I don't think so. His name is Ray McSnoo."

"That's great, Queenie. Good for you," Bunny said, looking slightly thoughtful. "Wow, I just never thought of you as the marrying kind."

"Yeah, I never did either, you know, you're going about your business, you're all independent, but then you meet the right guy, and everything changes."

Bunny nodded slowly. She was really impressed with Queenie's attitudes about marriage.

"So I'm not going to be able to see your show," said Queenie.

"That's okay—there might be a little tour of it in the fall. I could send you the info. What's your email address?"

"I don't have the email," Queenie said.

"Oh," Bunny said, stumped. "Do you know your street address yet, in Niagara Falls?"

"No, not yet. Look, I'll get in touch with you, okay?"

"Let me give you my cell number," said Bunny.

She whipped out a pen and wrote her number down on a napkin that said Las Hermanas in the corner.

"Here you go," Bunny said, sort of singing it, handing the napkin to Queenie. "Stay in touch. And congratulations!"

"Thanks," said Queenie, holding the napkin by the corner. "See you later, Bunny."

Queenie darted for the door and almost knocked over a waitress carrying three plastic baskets of chips, one on top of the other.

Queenie said, "Sorry," and kept heading for freedom. When she got outside she muttered, "Jesus," and she ran across the street and started walking south very quickly, just to put some distance between her and Bunny.

Queenie examined the napkin. There was a bunny face drawn next to the name—little stick whiskers and two cricket paddles for ears.

That's charming, Queenie thought. They should have every asshole draw little pictures next to their names in the phone book. That would be super.

The margarita was sweating in her hand, and she took a big sip; it was melting quickly, turning from ice into margarita water, which wasn't such a bad thing. Queenie shook the water from her palm and slapped Bunny's napkin, name and number and cute little sketch side down on the margarita cup. She slid it around a little for good measure.

Queenie came to Delancey and turned right and looked at the sun setting. She lifted her hand to her forehead to shield her eyes.

"Ah, Trig," she said for some reason.

She was getting a little drunk.

Then someone ran into her from behind, shoulder against hers. He passed her—a tall, dusty-looking guy, scratching the back of his head fast, like a Chihuahua. Then he slipped through a green door, and Queenie looked up. It was an OTB.

Fate! she thought. Fate that Dusty ran into her and just happened to be going to the OTB. Queenie peered though the glass window and admired the green counters and all the many TVs. There was a close-up of a brown horse; flashbulbs went off around it. Its eyes were huge. The jockey stood beside it.

What could be better, thought Queenie. Sweet fast horses and their friendly elfin sidekicks. What was a better way to forget your troubles, forget you saw a dead person today.

Queenie stood frozen, staring at the horse on TV. Straight from the horse's mouth. You can lead a horse to water. Don't look a gift horse in the mouth.

"Are you a gift horse?" she said out loud. A couple walking by stared at her.

The horse shook its head, and its lips wiggled; it stepped up and down in place.

That's it, thought Queenie. Enough of this pissing around. I'm going to the fucking races.

Wednesday

So the next morning she was on her way. She didn't quite remember going to bed, just that she'd walked to Fourteenth Street up from Delancey, first on Essex, then on Avenue A, and she stopped into one bar per every two blocks to have a shot of Jagermeister.

Now her mouth tasted like licorice and vomit. Wow, she thought, did I vomit? She looked briefly around the apartment, sniffing, looking for signs but found none. She looked in the refrigerator for food of some kind, and there was only an open can of pineapple slices. Popsicles in the freezer, of course, but she just wasn't in the mood for icy flavored tubes. They all tasted pretty much the same even though each had ostensibly one of Five Fantastic Fruit Flavors, with Real Fruit Flavoring. No matter, she thought. I'll get something at the track.

Queenie turned on the shower and let it run for a second, then put her hand under the stream. It was lukewarm. She stripped down and looked at herself quickly in the long mirror. Oh man, she thought, grabbing onto her belly. That's what you get when your primary staples are beer and cheese.

She stepped into the shower and scrubbed down, washed her hair with a bar of soap because she kept forgetting to buy shampoo, and soon the clear shower curtain began to fog up. The water was getting warmer. Queenie closed her eyes and breathed the steam in. When she opened them, she pressed her hand against the curtain and watched it make a print. Slowly she brought her face to the shower curtain and blinked hard. She stayed there for a few seconds, looking at the sink and the mirror, blurry. The plastic smelled like mildew.

Then the water became scalding hot like it did sometimes for no good reason.

"Yeoww," said Queenie, and she batted at the faucet spastically.

The water stopped coming out of the head but had gathered in a pool in the tub and was slowly trickling down the drain, and the reserve was still burning. Queenie stepped up and down like a sheep in mud.

"Ow, ow, ow," she said.

All of her skin was pinkish. She stepped out of the tub and pulled a towel off the bar, which rattled. She'd yanked the towel rack off the wall twice before because the wall was made of nothing, cardboard practically; cream cheese would've held better, and now one side was always loose. Always screws loose, thought Queenie, and she laughed.

Queenie wrapped the towel around herself and kicked the tub.

"Fucker," she said.

She looked at herself in the mirror above the sink briefly and examined her face. She saw a slightly reddish spot on her chin. Oh no, this has got to go, she thought.

Queenie scratched at the spot gently at first, like it was a mosquito bite, and maybe it was, what did she know? She was no Dr. Zizmor. Not that it made a difference—it had to go whatever it was. It began to feel tender, so she scraped a little harder. By then the area around the spot was becoming pink and irritated, then there was a pinprick dot of blood in the middle. Queenie tore a thin square of toilet paper off the roll sitting on the toilet tank and pressed it to the spot and let it hang there for a few minutes as if she had cut herself shaving. I don't have time to deal with this right now, she thought. I have to get to the track.

Then she put on some clothes and counted her money. She had a hundred and twenty-six dollars, twenty of which could go to bets, another twenty for beer, plenty for soup and a racing form. What a beautiful day, she thought. No, she thought, locking her apartment door, what a beautiful country.

It was probably ten in the morning. The sky was overcast and looked about to pour, but it didn't bother Queenie. She looked long-ingly at the Turkey Club down the street, already pouring red eyes for early risers.

What I wouldn't give for a mimosa, she thought.

She walked down Bedford and glanced at the old Polish lady on the corner who always sat on her stoop in a fur coat. Queenie won-dered how she could take it in the summer, although she suspected the old lady had been dead for some time. The old lady didn't like the young people in the neighborhood much. One time she called Meade a "son of a whore." Meade had said to Queenie, "How do you think she knows my mother?"

Queenie was almost at the deli on the corner that she was certain was a cover for a drug operation. They never had any food or other typical deli items—no cigarettes, no beer, no ice cream, no tiny packets of Advil. There were only cans of diced green chilies and some paper towels and pretzels, but most of the shelves were wooden and bare, and there was always a young strung-out Puerto Rican guy sitting in a folding chair against the soda fridge in the back, nodding off.

But they did have newspapers out in front, and Queenie sped up when she saw them. She'd forgotten—the *Post* and the *Daily News* were probably all over Trigger. Queenie imagined the headlines as she approached: STRIPPER SLAIN—no one was just killed in the *News* or the *Post;* everyone was "slain." New York was a town full of peo-ple getting slain; it was all very *Excalibur.*

There would have to be some kind of clever word play or alliter-
ation, though; it wouldn't just be STRIPPER SLAIN. It would have to be
something like STRIPPER SLAIN IN SUPPOSED SUICIDE, she thought,
but much better, and cleverly abbreviated (STRIP SLAIN—SUP CIDE).
The *News* and the *Post* would think of something good—they're
goddamn professionals.

She stopped at the red-wire stands which held the papers, and her
eyes scanned all of them quickly for a familiar picture or something
about someone getting slain, but she didn't see anything like that.
She picked up a *Post* and examined the cover: it was a photo of the
hapless president, doing the stern eyebrow thing. The caption read
in block letters: PREZ SEZ TO MIDDLE EAST: BRING IT ON.

Okay, thought Queenie, international affairs are important; it's
understandable that Trigger wouldn't make the front page. She
started flipping through. Page 2, page 3, page 4. Shit going down in
Northern Ireland, okay, thirteen people injured in Missouri acid
spill, okay, that's pretty serious business.

Then things started to get a little silly. Pages 5 and 6 covered an
impromptu fashion show in SoHo (COVERT COUTURE), and then the
obligatory twenty- or thirty-page assault on the liberals (DEMS SAY:
FREE BABY KILLER!) interspersed with various local news pieces.

Queenie's eyes kept jumping, and then in the corner on page 9, a
very small headline, just big enough for ladybugs to read: WOMAN
KILLED IN SPAN. HARLEM. Trigger didn't even get to be slain. The
story was two sentences long:

> A twenty-six-year-old stripper, identified as Tara Rote, was
> found shot dead yesterday at her apartment in Spanish
> Harlem. Police are currently following a number of leads but
> do not yet have a suspect in custody.

Jeez, thought Queenie, that's pretty piss-poor reporting on behalf of
the *Post*. She had really come to expect more from them. She
grabbed the *Daily News*, and there was almost exactly the same
photo of the president on the cover—very stern but really more like

a little kid trying to look like a gangster—tight thin lips and furrowed brow, and the headline read, TUFF LUV 4 MIDDLE EAST.

Queenie flipped through. I'm so fucking glad that this fashion show got so much coverage, she thought (SURPRISE SUMMER STYLE). People should really have all the facts about that sort of thing. God knows there aren't enough news items about handbags.

And then finally, on page 12 no less, another small column—not even a column, just a tiny box in the lower right hand corner with the headline: DEATH ON UP. EAST SIDE, and the story was a whopping three sentences:

> Police confirmed the death of twenty-six-year-old Tara Rote yesterday. Rote, a stripper and alleged prostitute, was found shot in her apartment on East 104th Street.
>
> In an unrelated incident, prostitute Prentice Hamilton, 22, of Crown Heights, was strangled by her boyfriend, Anthony Miller, 23, last night at Miller's home.

Queenie dropped the paper, frustrated. The Puerto Rican guy inside the store stared at her suspiciously through the window. Queenie kept moving.

Jesus Christ, thought Queenie, the *News* didn't even give Trig her own fucking story. They just lumped her in with the other hookers. If they're going to report the news like that, they should just make it a section like the page 6 spot or "The Word" or any of the idiot editorials. Dead Hooker Corner or something.

Queenie walked down into the subway station, and a train had just arrived, and a group of people got off, not rush hour people but at least twenty or thirty of them, and they mauled through all four turnstiles before Queenie had a chance to swipe in. Four turnstiles, assholes, she thought. You might leave one open for those of us going *this* way.

Queenie looked around for someone to roll her eyes at in solidarity, but there was only a bald man in a skirt, and he was smiling calmly.

Wow, thought Queenie. Whatever's going on for him in his head sure is working because he looks pretty damn relaxed.

Queenie finally swiped in and began to sift through the stragglers who'd exited from the far end of the train. She walked down the stairs and heard the accordion guy. Thank God it was the accordion guy and not one of those long-hair hippie bastards, or the Kate Bush girl. Queenie knew on an intellectual level that they were all expressing themselves, and that was indeed a beautiful thing, but did they have to do it so loudly? One time Queenie thought about punching one in the face, the short skinny guy who screamed all his home-grown lyrics about how he saw faces in the crowd and he wondered if they see him, and Queenie thought she could easily punch him in the face and no one would care, she might even get cheered on. Hell, she might even get a date out of it.

Queenie could hear the Manhattan-bound train coming. She needed to go the other way and figured she just missed hers. I don't even care, she thought. I'm going to the races. *A Day at the Races.* She used to watch that movie with Uncle Si, and he'd make her fast-forward through the "Who Dat Man?" number, when the Marx Brothers are all jumping around in blackface.

He'd tried to explain it in a nutshell: "People thought that kind of thing was funny." He also made her fast-forward through the "What Makes the Red Man Red" number in the *Peter Pan* cartoon.

She started humming "Who Dat Man" anyway, singing the lyrics in her head. All God's children got rhythm, all God's children got something else—she couldn't remember what. For the life of her she could not think of what else all God's children got. All God's children got speed? she thought. That doesn't make any damn sense, it can't be speed.

The Manhattan-bound train screeched to a stop, and the doors opened. Queenie kept staring at the accordion guy, his music drowned out by the train and the scraping rails.

Then there was a hand on her arm, yanking her.

"Come on," Hummer said, into her hair.

"Dude," said Queenie. It was a funny thing—Queenie only

called people "Dude" when she was surprised. "What's going on? I'm going the other direction."

"We have to get on this train now," Hummer said, his voice low. He looked above Queenie's head at the people getting off the train.

"I'm going to Aqueduct," she said, turning around to see what Hummer was looking at.

"I have to talk to you—look, I'll pay you for your time, you just have to get on this train with me right now," he said.

Queenie didn't think. She couldn't immediately argue in the face of money. She let Hummer lead her.

"Okay, you can let go though," she said, trying to unclasp his hand.

He didn't let go and led her quickly into the subway car as the doors slid shut.

"Let go, Hummer," she said, and she poked him in the ribs.

Hummer let go of her, and said, "Ow."

"Well, I'm coming with you," she said, holding her arm.

Queenie found a seat and sat down and watched Hummer approach her. His eyes darted around, casing the joint, and he looked tired and pale.

"Would you sit?" said Queenie.

He sat down next to her as the train shook from side to side. It always shook in the tunnel.

"Hey, why aren't you at work?" said Queenie.

"I called in sick," he said.

Queenie's ears began to plug up. She didn't like to think about this part of the ride, when they were underwater; it made her feel like everything was closing in. She opened her mouth wide so her ears would pop.

"What, you find that so surprising?" Hummer said, almost cocky.

"No, no, my ears are plugged. That wasn't a surprise face. You'll know when I'm surprised," she said. She didn't know what the hell that was supposed to mean.

Hummer leaned forward and looked to the right, through the door to the next car.

"What's going on?" Queenie said, not at all urgently.

Hummer didn't answer. He kept staring into the next car.

"What the hell are you looking at?" Queenie said, leaning forward.

"Lean back," he said tensely, pulling her arm. "I think I'm being followed."

Queenie laughed, and Hummer appeared offended.

"Who's following you?" she said.

"I don't know."

"Then how are you going to recognize them, say, in the next car?" Then her heart dropped and she whispered, "Wait, is it a cop?"

"I don't think so," said Hummer.

"Who then?"

"I don't know."

Queenie nodded. Hummer is being pursued by ghosts, she thought. Maybe one in particular.

"Hey, I'm sorry about your girlfriend," said Queenie.

"Shh," said Hummer fiercely, holding his finger to his lips. "Not here," he whispered.

Of course not here, thought Queenie. What a drama queen.

"Have the police talked to you yet?" she said.

"Not. Here," Hummer snapped.

Queenie sighed loudly.

The train pulled into First Avenue, and Hummer stood, so Queenie did, too. The doors opened, and Hummer bolted out. Queenie caught her breath and ran after him.

They came above ground, and Hummer took off immediately, Queenie right behind.

"Where can we talk?" said Hummer, walking quickly across the street.

Queenie looked on the corner, at Blimpie and Mackey's bar. The clock above the drugstore read 11:07. Mackey's wasn't open yet. Queenie remembered she was hungry.

"Let's get some sliders," she said.

"What's that? What's sliders? What does that mean? Is that drugs?" Hummer said nervously.

Queenie closed her eyes. "No, they're hamburgers. We can put drugs in them, though, if you'd like."

Hummer shook his head quickly, and they crossed Fourteenth Street and headed south.

"I don't eat red meat," he said.

Queenie rolled her eyes. "They have chicken, too," she said. "Hey, so have you talked to the cops yet or what?"

"*Shhh,*" Hummer snapped, and he placed his hand on her back and pushed her gently, scooting her along.

"Where is this place?" he said, impatient.

"It's right there," said Queenie, pointing to the corner of Twelfth and First, at Jaffee's Sliders.

Queenie felt a drop on her face and couldn't tell if it was rain or water from an air conditioner. Hummer took her arm again and ran across the street, against the solid DON'T WALK. Cabs and cars honked. Usually Queenie enjoyed flipping drivers off, or even hitting the hoods with her palm if they were close enough—that was really her favorite; it gave her a little rush. She had to take her thrills where she could get them. But Hummer shuffled her along too quickly.

"Can you hold on a goddamn minute? I really don't have much trouble walking by myself anymore," she said, starting to get pissed.

Hummer let go and walked ahead of her into Jaffee's, letting the glass door shut in her face. She sighed, and said, "Classy."

She pushed the door open again and saw that Hummer had sat down at a table in the corner, trying to appear calm—for who, Queenie didn't know; they were the only customers. She guessed not many folks wanted sliders at eleven in the morning, and she thought that was just plain crazy.

Queenie turned toward the counter.

"Queenie," Hummer whined, exasperated, gripping the ends of the table.

"Lemme get some food," she said. "You want anything?"

"No," Hummer said, pouty.

Queenie shrugged and turned around again.

"Wait," said Hummer. "Do they have Shasta?"

"I don't think anyone's had Shasta since 1985," Queenie said.

He folded his arms, and said, "Then, nothing."

Queenie nodded. Shasta or bust, she thought.

She walked up to the counter, and a young woman with long black hair that looked wet, probably Queenie's age or a little younger, stood there and managed to look bored and real pissed off at the same time.

"Hi there," said Queenie.

The girl said nothing. A goddamn oil painting.

"I would like four cheeseburger sliders, please," said Queenie.

The girl pressed buttons on the electronic register and made them beep.

"Would you like to try our special Cajun fries?" the girl said, with absolutely no intonation. The computer in *War Games* had more vocal color, thought Queenie.

"Not today, thanks. Can I also get a Coke?"

"Size?"

"What are the sizes?" said Queenie.

The girl sighed. Now Queenie was in real trouble. The girl pointed to the chart above her head that displayed the three sizes. She must think I'm some piece of work, thought Queenie. But really, who can blame me, she thought, what with all these places that have a huge small, and then the large is just outrageous. It's like the size of someone's neck. Not to mention all those places that just did away with medium altogether.

"Sometimes they don't have medium," Queenie said quietly in her defense. "I would like a medium Coke, please," she said meekly.

"Five-thirteen," the girl said.

Queenie handed her a ten, and the girl plucked the bills and the coins out of the register like she was going to throw them. Then she handed the change to Queenie. Her hands were wet and cold.

"Thanks," said Queenie, and she dumped the massive amount of change into her right pants pocket. She stood there patiently.

"I'll call your number," the girl finally said.

"Fantastic," said Queenie, and she went to sit down.

"So, Hummer," she said, cheery, like she was interviewing him for a job. "Have you talked to the cops yet?"

"I'm supposed to go up there later," he said. "But I needed to talk to you first," he said, and he paused.

"Okay," said Queenie. "Well, here I am. I'm not at Aqueduct or anything, so why don't you lay it on me."

"I need you to find someone else," he said.

"Excuse me?"

"I need you to find someone else." Then he leaned across the table, and said, "I'll pay you to find someone else."

Queenie stared at him for a second, and said, "Is this person going to be dead?"

"Queenie—"

"Because I'd just like to know ahead of time so I'm a little more prepared."

"Queenie," he said, closing his eyes, like she was so silly for asking.

"No," she said emphatically. "You're out of your mind, man. I realize you're probably kind of emotional and everything, and don't think I'm being insensitive, but I'm still going to have to say no."

"Queenie—" he began.

"Actually I'm a little torn between No and No Fucking Way."

"Thirty-seven!" the girl behind the counter screamed so loud both Queenie's and Hummer's shoulders shook.

Queenie stood and walked to the counter and thought, How can I be number thirty-seven? Have there been thirty-six people who got sliders between eleven and eleven-thirty on a Wednesday? She just couldn't believe that was the case.

Queenie grabbed her tray and stared at the cute little burgers sitting side by side in the basket. Grease pooled into spots on the tissue paper below. If only they had bacon here, thought Queenie. If only every restaurant had bacon.

She sat down and didn't look at Hummer, just picked up the burger closest to her and bit into it, and it was goddamn good. Queenie made a kind of grunting noise.

"What was that?" Hummer said, looking at her like she'd just coughed up phlegm.

"This is goddamn good," said Queenie.

"Can I talk to you while you eat? Just hear me out a little," said Hummer.

Queenie rolled her eyes but figured she'd sit with him as long as it took to finish her sliders, which would not be very long, so why not. She nodded and kept chewing.

"Okay," Hummer said, and it took him a second to get his bearings. "Trigger had a guy out in Coney Island. I saw a picture of him once." Then he sat there, waiting for a response of some kind.

Queenie swallowed.

"I'm . . . sorry?" she said.

Hummer shrugged and stared off. "He was kind of a weird guy. He looked a little . . ." Hummer bounced his head from side to side. "Strange."

"Strange, how?" said Queenie, her mouth full.

"You know," Hummer said.

"No, I don't. Do you mean gay? Did he look gay?"

Hummer sighed. "No, he looked shifty—he had tattoos up and down his arms, and well, he was a little bit of a frightening guy."

Queenie started on the second burger.

"Were the tattoos of like, really scary animals and clowns and stuff?" she said.

"What? No."

"So how exactly was he frightening?"

"Look," said Hummer, rubbing his eyes. "I don't know. It was just a feeling I got. That's not what I'm getting at," he said, getting louder. Queenie put her finger to her lips. Hummer looked around, paranoid. Then he leaned forward and began to whisper. "He has something of mine."

Then he stopped. Queenie leaned forward, somewhat intrigued. "What?" she said.

"A ring," whispered Hummer.

Queenie burst out laughing. "A ring—like in *Clash of the Titans?*" she howled.

"Would you shut up?" said Hummer.

"Sorry," said Queenie, even though she wasn't at all sorry. A missing ring with the magic crest and potion inside to destroy the dragons. Queenie laughed again, a little quieter.

"Yes, I don't know why that's so funny, but I had a ring, and Trigger liked it for some reason, so I let her wear it. The last time I talked to her, she said, 'I left it at a friend's house,' and I said, 'The guy in Coney Island?' and she told me not to worry about it, and that all she had to do was go out there and get it."

"So—what? Is the ring really valuable?" said Queenie.

Hummer exhaled. "No, not very much so."

Who the fuck says, Not very much so? thought Queenie.

"So what's the problem?"

Hummer stared and gave her what Queenie liked to call "why aren't you getting this—you are an idiot" eyes. Or just "idiot eyes" for short.

"Don't look at me like that," Queenie said, picking up the third slider. "Speak."

"It's not a good idea for something that belongs to me to be in the possession of someone else who . . . knew Trigger," he said softly.

"Oh," Queenie said loudly. "Oh, I get it. You want to cut yourself off from her so you're not a suspect."

"No," said Hummer sternly, pointing at her. "I just want to remove anything that's unnecessary." He paused. *"And* I don't want this freak to have my Dartmouth ring."

Queenie nodded and tried hard not to laugh.

"So you want me to go to Coney Island and find this fella and get your ring back," she said definitively.

"Just try to get it back. That's all."

"Oh, yeah, okay," said Queenie, pretending to consider it for one full second. "So I've decided I'm still gonna have to go with no."

"I'll pay you."

"Hey, I realize those are three pretty important words to you, but they don't have magic powers."

"I'll pay you a lot."

Queenie gritted her teeth and sighed.

"Just tell the fucking police," she said. "Tell them you gave your girlfriend a ring, and she gave it to her other boyfriend. They'll take it from there; they'll figure out what happened. That's their job. That's why we pay taxes," said Queenie.

Hummer shook his head. "I don't want any more strikes against me here. Look, I'll pay you more than you'll make in a pay period at some temp job."

Queenie was getting cross. She half dropped, half threw the slider into the basket for effect, to show that she was getting cross.

"Does it occur to you that maybe your friend was in some kind of deep trouble with some deeply troubled people, and that maybe you, and definitely me, shouldn't go around sticking our asses into other people's problems?"

"We're not sticking our . . . asses anywhere," he said awkwardly.

Queenie felt sorry for him for having so much trouble with the metaphor. She picked her slider back up, and Hummer grabbed her wrist in midair. They stared at each other. His grip was tight.

"Let me eat my slider, Hummer," she said softly.

He let her go and ran his hands through his hair and scratched his scalp. They were quiet for a few seconds.

"The cop's name is Olds—did he call you?" Queenie said between bites.

Hummer nodded.

"Did he break the news about Trigger?" she said.

"No," said Hummer. "You did."

Fucking hell, thought Queenie. He found out from my dumb-ass message.

"I'm sorry," Queenie said. "Sorry you had to find out from my dumb-ass message."

Hummer shrugged. Queenie stared at the last burger and felt sad about it. She always felt sad at the end of a meal; it was like saying good-bye.

Then Hummer said, "I'll pay you to go out there and just see if you can find him."

Queenie tried to open her mouth but it was too full; there was a pickle slice teetering on the edge. She didn't care too much what Hummer thought of her, but she didn't want to start spitting up food arbitrarily.

"And if anything at all weird goes on or you panic or anything, just forget about it. Go home and keep the money."

Queenie geared up to say, What part of NO don't you understand, but it was so overused, she thought. It was probably funny the first time someone said it, but the gild had definitely worn off that lily. It was on a T-shirt for chrissake. You can't like anything once it's been put on a T-shirt, she thought, though she remained fond of I'M WITH STUPID. She always got a bang out of that.

"If it gets ugly in any way, if anyone starts asking questions, I'll take responsibility. There's a good chance you can just go out there—I know where the guy works, and you can talk to him and get the ring back. Nobody will bother you, and you'll go home five hundred dollars richer," he said.

"Five hundred dollars?" said Queenie.

Hummer nodded and smiled.

"Five hundred *American* dollars?"

"Yes."

"Just to talk to this guy and try to get the ring?"

"Yes."

"How would I get him to give it to me?"

"It doesn't matter to me—you can buy it from him if you'd like. I'll reimburse you, of course."

"Of course," said Queenie.

Queenie put her slider down and thought about it.

"It'll take you an afternoon," he said.

Queenie still thought about it.

"You haven't gotten a job since the last time I saw you, have you?" he said, smug again. "This could pay, what, a couple of months rent?"

"I live in Brooklyn, not Thailand. But yeah, it would pay some rent," she said. "How do you know I wouldn't just go home and sit on my ass and spend your money on those nice Murad skin products from the television?"

Hummer smiled and looked fairly unsavory, as unsavory as he could wearing a sweater vest.

"I don't know, Queenie," he said. "I trust you for some reason. Maybe because we were kids together."

Queenie looked down at the half a slider left. You wouldn't have to be sad at the end of a meal, she thought. Five hundred dollars could buy a fuckload of sliders. Not to mention beer and Barn-Pons and coffee and other necessary items.

Queenie leaned back in her chair and stretched her arms over her head. She yawned a little, and said, "What's he look like?"

Queenie got off the F train at the Coney Island/Stillwell Avenue stop and started walking toward the boardwalk. It had begun to drizzle, even though it was muggy, and the sky was dark. Queenie pulled up the hood of her sweatshirt.

FUN & GAMES read the sign near the next cross street, with a huge arrow, blue and red and green with yellow stars glittering around the words, pointing to the booths and the rides. The Ferris wheel was turning slowly, and Queenie could hear the rattle of the old wooden roller coaster, strange muffled screams of the patrons, soft then loud, howling like ghosts. There weren't many people around. Many of the booths looked closed up. The guys who ran them stood with their arms crossed in front of huge cartoony stuffed animals, hanging around the borders like vines.

Queenie walked up the ramp leading to the boardwalk. She was sweating already and could feel the drops on her waist, her love handles. Wow, she thought, this extra layer of flesh will really come in handy during winter, or maybe if one day I live in the woods, a cute bunny or a rascally chipmunk will have a place to sleep.

She stepped up to the boardwalk and listened to the hollow sound her feet made on the planks. There were some schoolkids on the beach, girls in shorts and bikini tops listening to the radio, and some boys roughhousing in the water. There were also many old people—a man with a cane sitting on a bench and a frail woman inching along the boardwalk wearing thick orthopedic shoes. She wore geriatric cataract shades.

Queenie made a wish that when and if she ever got that old, she would be medically forced to wear sunglasses.

She pulled the napkin from Jaffee's Sliders out of her pocket, and next to the cartoon cheeseburger (who had legs and curly hair and pouty lips and was generally pretty sexy, especially for a cheeseburger) was written, "Clam bar. Shark on neck." This is what Hummer knew, that the man who had his ring had a shark tattoo on his neck and worked at a clam bar. Hummer had told that to Queenie right before they went to the ATM.

Queenie came to the food stands. They were all open, but there weren't many people inside. It was usually jammed at the Nathan's during the summer, but now there was only a couple with a baby wearing just a diaper, sitting in a stroller. There were some rough-looking characters, older, leathery-faced, sitting at the bar, drinking beer.

Queenie passed a stand with a sign that read, CLAMS! SHRIMP! OYSTERS! There was an old sunburned man behind the counter with a dishrag over his shoulder. A large woman sat at the stand, with three little kids milling around under her feet like mice.

Then she came to a stand with a sign that read, CLAM BAKE, and there were clams drawn with little motion lines around them, as if they were dancing. Were clams who were about to be baked really that happy? thought Queenie. Maybe they were trembling with fear.

No one was at the bar except a younger fellow with dark hair wearing a black T-shirt behind the counter. He had ink up and down his arms. Queenie sat on one of the stools and looked at the clam strips in paper trays under the glass. Her stomach hummed. You just had four sliders, she told it.

The young guy glanced at her. He had a thick neck and thick arms. It was also plain to see the dark outline of a small shark on his neck. It didn't really look like a dangerous shark; it wasn't baring its teeth or anything—it just seemed to be resting. And when Queenie stared at it, she really couldn't be sure it was a shark at all—it could've been a dolphin. But she thought it was too much of a coincidence—this had to be him.

Queenie thought he was around her age, and she thought it was strange—a young tough punky guy working a clam stand. They were usually the old guys with the dishrags over their shoulders, or Russian or Dominican families. Mom and Dad with all the kids working.

"You know what you want?" he said.

"Not just yet," said Queenie, and she looked up at the posterboard menu. "Do you have beer?" she said.

Shark shook his head. "Down the boardwalk—Rosie's."

Queenie looked back to the posterboard. Clam dip, clam chowder, fried clams.

"Clam strips," she said definitively.

"Large or small?"

"Small," said Queenie, and almost patted herself physically on the back. See? Already eating better. Went with the small and not the large.

Shark reached under the glass for a paper tray of preprepared strips and turned around to put them in the microwave. Queenie looked at his back and his arms; he wasn't just big-boned but strong, too, and not Hummer's Bally Fitness strong, just strong naturally, peasant big, like Uncle Si and Queenie's father, strong from being in fields for a few centuries.

He pressed the buttons on the microwave, and it started to hum. He turned to face Queenie and wiped his hands with a paper towel.

"Three-fifty," he said.

Queenie shelled out five and laid them on the counter. She glanced down and saw a pack of Reds next to the microwave.

"Could you spare a cigarette?" she said.

He looked confused for a second. Then he said, "Sure."

He picked up the pack and shook one out and handed it to her. His hands were huge and warm. Queenie looked down and saw it, on his pinky, a chunky purple ring with a thick gold band. He gave her a wrinkled pack of matches. Queenie lit it up.

"Thanks," she said. "That really hits the spot."

Shark didn't say anything.

"So tell me," said Queenie.

Shark rested both his hands on the glass and leaned forward. He looked fairly unimpressed. He raised his eyebrows slightly.

"How do you get a gig like this? Seems like there's mostly old-timers around here, and I'm not too good guessing people's ages, but I'd say you can't be a day older than twenty-seven," she said, in one long stream.

Shark narrowed his eyes at her. He didn't speak.

"Well?" said Queenie. "Am I close?"

He paused, and said quietly, "Twenty-nine."

"That's what I'm talking about," said Queenie, shooting a finger gun at him. "Twenty-nine and never been kissed," she said, and she laughed abrasively.

Shark didn't laugh. He kind of smirked. Then the microwave dinged, and Shark turned around and pulled the clam strips out and placed them in front of Queenie. Then he opened a small refrigerator and pulled out a tiny plastic container of tartar sauce.

"Oh boy," said Queenie. "Thanks."

She peeled off the top of the container and sniffed. It smelled like relish, and her mouth watered. She picked up a clam strip and dipped it and bit off half. It burned her tongue.

Shark watched her. Not a big talker, she thought.

"You a Dartmouth man?" she said, nodding toward the ring.

There was a brief flash of something in his eyes, but it wasn't panic. Queenie got the feeling he didn't panic too easily. Just calm recognition.

"No," he said. "Did you go to Dartmouth?"

"Oh sure," said Queenie. "Class of ought-five."

Shark didn't react. Nothing on his face moved.

Queenie smiled. "I'm just kidding with you. No, I knew a guy who went there. Kind of a sad story—met the wrong girl, got in some trouble. You've heard it a thousand times."

Queenie swallowed another clam strip and felt the oil glaze her lips and drip on her chin.

"So how'd you get ahold of a Dartmouth lacrosse ring?" she said.

Shark looked confused and glanced down.

"See those two lines on the side?" said Queenie. "They're lacrosse sticks. See the little pooper-scoopers up top?"

Shark held his finger up to his face. "You can see that from here?"

"I have good eyes," she said. "So where'd you pick it up? Bust it out of a piñata?"

He crossed his arms.

"My girl gave it to me," he said, without inflection.

"Yeah?" said Queenie. "She must have big fingers."

Now he smiled. It lit up his whole face. Wide features, wide cheekbones and a high forehead, but boy, did he have a nice smile, thought Queenie. Maybe Trigger had okay taste after all.

"Was it an anniversary present?" said Queenie.

"No. She just gave it to me."

"What'll it take for you to part with it?"

He tapped his fingers on the counter and said, "It's not for sale."

"Fair enough," said Queenie. "I guess if my girlfriend gave me another guy's ring, maybe I wouldn't want to sell it either."

"Who said it's another guy's ring?" he said, only a little interested in the conversation.

Queenie shrugged. "That's just not the kind of thing you find at a garage sale."

"Or in a piñata," he said.

"Right."

Queenie put out her cigarette. She didn't feel like double-fisting with food and smokes today. She coughed.

"You sure you don't have anything of an alcoholic nature back there?" she said.

"I'm sure," he said. "We have soda pop if you like."

"Nah," said Queenie. "Never touch the stuff."

He smiled again now and rubbed his chin. That's it, Queenie, she thought. You're growing on him.

"Say, can I see that ring up close?" she said.

The smile disappeared. Uh-oh, thought Queenie. Too much.

He placed his large hand palm down on the glass in front of her. The ring was purple and clear and really thick. Trigger couldn't've worn that on her skinny fingers. She must have worn it around her neck, thought Queenie. Must've weighed her head down.

Then she noticed dark red marks on his wrists, like his skin was rubbed raw. Queenie touched his right wrist gently with her index finger.

"What happened to you?" she said.

He leaned in close to her. She could feel his breath.

"I got caught up," he said. "In some rope."

"Yeah?" Queenie said, staring him in the eyes. "Your girl like to do that, too?"

He smiled and said, "She used to."

Queenie sat back and pulled her hand away. "Well," she said, her mouth dry, "it must be nice to find someone who shares your interests."

"It is," he said. "It's a real relief."

Queenie tried to get some saliva going in her mouth. Her throat felt like bark. She coughed again.

"You sure you don't want something to drink?" he said again.

"No thanks, I'm fine," she said.

She ate another clam strip and forced a smile.

"So," she said, cheery. "You sure I can't buy that ring off you?"

"It's not for sale. I already said that."

"Yeah, I know you did. I'm a little funny in the head," she said, tapping her temples with two fingers. "Do you play cards? We could play a game of Old Maid for it."

"No."

"How about if I flash you?" she whispered.

"No."

"Well, that doesn't do a whole lot for my self-esteem," said Queenie. "You just say, No, bam, just like that, not thinking it over, not even thinking about what I might have under all this," she said, gesturing to her T-shirt and Dickies. Then she said, "How about rock-paper-scissors? Have you ever played it? It's a blast."

Shark leaned over the counter, and said slowly, "What part of No don't you understand?"

Queenie opened her mouth in shock. She couldn't believe he actually said it! It wasn't just on T-shirts after all.

"Pretty much the whole thing," she said.

Then she started thinking about the I'M WITH STUPID T-shirt, and she started giggling. Shark looked at her like she was insane.

"Sorry," she said, just barely regaining composure. "You ever see those shirts that say, I'M WITH STUPID? That really sends me."

"Why do you want this ring so bad?" Shark said, leaning against the microwave table.

"All right, I'll tell you buddy, I'm not pulling anything over on you," Queenie said, wiping her eyes. "The guy who owns it wants it back. The guy your girlfriend got it from."

Shark remained stoic. He cocked his head to one side, and said, "How does he know who I am?"

"I don't know. He saw a picture of you once, knew you worked out here, heard your girl talking to you on the phone." Queenie bit into another clam strip. They were cooling down. They were pretty disgusting when they weren't piping hot, as it turned out.

"So who the fuck are you?" Shark said, tensing his mouth up. "You a friend of his?"

"No. I'm just working for him."

Shark looked away. Then he said, "You know Trigger?"

His voice sounded different when he said her name—soft and sexy.

"No, I don't know her. I just *saw* her—" Queenie said.

"What do you mean, you saw her?"

Queenie stopped chewing. He didn't know. Jesus Harry Carey, he didn't know. And now you have to tell him, Queenie thought. Way to go, genius.

"She's dead, isn't she?" said Shark.

Queenie nodded slowly. Shark blinked a few times very quickly and rubbed his chin.

"Do they know who did it?" he said.

Queenie cleared her throat. "I don't know—they, the police don't know," she said. "Look, I'm real sorry," she said, almost reaching her hand out to touch him.

"Hey, *who* the fuck are *you?*" he said roughly.

"Hey, nobody, all right, just some girl who's gonna take that ring off your hands because maybe you don't need any more connections to Trigger Happy besides the rope you tied her up with for fun," Queenie said in a stream. "You dig?"

Shark squinted at her and sighed, spread the fingers of his right hand, and screwed the ring off, still staring at her. Then he took her hand and pressed the ring into it so hard it hurt her palm.

"Go away," he said, dropping her hand, not aggressively. He fixed his dark eyes on her.

Queenie slid off the chair and backed away, not finishing her clams. She kept backing away and finally turned around and felt light rain on her face. The sky looked brown, muddy. Queenie headed toward the subway and heard her heart beat. That's all she could hear for a moment, not even the waves.

"Hey!"

Queenie turned around, and Shark was running toward her, not in an alarming way, just trotting, his big limbs looking gangly. Queenie found it endearing. He stopped in front of her and breathed hard, his shoulders hunched over.

Queenie looked him up and down and thought, Man, he is sexy. She didn't even want to try to remember the last time she'd been naked in the same room with a guy; it might spill into dog years.

He reached out and took her left hand, the one that held the ring. She let it go limp against his palm and imagined for a second that he was putting the old moves on her.

Sometimes Queenie had a rich fantasy life.

He pressed something else into her palm, something small and flimsy and smooth. He took his hand away, and Queenie looked. It was a matchbook from the Dark Horse bar. There was a dark horse on it.

"Trigger liked that place. She used to meet her friends there," he said.

The wind blew and screwed up his hair. Queenie tried to maintain her composure and not throw herself at him. She just barely succeeded.

"Friends like you?" Queenie said coyly, dropping the ring and the matchbook into her pants pocket.

"No. Friends like your boss," he said.

For a second Queenie thought he was referring to Roy Cohn. She must have looked confused because he closed his eyes like she was trying his patience.

"Your Dartmouth boss," he said.

Queenie nodded and was embarrassed. She wondered why he was telling her this.

"Why are you telling me this?" she said.

He smiled, and it drove Queenie crazy.

"I don't trust cops," he said.

Queenie was going to say, Well, okay, but what the hell am I supposed to do with that? and then maybe slip in something like, Hey do you want to go on a date with me sometime? but she was too caught up in his fucking smile.

"Oh," was really all she could get out.

Shark turned around and jogged back to the clam stand. Queenie watched him go. Oh well, she thought, one step closer to dying alone.

She usually said that to Meade when she had a less-than-positive experience going out with a guy. It was always funny, but now when she thought it, she thought about Trigger, and she shook her head and tried not to think about it anymore.

Something about the brown sky and the water on her face even though it was June made her feel very depressed.

The F train hummed along, and Queenie was one of five people on the car, sitting on one of the two-seaters at the end. She was thinking she could get off at Bergen or Smith and then she could transfer to the G, and then to the L, but jeez Louise, she thought, that's *three* trains. Three trains is absurd. But the alternative was she would have to ride into Manhattan and get the L, only to go back to Brooklyn, which was also absurd.

The car-to-car door slid open, and a young woman, probably about Queenie's age, came in and smiled at her.

Queenie smiled back.

The woman sat down next to her.

Oh fantastic, thought Queenie.

The woman wore a navy blue skirt that went to a little below her knees and a navy blue blazer, and a white button-down blouse with a Peter Pan collar. She had a short conservative haircut and no makeup on, as far as Queenie could tell.

"I'm Michelle," she said.

"Hiya, Michelle," said Queenie. "What's going on?"

"Not much, thanks," she said. "What's your name?"

"Queenie."

"That's an interesting name. Where did you get a name like that?" said Michelle, sounding genuinely interested.

"My uncle used to call me Beauty Queen," said Queenie.

"That's so sweet," said Michelle. "Where does your uncle live?"

Where is this going? thought Queenie. She can't be hitting on me, not in the flight attendant outfit.

"Massachusetts," said Queenie. Then she added, "Where does *your* uncle live?"

Way to turn the tables, she thought.

Michelle appeared surprised.

"I don't . . . have an uncle," she said.

"That's too bad," said Queenie. "Uncles are great."

"Mm-hmm," said Michelle, smiling. "Is that where you're from—Massachusetts?"

"Yes, it is."

"That's great," Michelle said earnestly. "New York can be pretty overwhelming, huh?" she said, nodding to Queenie, like she really understood.

"Yeah," said Queenie.

"I don't know about you, but sometimes I feel like it takes all the energy I have in the world to get up in the morning and get on the subway," Michelle said, sounding wistful.

"Yeah?"

Queenie still couldn't read her. She didn't think Michelle was crazy. A little ditsy maybe, but not a hundred percent fruit and nuts.

"Yeah, sometimes it really helps to talk to other people who might be feeling the same way," said Michelle.

Maybe she's AA, thought Queenie, but how does she know? Do I smell like beer? And since when does AA start recruiting like Mormons?

Oh shit, she thought, maybe Michelle's a Mormon!

"Do you ever feel like you need to talk?" asked Michelle.

"No, I generally express myself through song."

Michelle closed her eyes and nodded. "That must be very relaxing for you," she said.

"Yes, very much so. Sometimes, I cut people's hair to relax—that also helps," said Queenie.

Again, more understanding nods from Michelle. Then she reached into her small navy blue handbag and pulled out a pamphlet. It had a picture of the earth on it. Ha, thought Queenie, bad religion, I should have known.

"Queenie," said Michelle seriously. "If you ever need to talk to anyone, you should call us," she said, handing Queenie the pamphlet.

The word, "Rebirth," was underneath the picture of the world. Queenie opened the pamphlet, and read, "If you find yourself worn down by life, angry and sad at the littlest things, what you need may be STABILITY™."

"Hey," said Queenie. "Is that the thing all the movie stars are into?"

Michelle smiled knowingly. "A lot of celebrities have found peace in STABILITY™," she said. "They find it promotes a calm alternative to the rigors of public life."

"Uh-huh," said Queenie, glancing at the pamphlet. "So have you really trademarked the word, STABILITY™? I mean, will you sue me if I used STABILITY™ in everyday conversation, like if I were to say to my husband, 'Ray, I need more STABILITY™ in our marriage,' would I have to check with you guys first?"

"No, that wouldn't be a problem. But no other group can call themselves STABILITY™," Michelle said patiently.

"Lucky for me then, huh?" said Queenie, grinning.

"Yeah," said Michelle, trying to keep her smile going.

They probably tell them to just roll with the punches, thought Queenie. Listen to whatever the nut jobs on the street have to say no matter what kind of nonsense they spout because what we teach here at ZOMBIE CAMP is so much more rational.

"There's an informational film that screens in the STABILITY™ theater up by Madison Square Garden twice a day. Would you like a free ticket?" said Michelle.

"Oh, yes, definitely. Are there any people I'd know in it? Anyone who's on TV?" said Queenie.

"No, it's more of an introduction to the organization."

"Right, right, right," said Queenie. "Are you sure the blind guy from *Gimme Five* isn't in it? He's pretty talented for a blind guy."

"No, it's more of a documentary," said Michelle.

"Right," said Queenie. "You should really try to get that blind guy—I don't even think he needs a dog. He'd be a great rep for you guys."

"I'm sure he would, but this film is more of a documentary with some dramatizations," poor Michelle squeaked out.

"Oh, dramati-*za*-tions," said Queenie. "Like *Unsolved Mysteries.* Are there missing persons or killers on the loose in this film, though?"

"No," said Michelle, standing up.

Looks like I wore you down, didn't I, sweetheart? thought Queenie.

"Here's two tickets for you," said Michelle, handing them to Queenie. There were stars and a Milky Way blob in the corner. "Maybe your husband would like to go with you."

"Oh, sure—Ray loves the movies."

"It was nice to meet you, Queenie," said Michelle, holding out her hand.

"Nice to meet you, Michelle," said Queenie, shaking it.

Michelle started to walk away. Queenie almost felt sad.

"Hey, Michelle," Queenie called.

Michelle turned and came back.

"Hey, you know, Michelle, I was just thinking, I have a friend who I think would really benefit from STABILITY™—do you have a mailing list?"

Michelle's face brightened , and she reached into her purse again.

"Oh, sure," she said.

She pulled out a small card and handed it to Queenie. It read, "Want the 411 on STABILITY™? Fill out the information below and we'll send you an Introductory Package!"

They say, '411' to sound hip, thought Queenie. For the kids. She was about to check her pockets for a pen she knew she didn't have when Michelle held one up in front of her.

"That's what I like about you, Michelle," said Queenie. "You're always prepared."

Queenie filled out the card in the following way: Name: Roy Cohn. Address: 245 W. 44th St., Ste. 820, NY, NY. She then checked the Yes box that followed, "May we share your information with other organizations like ours?" Then there was a space for comments at the bottom. It asked, "Is there any specific issue you need to focus on in your life?" Queenie wrote, "I'm trying to come to terms with my sexuality."

She handed the card back to Michelle.

"Thanks a bunch, Michelle," said Queenie.

"No," said Michelle gently, and she placed her hand on Queenie's shoulder. "Thank *you.*"

Queenie smiled and nodded sagely. Michelle turned and walked away.

Queenie leaned back and closed her eyes and listened to the train rumble. It was approaching Manhattan. She wasn't quite asleep but she was breathing deep and picturing the Paper Doll, except it was all in pink for some reason, like pink powder was sprayed on the tables and chairs and floors and on the bar and the stage. Trigger was on the stage dancing slowly, and she was not pink. She was wearing the purple garter belt from the Frederick's of Hollywood catalogue and a purple bra, and laid down in front of her, flat on the stage were a folded-up shower curtain and a New York sweatshirt. Shark stood at the front of the stage, and wasn't pink either. He smiled that killer smile and reached his hand up to her and she took it. She smiled back and winked, and little silver flakes tumbled from her eyelashes down onto Shark's face like rain.

Someone nudged Queenie.

"Sorry," said a Chinese woman with a red shopping bag, squeezing into the seat next to her.

The train had gotten a little more crowded. Queenie reached into her pocket and pulled out the matchbook for the Dark Horse. Sure Queenie had been there. Queenie had been to every bar below Fourteenth Street that served Bud or Miller on tap. From what she remembered of the Dark Horse, it was very old New York—big wooden tables and paintings of horses and carriages on the walls. Funny place for Trig to meet her johns, thought Queenie, but then again, maybe not. Maybe it was perfect. It wasn't quite a dive, not a sports bar, not upscale. Close enough to the downtown area to meet up with businessmen, but also a good place to drink your shit off.

In her head, Queenie heard Shark say, "She used to meet her friends there." Queenie flipped the matchbook over in her hand and squeezed it, and she rode the train to West Fourth.

* * *

The Dark Horse was crowded for 3 P.M. They also served food, mainly different fried things and some old-ey English-ey type dishes like shepherd's pie. Dark wooden walls and wooden tables—it looked like the kind of place where people would be sitting in long rows, singing and toasting and clinking big tin cups. Like that scene in the old *Robin Hood* where Errol Flynn sidles in with the deer over his shoulders.

Businessmen were already filing in—young preppy guys with starch in the collars talking about hedge funds. Also some tan healthy women with tank tops and sculpted abs. Queenie could not hear what they were talking about but assumed it had something to do with how their abs became so sculpted.

Queenie walked up to the bar and sat down. Two young men next to her were having a conversation about the new subways. "It's like *2001*—like you're in a space station," Queenie heard.

She caught the bartender's eye and nodded. He held up a finger—one minute. Solid bartenders, thought Queenie. Total professionals, none doing shots behind the bar, moving quickly, not getting into conversations with patrons. It wasn't a good place for crying in your beer but perfect when you wanted to get served fast.

"What can I get you?" he said.

"Pint of McSorley's."

He nodded and pulled a glass from under the bar and drew the pint slowly from the tap. He gave it a nice little head, too, creamy like a milk shake. When he was done, a little drop crawled down the glass, and he wiped the bottom with a napkin.

"Four dollars, please," he said, and Queenie put down a five.

"Hey," nodded Queenie. "Do you know a gal named Trigger Happy—she comes in here a lot."

The bartender shook his head. "Can't say I do. I think I'd remember a name like that."

"I'm sure you would," said Queenie. "She's thin, real good-looking." Queenie thought of the picture with the blond boy in

Trigger's apartment. "Got a great smile, real big, takes up her whole face."

The bartender thought about it and shook his head again, slowly. "Sorry. I haven't been working here long, though. You might want to ask Helen Keller," he said, nodding to the far corner.

Queenie turned and saw a guy in his late fifties with a ring of silver hair, kind of chubby, sitting in the corner at a table next to the jukebox, alone. He had a cane in his hands and was staring out the window.

"He's here almost every day," said the bartender.

"Thanks," said Queenie, and she looked at him like she wanted to ask something else, but neither of them quite knew what it was.

"Was there something else?" asked the bartender.

"Yeah," she said slowly. "Can I get one of those bread bowls with the soup in it?"

"You want clam chowder or cream of broccoli?"

"Cream of broccoli," Queenie said, knowing it was a bold choice, bordering on healthy, which was against everything she believed in, but she'd already eaten clams once today.

"They'll bring it to you," he said, looking toward the corner.

"Thanks."

Queenie picked up her beer and walked over to Helen Keller. She stood there for a moment and watched him stare out the window, not at anything in particular. He didn't seem to be tracking people or cars, just appeared to be staring at the glass itself. He didn't acknowledge Queenie either.

"Excuse me, do you mind if I sit here?" said Queenie.

Now he looked up, but still not directly at her.

"Not at all," he said.

"Thanks," Queenie said, sitting down.

Helen smiled and blinked hard a couple of times, then reached for his beer. His fingers traveled along the tabletop until they hit the mug gently, then he grabbed the handle.

"Hey, friend, can I ask you something?" she said.

"Surely," he said, looking back toward the window.

"I'm looking for my cousin. She's around my height but real skinny and good-looking, brown hair."

Helen turned to Queenie and smiled.

"Sweetheart, telling me how she looks isn't gonna help," he said.

Queenie looked into his light eyes. Then she realized he was blind and almost blurted out, Hey, I was just talking about the blind guy from *Gimme Five*—small world! Then she just felt like a real asshole for not noticing sooner.

"I'm sorry," she said. "I feel like a real asshole."

Helen shook his head. "Not a tragedy," he said. "How do you like the McSorley's?"

"It's perfect. How'd you know that's what I'm drinking?"

"I heard you order it," he said.

"Oh yeah?" Queenie said, glancing back at the bar. "Your hearing's pretty incredible. It's loud in here."

Helen nodded and sipped his beer. "Hearing's better than most," he said. "Like a bat that way."

"That must be really neat," said Queenie.

"Sure it is, except for the part where I'm blind."

Queenie burst out laughing, and Helen smiled.

"I would imagine," said Queenie. Then she placed her hand gently on his and squeezed it softly. "My name's Queenie."

"I'm Helen," said the man. "Barry told you that."

"Yeah."

"So Trigger's your cousin?"

"Yeah, you know her?" Queenie said, perking up.

Helen scrunched his lip up. "Little bit. I know she comes in once or twice a week and we say hello. Why you ask?" he said, not particularly suspicious.

Queenie shrugged.

"I'm having trouble locating her."

"She works at a place downtown, I know that."

"I've been down there," said Queenie. "She hasn't been at work for a few days."

"Are you worried about her?" asked Helen.

Queenie paused and became sad. He knew her, who knew how well, but Queenie couldn't imagine breaking the news to yet another person.

"Not yet," she said. "Do you remember when she was here last?"

"I think it was Friday," he said.

"Friday—are you sure?"

Helen grimaced. "Yeah, I'm sure. I know it 'cause she brought me a beer and I asked her what she had on tap for the night, painting the town red and whatnot, and she said she had to work, 'cause she always works Fridays. Fridays and Saturdays."

"Did she say anything else?"

"She said she's waiting for somebody."

"Did she say who?"

"Nah, but then he showed up, and they went to a table over there," he said, nodding toward the bar.

"Did you talk to this guy at all?"

"Nah, she never introduced me to her friends like that, but I'll tell you, when he showed, she sounded nervous, all hem and haw, which isn't like her, you know, she's ballsy," he said, smiling.

Queenie smiled, too. Tough Trigger.

"You didn't happen to hear what they talked about, did you?" said Queenie.

Helen smiled again and looked like one of the wise men in a Nativity scene, but also kind of drunk and loopy.

"I always happen to hear what folks talk about around here," he said. "Far as I could tell, they were having some kind of argument. She kept saying, 'Don't ask me to do that, you can't ask me to do that,' so forth."

Then a waitress with springy hair brought a steaming bread bowl that smelled like onions and warm milk.

"Bread bowl," she announced, and set it down in front of Queenie.

"Wow, thanks," said Queenie.

"What you got there?" said Helen. "Cream of broccoli?"

"Yeah. Like some?"

"Nah. I prefer clam chowder myself," he said, wrinkling his nose.

"Me too. I already had clams today is the thing," said Queenie. God that sounds stupid, she thought.

Helen was quiet for a moment and Queenie looked around the room a bit. She watched the springy-haired waitress stand by the front door, looking disappointed. Then her face changed suddenly—she lit right up, and her mouth became wide and made her whole head look like a pumpkin. She pushed the heavy wooden door open, and a blond woman came in pushing a huge stroller, big as a grocery cart, huge plastic wheels and compartments. There was a blobby baby inside with its little eraser tongue poking out.

"Oh, he's bee-yu-tiful," said the waitress, leaning over to get in the baby's face.

The baby looked fairly unimpressed. He looked away, upward, like there was something on the ceiling.

The mother wiggled her nose and smiled. Then she said definitively, "He's wet," and she walked around to the front of the stroller and pulled the baby's pants off.

What indignity, thought Queenie. It must be really shitty being a baby.

Queenie turned back to Helen, who sat there quietly, as if he had been put on hold.

"So could you make out what this guy was trying to make her do?"

"Not so well," said Helen, pulling his cane toward him. "They quieted down some." He folded his hands over the top of his cane.

Queenie lifted a spoonful of the soup to her lips and saw tiny folds of milk curdling on top. She drank it, and it burned her tongue, but she didn't let that stop her. She jimmied the spoon into the bread wall to scrape some dough off. Ah, the bread bowl, she thought. Where is the genius who thought up the bread bowl, because I would like to shake his hand. And so resource-conscious as well. It all went back to Queenie's theory that really everything should be made sturdy and edible—bowls, cups, chairs, phones, hair clips.

"How do you like the bread bowl?" said Helen.

"It's really good," said Queenie, chewing a piece of soft hot broccoli. See? she said to herself. Veggies. You're a regular health nut. "What else about my cousin?" she asked. "I just knew her when we were kids, you know?"

"Oh, sure," said Helen. "She always, she puts on the Rolling Stones. You know that song, how's it go—'Paint It Black'?"

"Yeah, 'Paint It Black'," said Queenie, suddenly excited.

"Number's 8906. I punch it in, and she comes over and puts her hands on my shoulders, and she says, 'You know I love this song,' " he said, quietly, smiling.

Queenie smiled, too. She didn't say anything for a few seconds, then she said softly, "Yeah, Trig always liked the Stones."

Then she looked back down at her soup and drank it, and she and Helen sipped their beers, and didn't talk about Trigger for a while.

Instead they shot the shit about the Mets and how the Russian Mafia runs everything (even the subways). Soon the Dark Horse started to become crowded with the after-work crowd, and Queenie felt nervous for some reason, like she was being watched.

She said good-bye to Helen, stood up, placed one hand on his back, and shook his hand with the other.

"Nice to meet you, Boss," said Queenie.

"Thanks for the company. And tell Trigger to get on back here," he said sweetly, gripping Queenie's hand.

"Will do," said Queenie.

And then she left the smoky bar and stood on Hudson for a few minutes with her hands over her face, breathing slowly.

Then she shook out of it and headed to Fourteenth Street, looking through the window of the Dark Horse and seeing the blond mother with the humiliated baby on her lap. The baby didn't seem to mind being there. Mothers, mothers, mothers, thought Queenie as she crossed the street. Motherfucker—one who fucks one's own mother. Is the implication that the motherfucker is fucking his own mother or mothers in general?

Did Trig have a mother? Of course she did, thought Queenie. Of course Trig had a mother, but she was definitely out of the picture. Only the sophisticated estranged father comes to the funeral.

Small and fragile, thinks Queenie. That's where Trig gets her bone structure—from her tiny fragile leaflike mother. So fragile that little Trigger-Tara's afraid to hug her. Her bones are brittle and crispy like old newspaper. And she's always cold, Trigger's mother. Little Trigger wants to be carried by Mom, but Mom's too tired.

A disease! thought Queenie triumphantly. Maybe she has a disease. No, she doesn't need one. She always *thinks* she's getting sick. She spends many days in bed. She likes old movies where the couple breaks up in the end—*Gone With the Wind, Casablanca, Roman Holiday.* She doesn't like it when they stay together.

Then one day she leaves. No, she doesn't leave. She dies suddenly. In an accident. Probably of the car variety.

Little Trigger's sophisticated father handles his wife's death with sophistication. He explains to Little Trigger that there is a heaven, and now Little Trigger's mother is in it. He's not sure if he believes it, but Little Trigger is only six or seven so you know, you have to tell kids something. No, thought Queenie, he definitely doesn't believe it; he's too sophisticated.

One day he comes home from work and calls for Little Trigger, and she doesn't answer. He walks upstairs to her room, and she's not there. He begins to get nervous. He looks frantically out their back window—no—sliding glass doors into their small backyard where there's an old swing set. It's too cold. It's winter. There's ice on the ground. No Little Trigger.

He runs all over the house. His pulse rises, which is no good for his blood pressure (his diet is okay; it's just that he doesn't really exercise and there's a history of heart disease in his family). He climbs up and down the stairs two or three more times, looks in his bedroom, and sees the blankets clumped up in the way he left them. He checks the basement, the attic.

Finally, he returns to his bedroom and sits on the edge of his bed and puts his head in his hands and tries to think logically. Call the police, he says to himself.

And just then he feels tiny feet kicking him from behind, and he turns around and pulls the covers away, and there's Little Trigger, pretending to sleep, hands at her sides, toes pointing up.

"Tara," he says, breathless. "What are you doing?"

Little Trigger opens one eye, and says, "I'm Mommy. Get it?"

Now someone pushed Queenie down the stairs of the subway station. It was a kid with a do-rag on his head.

"Jesus, watch it," said Queenie.

She heard the train coming and started to run. She swiped through the turnstile and slid into the car right before the doors closed. It was crowded and full of hot, sticky, angry people. It hadn't ever poured outside—it just seemed to get muggier and muggier. Queenie smelled like beer and sweat and smoke, but on the inside, she was great—that bread bowl really hit the spot. Burping was kind of a pleasant experience.

She leaned against a pole and tried to read the *Daily News* over a burly fellow's shoulder. He kept looking around, turning his head, trying to curve his paper so Queenie couldn't see. Oh yeah, I know how it is, thought Queenie. It's so inconvenient. You should just get over it, Mr. Privacy, thought Queenie. People will read over your shoulder in this town.

Queenie looked up at the ads. Some trains got all the props, she thought, her sense of social justice kicking in. Some trains got the two-themed cars, with only two Super-ads that ran down each side and in the little squares above people's heads, next to the doors. Queenie liked to read them all the way down to end. Sharpshooter eyes.

But unless it was one of the Outer Space Ls, and usually it wasn't, most of the ads were out of date, and there were always huge spaces with no ads at all, just the blank gray light sheet.

Queenie stared at the one for Captain Morgan's Spiced Rum. The Captain was here. Apparently you knew the Captain had been someplace when you had a Sharpie red mustache painted on your upper lip. That's funny, thought Queenie, *I* know the Captain's been here when my throw-up tastes like IHOP.

She guessed that probably wouldn't make the best slogan.

The train screeched into the Bedford Avenue station. Queenie liked being on the train when it screeched on the rails because then she could watch the people on the platforms cover their ears. They always made a big show about it, too—so dramatic, like it was the goddamn nuclear fallout siren. Drama queens, thought Queenie.

She stepped off the car with a throng of assholes and moved toward the exit with them, like a bunch of cows. The train screeched away, and she thought, That's not so bad, not so much worse than baby nails on a blackboard. Really, folks, let's all get a grip. She found herself thinking, If that's the worst thing that'll ever happen to you, you'll be lucky. She remembered her father saying that to her once when Queenie told him her feet were cold. She was probably five.

When she came above ground, she stood on the corner and made a pro and con list, which is what you're supposed to do if you're wrestling between two things. It went like this:

Pros of going home:
1) You'll be at home.
2) There are Popsicles at home.

She couldn't think of any more pros for home. So she went to:

Pros of going to Big Styrofoam Cup:
1) They have big Styrofoam cups full of beer there.
2) They always have such nice seasonal decorations.

The biggest and most important con of going home was that there were not big Styrofoam cups of beer. Queenie really didn't need to go any further than that first con for home. She could think of no cons for Big Styrofoam Cup.

So Queenie crossed the street and walked into Big Styrofoam Cup and didn't regret it for a second.

There was a Mets game on the television, and most of the denizens were watching intently. Queenie had met them all at least ten times but only remembered a few names.

"Hey, Jill. Hey, Stacee. Hey, Fella with the Neck Growth. Hey, Unbelievably Tall Guy."

Queenie bummed a cheapo cigarette from Unbelievably Tall Guy and sat at the far end of the bar. She looked up at the streamers—all summer décor. Little crepe paper suns dangling and strings of plastic pink flowers everywhere.

Leave it to the folks at Big Styrofoam Cup, marveled Queenie.

The barmaid was an older Polish lady with hair like Wilma from *The Flintstones*. She shuffled over to Queenie.

"Ya-yes?" she said, low then high, like it was two words.

"Can I get a big cup of Bud?" said Queenie, lighting her cigarette.

"Big cup of Bud," Wilma repeated.

Queenie watched her pour it. "Sympathy for the Devil" played on the jukebox. Someone always plays "Sympathy for the Devil" in here, thought Queenie.

Wilma brought the Bud over, and said, "Three-fifty."

Queenie gave her five, and said, "Thanks."

It was huge! It was an absolutely outrageous size for a beer, and that's what Queenie loved about it; it was as if she saw it in a dream, as if she held up her hands to the sky and wished for a gigantic vessel of beer, and here it was. She took a sip and it was a little watery but so cold and good she couldn't complain.

"Uh, hey, hey," said Old Crazy Polish Guy 2.

Usually he was not seen without Old Crazy Polish Guys 1, 3, and 4, but he seemed to be solo today. His lips were wet, and he was teetering back and forth, holding a mug of beer. How conservative, to get a mug, thought Queenie. She'd been there, though. She'd come into Big Styrofoam Cup before saying to herself, I will not get a big Styrofoam cup of beer because then I will be drunk before nightfall and it will be all over for me. So in the spirit of moderation, she'd get a pint or a mug, but then she'd just end up having twice as many and paying through the nose. So you see, she told herself in a stern but wise tone, it's foolish to get anything but a big Styrofoam cup of beer straightaway.

"Hiya," said Queenie to Old Crazy Polish Guy 2.

"Will you dance?" he asked, his eyes red, still wobbly.

"Not right now, thanks," said Queenie.

He winked at her, and she winked back. Then he moved on and asked the Puerto Rican lesbian to dance. She told him to lie down.

"Lie down, George! Lie down!" she shouted.

He just giggled.

Queenie finished her cigarette and put it out and looked up at the television, at a beer commercial. A lot of tits. You really don't need tits to sell beer, she thought. Everyone in this bar would still be here drinking lots of beer, regardless of the tits. The Old Crazy Polish Guy demographic would still be going strong with or without tits.

Queenie nibbled on the edge of the big Styrofoam cup. She glanced around for more smokers, someone to bum from. The only people she could see smoking were sitting too far away, meaning she would have to stand up, and that just wasn't in the cards.

"Anyone sitting here?" a man said to her.

She turned, and said, "No. Go ahead."

He sat next to her and she looked at him and thought, Please have cigarettes, mister, please. He looked like a smoker. His face was tan and weathered and had a bunch of lines. He was probably somewhere in his forties, early or late, Queenie couldn't tell. He had clear light blue eyes and brown hair with a little gray here and there and he wore a green polo-ey-type shirt, but it had no logo, and khaki pants, and a light summery tan blazer. He smelled good, too, like a nice cologne, but not like smoke, unfortunately.

Wilma walked up and gave him the once-over. She wasn't as nice to men as she was to women. Queenie thought it was because it was always men she ended up having to kick out.

"Can I get a Coca-Cola with lemon, please?" he said with a Brooklyn accent.

Wilma appeared to be very disappointed. She brought him a Coke and reluctantly set it down in front of him.

"One-fifty," she said, grimacing. No big sales here.

Queenie laughed without realizing it.

The Coke drinker put two dollars on the bar, and Wilma swept them up and stuck them in the register.

"I guess you're wondering why I come to a bar and order Coca-Cola," he said to her.

Queenie sniffed. "I guess I am wondering that, yes."

"I enjoy the atmosphere."

He wasn't looking at her. He was watching the TV but wasn't invested—Queenie could tell.

"Excuse me," Queenie said, as flirty as she could be, which wasn't very flirty—all she did was smile big. What would Trig do? she thought. Trig wouldn't have to do anything, Queenie thought. If you were Trigger Happy, he would come to you.

"Do you happen to have any cigarettes?" she said in a high, unfamiliar voice.

He turned to her and smiled, and his laugh lines moved and creased. He wasn't bad-looking, thought Queenie. Probably a knockout when he was younger. Nice blue eyes.

"I don't smoke," he said sweetly. "I'd like to buy you a beer, though, if you'd like another beer."

All-fuckin'-right, thought Queenie. She couldn't remember the last time a guy had bought her a beer, and sure, this fellow was a little older than she would've preferred, but a beer's a beer.

"Why wouldn't I like another beer?" said Queenie, smiling.

The Coke drinker shrugged.

"In case you'd prefer something else," he said.

"Like a shot on the side?"

He nodded and looked a bit surprised. "Sure. I was thinking more along the lines of something sweet."

"What—like Baileys?" scoffed Queenie.

He shook his head gently and waved Wilma over.

"A beer and a shot of Jameson's for the lady," he said.

The lady! thought Queenie. Now I'm a lady. Even Wilma cracked a smile as she pulled a brand-new Styrofoam cup off the stack.

"My name's Queenie," Queenie said, extending her hand.

"I'm Reynold Little," he said, shaking her hand. "People call me Rey."

"No kidding!" said Queenie, genuinely surprised. "My imaginary husband's name is Ray!"

"Really?" he said, amused. He appeared not to know quite how else to respond.

Wilma set the beer and the shot down in front of Queenie, and Rey handed Wilma a five and three ones. Good tipper, thought Queenie. I could do much worse. She took a sip of the beer and smiled.

"So what's wrong with Baileys?" Rey said.

"Nothing," said Queenie, as she lifted the shot to her lips. She tilted it to Rey in a mild toast. "If you're eighty years old." She drank the shot down, and it made her chest warm.

"How was that?" asked Rey.

"Tastes a lot better when someone else buys it," said Queenie.

"Better than Baileys, huh," he said.

"Not better, necessarily," said Queenie. She suddenly felt bad for speaking ill of Baileys. She didn't want to offend Rey personally. "It's a different thing."

Rey smiled slowly and sipped his Coke.

"I suppose you're right about that. My mother drinks Baileys," he said, matter-of-factly.

"That's what I'm talking about," said Queenie. "Everyone's mother drinks Baileys."

"Does yours?"

Queenie shook her head lightly.

"I don't know," she said vaguely. "We're not on speaking terms."

"I'm sorry to hear that," Rey said genuinely.

They were quiet. Queenie stared into the mirror behind the bar, at her face between the bottle necks. She thought of the mother at the Dark Horse wiggling her nose.

"Did you have a falling-out?" Rey asked gently.

We just never understood each other, Queenie was about to say, which is what she usually told people if they asked about the mother. She wanted me to go to typing school and get manicures and receive callers, but all I did was hobble around on my bum leg and play with my glass animals.

But she didn't say that.

"No, I've never met her," she said instead.

That left Rey quiet.

Queenie laughed under her breath, staring at the bar.

Then she said, "You know, when I was about seven or eight, my friend Jimmy said to me, 'How come you don't have a mother?' And, I couldn't answer him, because I didn't really know, and then he said, 'Maybe you were like Jesus,' which you know, really scared me because, even though I wasn't religious or anything, I knew Jesus had his work cut out for him, and I was thinking, I'm just not prepared for that kind of responsibility. And then Jimmy said, 'Nah, Jesus wasn't a girl,' and I was like, 'How do you know? You weren't there.' "

Rey laughed, and so did Queenie, and she was very far away for a few seconds. She was lying on Jimmy Schaw's sleeping bags. His parents were so poor he didn't even have a bed, just three sleeping bags stacked up. His big brother had pitched a tent around them, to make it a fun thing. That was the first time anyone had asked her about the mother.

Of course Queenie had wondered about the mother since then. She wasn't blind—of course she'd noticed most people had one, and she didn't. But that was rarely; most of the time, she honestly didn't think about it.

But when she did, when it crept into her body like a germ, she didn't get angry or sad. When Queenie imagined being face-to-face with the mother, she didn't think she would yell at the mother and curse her for leaving. She did not want to scream and beat the mother with her fists. There was only one thing she wanted to do, that she never told Jimmy Schaw or Uncle Si or Meade or anyone.

All she wanted to do was touch the mother's lips. All she thought about when she tried to conjure a picture in her head were the lips, not smiling or laughing or talking, just resting gently over the teeth, sealing her body closed.

Rey rattled the ice gently in his glass. Queenie turned to him and shook herself out of it.

"So why don't you drink?" she said.

Rey wiped the corners of his mouth with his fingers.

"Is it a problem for you?" he said.

"No," said Queenie, and then she thought about it. "Actually, yes. I can't trust people who don't drink."

"I guess you're not going to trust me, then," he said softly.

"I guess not."

They were quiet for a minute, and both looked at the TV.

Then Rey turned to her. "I quit drinking eight years ago," he said, without any kind of a bent at all—not regret, not pride, nothing at all that Queenie could detect.

"That's too bad," Queenie said earnestly.

Rey smiled. "That's one way to look at it."

"You do drink coffee, though, right?" she said hopefully.

"Yes, I drink coffee. And," he said, lifting his glass, "soda pop."

"Thank God. I mean, no offense, but you don't drink, you don't smoke—People might think you're a monk or something. You're not a monk, are you?"

"No," he said, still smiling.

"Good," said Queenie, putting her hand to her chest, fake-relieved.

Goddamn you're charming, she thought to herself. You've got him eating out of the palm of your hand.

"So what are you—if you're not a monk, I mean?" she asked.

He continued to smile. "I'm a surveillance specialist," he said.

"What does that mean?"

Rey reached into his breast pocket and pulled out a card. He handed it to Queenie.

It read:

Reynold Little, Private Investigations
Trailing   Locating   Missing Persons   Asset Searches
59 Gelston Avenue, Bay Ridge, Brooklyn
718-555-3959

Over 20 years experience in NYPD

"Is that true?" Queenie said quietly, slowing down the flirties. "About being with the police?"

"Yes, it is," said Rey.

"What are you—retired?"

"No, I didn't quite make it."

"They fire you?"

"Not exactly."

"Then what exactly?"

He grinned. "I'll save that story for when I know you a bit better," he said.

Wa-hell, wa-hell, thought Queenie. We certainly are confident.

"So what do you do—follow cheating husbands?" Queenie said.

"Sometimes," said Rey. "Sometimes I follow women who might be sleeping with them."

Queenie laughed. "Well, what's the point of that? If you don't mind my saying, why wouldn't you go right to the source?"

"Sometimes the client just wants to know who the other woman is."

Queenie began to get nervous. She gripped her big Styrofoam cup with both hands and started scratching her nails into the sides.

"And then what?"

Rey shrugged. "I turn the information over."

"To the client . . . the wife?"

"If that's the situation," Rey said, looking up at the TV. Without shifting his gaze, he added, "They may not even be married yet. She may be noticing small changes in his behavior—maybe she has for some time; she has suspicions. And you can believe me, people do all kinds of things they never imagined they would do when they have suspicions. She might find a paper napkin in the trash, for example, which her fiancé just now used, and sees a woman's name and a phone number on it—smudged and backwards, you see, because it was written on his hand. She may bring it to me."

He turned to Queenie. He had stopped smiling.

"And that's where you come in," Queenie said quietly.

"That's where I come in," he said.

Queenie stared at him, and her heart started to pound.

"What do you want?" she said gravely.

"I'm sorry," said Rey. "I didn't mean to scare you."

Queenie believed him for some reason.

He opened his jacket and reached for the inside pocket. He pulled out a manila envelope which was folded in the middle.

"I shouldn't be doing this," he said, facing forward. "I'm breaking a contract with a client by doing this." He slid the envelope across the bar to Queenie.

Queenie stared at it but didn't touch it.

"Two days ago I was hired to follow you. My client suspected her fiancé was having an affair with you," he said calmly.

"*What?*" Queenie said.

"Let me tell you what I have to tell you. Then I'll answer your questions to the best of my ability," he said, in the same even tone.

Queenie was speechless.

"I've been trailing you for a day and a half, and I'm fairly certain you're not sleeping with my client's fiancé. I took these photos of you yesterday," he said, tapping the envelope. "And the only reason I ever break a contract with a client is if he or she, or a third party, is in danger."

He took a sip of Coke, and then said, "And I think you may be in danger."

He pushed the envelope closer to Queenie, so it was next to her beer. She stared at it. Then she peered down to the end of the bar.

The patrons seemed to move in slow motion, lifting beers to their lips, talking, yelling at the TV screen. Queenie's heart beat in her throat.

"Go ahead. Open it," said Rey softly.

Queenie picked the envelope up and stared at the flimsy silver clasp. Her hands shook.

"Would you like me to open it?" said Rey.

Queenie nodded.

Rey tugged the envelope gently from her hands. He bent the tin clasp and opened the flap, and he pulled out a thin stack of shiny color photographs. Queenie stared, transfixed. The first picture was of her in front of her apartment, leaving. She stared at the image of herself—she was holding her hand to the side of her head, where she'd been hit.

Now she lifted her hand to her head above her ear and still felt the tiny bumps, not as pronounced as the day before but still there. There was a small stickie note in the corner of the photo which read, "6/19—5:47pm." She flipped to the next picture. It was of Queenie at the counter at Zia Maria's, taken through the large window, taken from across the street—6/19—5:59pm. Queenie stepping onto the L—6:07pm. Queenie walking on First Avenue, from the subway to Wintertown—6:19pm. Queenie coming out of Wintertown—7:13pm. Queenie talking to Meggy Bunny, taken through the window at The Sisters—that was a funny one. Queenie actually looked as bored as she'd felt. She inadvertently smiled now, seeing Bunny's big mouth wide-open.

"You didn't seem to want to talk to her too much," said Rey, noticing, grinning.

Queenie squeezed the pictures between her fingers and stopped smiling, and so did Rey.

Then Queenie waved to Wilma, and Wilma raised her eyebrows.

"Double Jameson's, neat," Queenie called. Then she turned to Rey. "You can pay for this one, too."

Rey dipped his head down a bit and appeared to feel bad. Well that's just a crying fucking shame, thought Queenie.

Wilma put down a snifter so big it looked like it should be holding fruit. It was full to the rim. Good old Wilma, thought Queenie. Never one to skimp.

"He's paying," said Queenie, barely cocking her head in Rey's direction.

"Four," said Wilma harshly.

That's it, Wilma, give him the old cold shoulder, thought Queenie. She lifted the drink to her nose and smelled it gently before she drank the whole thing down without blinking. She closed her eyes and felt it in her chest.

"Look, I realize this is a little strange—" Rey began.

"You don't realize shit," said Queenie. "Anyone ever follow you, Rey? Anyone ever take pictures of you outside your goddamn apartment?"

Rey put his hand on Queenie's shoulder, and for some reason, she didn't shake it off. He leaned in to whisper.

"I realize this is a little strange," he said again. His breath smelled like mint. Mint and Coke. "But you need to listen to what I'm going to tell you. May I?" he said, gently tapping the pictures.

"Oh, *sure,*" said Queenie loudly. "Be my guest, Rey."

Rey smiled genuinely. He had nice straight teeth, too. They're probably all crowns, thought Queenie, full of spite.

He started with the picture of Queenie at Zia Maria's. It was taken from across the street, Queenie thought, right outside the Salty Dog.

"Were you outside the Salty Dog?" said Queenie.

"Yes," said Rey.

He tapped the picture closer to the bottom, the forefront, where various types of people were gathered at the bus stop. Some were gazing down at the street, some reading, some looking south, for the bus presumably, most looking tired and washed-out. Frozen forever, with Queenie on the other side of the window, people in midbite inside the restaurant, lifting wedges to their lips, mouths open, black holes.

"Look here," said Rey, tapping the picture again.

He pointed at a man with thick glasses and unkempt hair that poofed out under his gray baseball cap. He wore a bright green New York Jets windbreaker.

Rey looked at Queenie expectantly.

"I don't know who that is," she said.

Rey nodded and put the picture in the back of the stack. He skipped the subway picture and pulled out Queenie on First Avenue. It also appeared to have been taken from across the street. Queenie was looking down. Rey pointed to a figure on the left, the same figure, with the bright green jacket.

Then he flipped to Queenie talking to Bunny in The Sisters. It was taken from outside somewhere, across the street as well, through the front glass doors and large windows. Rey tapped it— the same figure appeared by the door of The Sisters, squinting behind his glasses.

The next: Queenie from the back, staring into the window of the OTB. Her margarita-to-go dangled at her side in one hand, her other hand pressed to the window. And again, the guy in the bright green jacket stood a few feet away, leaning on a phone box awkwardly. Queenie could make out tiny beady black specks for eyes.

The next: Queenie exiting the first bar, off of Delancey, after the first Jager shot. The green figure was in the corner of the picture, standing next to a street-cleaning sign.

How could I have not noticed this freak? thought Queenie. Then she looked at Rey and thought, Either of them.

Rey kept flipping to pictures which showed Queenie either entering or exiting seven other bars. Queenie covered her mouth; she tasted the licorice of the Jagermeister in the back of her throat.

"I don't even remember this one," she said, picking up the last of the bar photo series.

It was of her coming out of a new French bar that she swore she'd never go into. She was also smoking a cigar and holding the doorframe for support.

Rey pointed to a green blur behind her.

"I think that's him," he said. "See, there's a glare off his glasses."

"I see it," Queenie said defensively.

"He's not quite in all of them, but most," Rey said.

Queenie nodded. Then she got pissed.

"So if you used to be a cop and everything, why didn't you take this guy down? Or hold him for questioning at least? That's what you're supposed to do, right? Hold them for questioning?"

"I'm not a police officer anymore. I can't hold anyone for anything," said Rey patiently. "And though it's a bit embarrassing, I didn't notice the guy until I printed the pictures up. I was too busy watching you."

"Wow," said Queenie. "You're a pretty shitty detective."

Rey smiled again. Why is he smiling so much? she thought. Because he's laughing at you, she said to herself, but she didn't quite believe that.

"Some folks think so," he said.

"Yeah, well, you can put me on the list," she said. "So, wait, how did you find me, here?"

"I trailed you today as well," he said, matter-of-factly. Just another day, you know.

"Oh, really," said Queenie, nonchalantly. "Well that's just fuckin' great. Where's the spread from today?"

"I didn't take pictures today. And I didn't see our friend anywhere," he said, tapping the photos. "And I already suspected that you weren't involved with my client's fiancé on a romantic level."

"Your client," Queenie repeated. "Hummer's girl, right? The future Mrs. Fish? What's her name—Lydia?"

Rey said quietly, "Charlotte."

"Right. Charlotte. Charlotte Fish."

"Charlotte Fields right now," said Rey.

Queenie nodded angrily. "Right, right, of course. You must have a lot of integrity doing this kind of work," she said.

Rey smiled.

"I try to."

Queenie stared at him.

He kept smiling.

"So tell me, Detective," she said. "Do you know who Trigger Happy is?"

"No," he said. "Is that who Mr. Fish is having an affair with?"

"Was," said Queenie. "She's dead now." Queenie drank the rest of her beer down. "So yeah, keep me on the list—you're a shitty detective, all right." Queenie stood up and was a little dizzy. She held the end of the bar. "Thanks for the drinks, Rey. So you can tell Mrs. Fields and her cookies whatever you want to about me and Trig and whoever else you feel like talking about. In the meantime, I'll ask you to follow someone else and stay the fuck away from me."

She picked up the envelope of pictures and headed for the door and didn't look back.

"See you later, Wilma," she said loudly, waving her hand in the air. "Bye, Jill. Bye, Stacee. Bye, Unbelievably Tall Guy."

Unbelievably Tall Guy smiled and nodded. God, he had a big head. It was the size of a basketball. Queenie was surprised she didn't feel a breeze from him shaking it around.

She walked out the door, and the humidity seemed to clog her throat up and made her cough. There was no chance of rain now; the sky was just brown and still. Queenie held her hand in front of her face and watched it shake. She clutched the manila envelope so hard her fingers made sweatprints on it.

"Mother*fucker*," she said, crossing the street to the liquor store.

She glanced behind her. Bedford was full. People poured up from the subway. She scanned the crowd for Rey and didn't see him. Then she looked for the man in the green windbreaker and didn't see him either.

She slipped into the liquor store, and the door beeped at her. There were two young guys milling around, not counting the Indian fellow behind the glass. Queenie looked at all the fine wines. Always look for the upside-down cone in the bottom of the bottle, Uncle Si used to say. That means you're drinking classy.

Queenie walked to the tiny open window where the Indian guy was bored stiff behind the bulletproof glass. He stared at her. He knew who she was. Queenie came into the store quite a bit to buy little minis of Jack Daniel's for the L ride into Manhattan. Sometimes she came in on late nights and tried to convince him to give her samples.

Now she leaned down to talk through the tiny window in the glass.

"Can I get a fifth of Wild Turkey?" she said.

Why do they have the glass anyway, she thought. Were people so much more likely to rob liquor stores, and was it because liquor stores had so much more money, or did the thieves want the liquor? That'd be a good name for something, thought Queenie. *Liquor Bandits*, starring Ray McSnoo and the Blind Guy from *Gimme Five*.

Queenie noticed the Indian guy wasn't moving. He crossed his arms and stared at her skeptically.

"Let me see your ID," he said.

Queenie sighed. *"Dude,"* she said. "I'm in here almost every day."

He continued to stare and not move.

Queenie pulled her wallet out. "Je-*sus,*" she said loudly. She picked her ID out and slapped it on the glass.

The Indian guy inspected it.

"It's expired," he said, all snotty.

Queenie leaned her head against the glass and closed her eyes, exhausted.

"I know," she said. "But my birthday hasn't changed."

He looked at her, suspicious, and narrowed his eyes for good measure, then finally walked over to the Whiskey/Bourbon section and grabbed a bottle of Wild Turkey.

When he came back to the window, he said, "Twenty ninety-nine."

Queenie shelled out a twenty and a five and dropped it into the money tray. Just then one of the other customers decided to leave, and a breeze funneled through when he opened the door, and the bills blew back up at her.

"Fuck," she said.

The Indian guy seemed taken aback. She pushed the money

through firmly, and he picked it up and gave her change. He slid the bottle into a thin paper bag and opened the hatch next to the window—a tiny Plexiglas box like they had at the post office. Like for a really tiny mime, thought Queenie.

Then the Indian guy smiled, huge and genuine, and waved at her.

"Thank you!" he said.

"You're, uh, welcome," said Queenie, confused.

What the fuck, what the fuck? she thought. She left the store and got caught in a crowd coming from the subway, moving north. Every time someone roller-bladed past her or a horn honked, she jumped. Steady, girl, she thought. No one's following you now, yes yes?

She kept her head down and hustled home, held the bottle close to her chest as if someone was going to take it. She turned the corner of her block and pulled out her keys, opened the heavy front door, and ran up the stairs, almost running into one of the HeySitDown girls who lived upstairs.

"Heyyy, what's up," she said, stopping to talk. Every time one of the HeySitDown girls stopped to talk to Queenie, it was either about TV or pot.

"Not much," said Queenie, racing past her.

Queenie opened the door of her apartment and shut it behind her and leaned against it, breathing heavy, sweating.

She dropped the envelope to the floor and began to unscrew the cap off the Wild Turkey. She hadn't fully cracked the seal when a blurry figure appeared next to her, coming from the kitchen.

"Hi, Queenie," it said.

Queenie screamed and dropped the Wild Turkey. It hit the floor with a thud but didn't break.

"Look what you did," said Meade, squatting to pick it up.

Queenie fought back tears.

"You son of a bitch!" she yelled.

"What's the problem?" said Meade.

"Put the whiskey down," she said, her voice shaking.

"Why should I do that?"

"Put the whiskey *down.*"

Meade set the bottle on the floor, upright. Queenie started to punch his shoulder furiously, releasing a stream of profanity and nonsense.

"Sonofabitch goddammit what the fuck are you doing sneaking into people's apartments sonofabitch bastard cocksucker—" Queenie kept on, and a few tears eked out, and her voice became hoarse. Meade stood still. Finally, after wearing herself out, she stopped.

"Are you finished?" he asked calmly.

Queenie didn't answer. She walked like a zombie to her bed and flopped down on the mattress. She rolled onto her back and rubbed her eyes.

"I am a little tense right now," she said.

Meade paused.

"Yeah, I got that," he said.

He picked up the whiskey and unscrewed it and took a sip. He walked over to the bed and handed the bottle to Queenie. She stared at it.

"Come on, now," he said.

Queenie sat up and took a gulp.

"You know," said Meade quietly. "I've had a key to your place for quite some time."

"I know."

"You and I sort of go over to each other's places whenever we feel like it," he said.

"I *know,*" Queenie said, getting pissed.

"I'm glad you know," he said, taking the bottle from her. "Because all this," he said, waving toward the door, "this is not a normal reaction."

Queenie placed her hand over her eyes.

"I know," she said, quieter. "Just look at the pictures."

"What pictures?"

"Those pictures," she said, pointing blindly in the general direction of the door. "In the envelope. On the floor."

Meade gave her back the bottle and stood up and walked to the door and picked up the envelope. Queenie drank the whiskey and watched him open the envelope and pull out the photos. He flipped through them, dark eyebrows furrowed together. He looked like a Muppet.

When he was done, he put the pictures back in the envelope and came and sat down next to her again.

"It's you," he said.

"Yep."

"Who took them?"

"A private detective. Working for Hummer's wife."

Meade furrowed again, and then his face brightened up. "He thinks you and Humvee are doing it?"

"Yep."

"No shit."

Queenie took another gulp of whiskey and handed it back to Meade.

"And that's not all," she said, taking the envelope from him. She pulled the pictures out roughly. The one on top happened to be her in front of the OTB. "Look at this guy," she said, pointing to the green jacket. *"He's* following me, too."

She handed the photos back to Meade aggressively.

"Who is he?" said Meade.

"I don't fucking know. He's a Jets fan."

"Does he have something to do with the stripper?"

"I don't know. I don't know. Maybe."

Queenie's face was red. She sat there like a kid who got busted for fighting.

"Drink," Meade said, giving her the bottle.

Queenie drank.

"Maybe you should call the stutterer," said Meade.

Queenie shrugged. She clutched the bottle to her chest.

"I guess you're right," she said.

"Maybe you should drink more."

"I guess you're right," she said, sneaking in a smile.

"Maybe we should go to the Turkey Club and play darts."

"Meade, I don't feel like moving."

Meade rolled his eyes.

"God helps those who help themselves," he said, standing up. "Come on, now, let's move it out."

"Not now."

"Yes now. This is just what you need."

He picked up a balled-up sock and threw it at her.

"Quit it," she said.

He grabbed up Queenie's blue sweatshirt and threw it at her. A slip of paper tumbled out of the pocket and floated to the ground. Meade picked it up and examined it.

"Is there something you're not telling me?" he said coyly, turning his head slightly.

Queenie turned her head slightly as well.

"No. I don't think so. What is that?"

Meade handed it to her. He picked up a *Gourmet* magazine Queenie had stolen from the collective building mail trough.

"I just thought that if you thought you were pregnant, that I'd be the first to know," he said, pretending to be cold. "But no, that's cool. You don't need to tell me anything. You're an independent woman. You don't even need to tell me when you get laid anymore, that's fine."

"What the piss are you talking about?"

She stared at the paper. It was the receipt from Drug Barn, the one from Trigger's garbage can. 1 INSTKW. InstaKnow—Queenie remembered the commercials: "Know in an instant!" She covered her mouth.

"I know. It's shocking what you hide from me," Meade said, flipping gingerly through the *Gourmet*.

"Trig might've been pregnant," said Queenie, thinking aloud.

"Huh?"

"Maybe Trig was pregnant."

Meade shrugged, confused. Queenie shook the receipt in the air. "I found this in Trigger's garbage can. At her apartment." Queenie stared at it. "Maybe she was pregnant."

"That's too bad," said Meade, turning the magazine sideways, as if it had a centerfold. Then he dropped it, and said, clapping, "Come on, Slugger, let's move."

Queenie slumped against her flat pillow and stared at the receipt. "I don't feel like it," she said sadly.

"Aw, come on," Meade said, getting annoyed.

"No, Meade," Queenie said firmly.

Meade sighed. "So you're going to sit here and pout because some girl you never met *might* have gotten knocked up by one of her *many* johns," he said roughly.

"Fuck you," Queenie said, angry.

Meade held his hands up. "Okay, fine," he said, and headed for the door. "Why don't you call me when you feel like a normal person, whenever the hell that is," he said, and he left and slammed the door.

Queenie felt bad for a second, then took a swig of whiskey and stared at the receipt. She touched it gently with her thumb. Her eyes began to hurt, and she realized she was tired. You should put the bottle down before you fall asleep, she said to herself. No, wait, it's Wednesday; you have to call Uncle Si.

She got up and stumbled to the phone, picked it up and dialed and balanced it on her shoulder while still holding the Wild Turkey by the neck and the receipt in her other hand.

"Clear Skies," a voice said.

"Hi, Nancy? This Queenie," she said, slurring.

"Oh, hi. How are you Queenie?" said Nancy cheerfully.

"I'm Okay. Uncle Si around?"

"Hold on a second, let me check for you," said Nancy.

The phone beeped twice.

"Ha-low," Uncle Si said gruffly.

"Heya, Uncle Si. S'mee, Queenie."

"Aw, hi there, Queenie. Where you at?"

"You know, Uncle Si. I'm still in New York."

"New York? Where you live? You live near McSwiggans?"

"No, I still live in Brooklyn."

"Brooklyn?" Uncle Si said, almost shocked, like he'd never heard it before. "That safe out there?"

"Sure, Uncle Si, it's very safe. It's full of young people."

"That don't make it safe," said Uncle Si. Then he paused. "That in Brooklyn? McSwiggans in Brooklyn?"

"No, McSwiggans is in the city. Manhattan," said Queenie. "The city" was too confusing. In Lowell, Boston was "the city." "You know what I live near?" Queenie said, taking a sip of whiskey. "I live near the steak place. Remember the steak place where they serve the big steaks and the big slices of onion and tomato as an appetizer? Remember?"

Si was silent.

"Si?" shouted Queenie. "You remember the steak place?"

"Nah, I never been to that place," he said.

"Sure you have, sure you have," said Queenie. "Remember it looks like a big snow lodge and we ordered steak for two and we couldn't finish it and you said they should offer a prize for being able to eat it all? Don'tcha remember?" she said, lying on the bed.

Uncle Si said nothing.

"Si!" she said loudly.

"What's that, now?" he said, confused.

"Don'tcha remember that, at the steak house—remember how big the steaks were?"

Nothing.

Queenie covered her eyes.

"Uncle Si," she said slowly, enunciating. "Remember about five years back, when you came to visit me in Brooklyn, and I took you to that steak house, and we couldn't finish all the steak they gave us?"

Si breathed heavily and finally squeaked out a very small hoarse, "No."

Queenie balled up the receipt and hit her fist against her knee.

"Well, we were there, Uncle Si. It happened—it sure as shit happened even if you can't remember it," she said, almost laughing.

She heard Si smack his lips a little. She knew they were too dry, and he was out of soda water, the Canada Dry with the lemon lime twist built in, because he didn't like the pulpy parts of actual lemons. Then again, maybe he didn't even like the Canada Dry anymore, she thought. He probably couldn't tell the difference between his favorite seltzer water and the generic. He probably couldn't tell the difference between seltzer water and anything else.

"No," he said again, tired, worn-out.

"Right," said Queenie quietly, defeated. She rubbed her eyes, and they made a disconcerting squeaking sound. Then she realized she was crying. "You don't remember, I know you don't."

"No," he said, even weaker.

"I heard you the first time," said Queenie. "I'll call you on Friday, Uncle Si, okay? Okay?"

"No," he said.

"Okay, then, bye-bye," Queenie said, pissed, and she clicked the phone off and threw it on the bed next to her.

What was with the tears? Silent movie star tears with no sobs or breath-catching, just little glam beads crawling out in a steady stream. She sighed and reached for the phone and pressed REDIAL.

"Clear Skies," said Nancy.

"Hey, Nancy. S'Queenie again."

"Oh, hiya, Queenie. You get disconnected? You want Si back?"

"No, no, that's okay. We're done for right now. But I think he's thirsty. Could you have someone bring him that seltzer water he likes, the kind with the lemon lime twist built in?"

"Yes, no problem, I'll have Arlita bring one up when she's free," said Nancy.

Thank God you are so helpful, Nancy, thought Queenie. Thank God you always say what I want to hear.

"Thanks, Nancy. Talk to you on Friday."

"All righty then, Queenie. You have a good day."

"Right back at you, Nancy," said Queenie, and she hung up again.

A good day, she thought. Yeah, Nancy, this one's been a real winner. She stood up and opened all of the windows, even the one that opened onto the fire escape. If someone's going to rob this place, she thought, the joke will be on them.

"Ha!" she shouted.

She lay back down on the bed and hugged the whiskey. She kept all of the lights off, so the room was full of only the eerie street-lights, and all she could hear were incredibly loud trucks rambling through the street. Why was her corner such a pinnacle of industry, she wondered, and what were they carrying? They sounded like chain saws, like an army of the Mad Max vehicles.

She closed her eyes and tried to breathe deeply, but the breath kept getting caught in her throat.

Calm yourself, she thought. What would Trigger do? She proba-bly would've taken Mr. Bay Ridge P.I. home and had her way with him. Because she's just that kind of girl.

"She always liked it," Queenie said aloud.

Trig always gets a thrill from letting boys touch her, thought Queenie. She likes the look in their eyes—she likes them desperate and starving. She likes their bodies tightening up. She tries it out for the first time on a boy in seventh or eighth grade, and his name is either Jeff or Chris or Matt. No matter what she does with her hands, as long as she keeps them on his skin, Jeff/Chris/Matt is frozen. She likes it when he's a little scared.

Scared scared scared—what does Jeff/Chris/Matt look like naked? The most beautiful thing she's ever seen. He smells a little funny, though, like meat. Like sweat, whiskey, smoke, cream of broccoli soup, thought Queenie.

And then, eventually, who knew what time it was (she only knew she was halfway done with the whiskey), Queenie fell asleep sitting up.

Thursday

She had the other dream, the one she had most often besides the subway dream, where she was in high school at her locker, and she
couldn't for the life of her remember the combination, but it was
always on the tip of her fingers. It was either 32-18-45 or 42-30-35 or
something like that, but right when she thought she had it, the little
white numbers and lines on the face of the lock ran together and she
couldn't see them at all. And of course she was late for class—which
class she didn't know, and the halls of her ritzy high school were
extra long and dark, and the class she was late for was on the very
top floor, and the school had so many more floors than it actually
did, at least seven or eight, and Queenie pounded up the speckled
stairs with her arms full of heavy books. She could feel herself
becoming tired and her breathing become labored, and the bell kept
on ringing in her ears, getting louder and louder.

Queenie opened her eyes. She was all wet. Her shirt and the
sheets under her were wet, and she reeked of whiskey and felt sick.

She sat up panicked for a second. The phone continued to ring next to her. She held her breath and took her shirt off over her head and threw it. Then she grabbed the phone.

"Yeah," she said, breathless.

"Hello, is this Queenie Sells?" an energetic voice said.

"Yeah."

"Hi, Queenie. This is Tony Bradshaw from Higher Ground. How are you this morning?"

"Oh," said Queenie, glancing around her. "I'm super."

"I'm glad to hear that," said Tony. "We sent you some information on how to consolidate your credit debt and make one low monthly payment for ninety-three months, and I can't believe you haven't responded to this once-in-a-lifetime deal!"

"Yeah, well, I'm just full of surprises," said Queenie.

"Have you had a chance to look over the information?" said Tony hopefully.

"Tony, let me tell you what I've had a chance to do this morning," said Queenie, looking down at herself, in her bra and pants. "I've had a chance to wake up covered in Wild Turkey, right down to the mattress, and I may or may not have vomited in my sleep. So what I think my priority is right now is stripping my bed and taking a two-hour shower. Mm-kay?"

Queenie didn't wait for Tony to respond. She clicked the phone off and placed it on the floor. Then she proceeded to strip the sheets off her bed, and one corner was stuck and wouldn't follow.

"Fuck you," she said to it, and she walked around to the other side of the bed and yanked the sheet, snapping it free.

She balled up the sheets and threw them on the floor, and then she went into the bathroom and stared at her face in the mirror and touched the gray spots under her eyes; they were soft. Then she noticed the thing on her chin again. It was just a hard little blood dot now.

"Fucking fuck-fuck," she said, and she scratched at it roughly with her thumbnail for a second.

Then she brushed her teeth and was uncoordinated about it, stabbing her gums and lips, and she bent down and drank from the faucet and rinsed and spit. She looked back in the mirror and pulled tight fistfuls of her hair for a second.

She took off her clothes and turned on the shower, and the water was too cold, then too hot, then too cold again, but Queenie was tired of waiting so she stepped in. Even though it was summertime and generally warm no matter what, the ice-cold water was not particularly refreshing. Queenie's skin rippled with bumps, and she clenched her teeth but would not give in and adjust the temperature.

Sometimes Queenie liked to treat herself poorly.

She soaped up very briefly and rinsed and then got out. She wrapped a towel around her torso, tucking it tight above her breasts.

She shuffled into the kitchen and opened the freezer and pulled out a long Popsicle from the Popsicle box and unwrapped it. It was (supposedly) grape-flavored and covered with freezer flakes, but she didn't much care. Her tongue stuck for a second, and it didn't taste like grape or any other fruit really—just ice and sugar blended.

She went to her closet and pulled out her laundry bag and rifled through, looking for something that didn't smell terrible, and she settled on a gray tank top—nothing to write home about, but it smelled more like cigarette smoke than BO, and that was all Queenie needed.

She pulled it on over her head and changed into some loose-fitting rayon-type pants with a racer stripe and an elastic waistband. Queenie called them her "workout pants" which wasn't an accurate description in any way because Queenie had never worked out in her life. But she always thought if she were to work out, she would wear these pants.

And then the phone rang again. Goddamn it, Tony, she thought. Am I gonna tear you a new one.

"What?" she said when she picked up.

There was fuzz on the line.

"Queenie," a whiny voice said.

"Hummer," she said. "Hummer, I have to ask you something."

"I can't talk now," he said, muffled.

"Of course you can't," said Queenie, sighing.

"Meet me at eleven-thirty at the Four Seasons," he said.

"At the what now?" said Queenie, licking her Popsicle.

"The Four Seasons restaurant, on Fifty-second between Park and Lex," he said, sounding annoyed.

"Oh, right, the Four Seasons on Fifty-second, where I hang out all the time. Yeah, they know me there—they named a fucking sandwich after me."

"I'm sorry," he said, sounding distracted. "I'd meet you somewhere else, but my father's in town, and I'm having lunch with him there."

"Great," said Queenie.

"Bring the ring," he whispered.

"No shit, Hummer. Look, was Trigger pregnant?"

Hummer was silent.

"I can't talk about this now," he said, suddenly hoarse.

"Yeah, I figured."

"I have to go—eleven-thirty, the Four Seasons—Wait for me in the lobby."

Then he hung up, and Queenie hated him for a second. She hated him for more than a second. She hated that Trigger fucked him and let him buy her a Kate Spade bag and maybe let him knock her up.

Queenie got another idea as she bit into her Popsicle. Her teeth stung, and she held her hand in front of her mouth and breathed heavily for a second. Then she slid her feet into the three-dollar shoes and picked up the phone again and looked through the papers and cards and matchbooks on the phone stand. She found Olds's number and dialed.

After three rings, a pickup.

"Olds."

"Olds, this is Queenie Sells."

"Miss Sells," said Olds, sounding surprised. "I was actually going to . . ." he paused, "give you a call today."

I'm sure glad I could save the old NYPD a cool eleven cents, thought Queenie. "I have to ask you something about Trig," she said.

"I'm sorry?"

"Trigger. Tara. Look, is she, *was* she pregnant?"

The words hung there. Olds was quiet.

Then he said, "What makes you ask that?"

"I don't know. I have a gut feeling—you know how it is. Don't you guys get those sometimes?"

"Sometimes," said Olds patiently.

"So, was she? Do you know?"

She heard Olds take a deep breath in.

"Let me ask you this, Miss Sells," he said.

Fuckin' hell, thought Queenie. Come on, man, no hypotheticals, please.

"Why would that information be important to you?"

Queenie sighed. "Because I'm wondering. I'm curious. I'm a curious person. I know you have to do an autopsy, and I just wanted to know."

He paused.

"We don't have that information b-back yet," he said.

"Oh," said Queenie. "Is there any way you could let me know?"

"Typically, that information is confidential."

"Oh," Queenie said again, deflated.

They were both silent then, but Queenie thought it was weird that he didn't just hang up.

"Well, thanks anyway," she said. "Bye-bye."

"Miss Sells?" he said.

"Yeah?"

"I may be able to call you and let you know," he said, suddenly less gruff.

"Okay, that's nice of you."

"Because we can always make eck-eck-exceptions for nonfamily members."

"Okay."

"Because we have, in the past, given confidential information to nonfamily members."

He already said that, thought Queenie.

"That's great," she said.

"And you may qualify, but you may have to fill out some paper-work."

"Oh, no, that's okay. I just thought if you could tell me quick and easy over the phone, then that would be neat," said Queenie, looking out the window, at the asphalt piles.

"No, I couldn't d-do that, but you may be privy to that informa-tion as a nonfamily member."

"Great!" said Queenie, like she'd never heard it before. Nonfamily member, paperwork, exceptions. Got it.

A police car pulled up to the curb next to the lot with the asphalt piles.

"If you can establish that you were a f-f-friend of hers, and you fill out all the necessary paperwork."

"Uh-huh," said Queenie, staring at the police car.

Then a black unmarked pulled up behind it. Two blues stepped out of the prowler.

"Then we might be authorized to reveal that information," Olds said for the nineteenth time.

"Right," said Queenie, stepping back from the window a bit. "Actually, I'm a little unclear. Could you walk me through the steps of that process again?"

"Well, you'd have to come up here and fill out some paperwork," Olds began.

Then Queenie watched Detective Miner step out of the unmarked car and readjust his pants above his waist. There was another guy in a suit with him. Queenie began to panic.

"Hey, Olds," she said, trying to sound calm. "I have to go— there's someone at the door."

"All right, then," said Olds. She could almost hear him smiling. "See you s-soon, Miss Sells."

"Okey dokey," she said. Uncle Si used to say, Okey dokey, Artichokey, but Queenie didn't feel that sentiment was particularly appropriate, so she said, "Bye, now," and hung up.

She watched Miner and the others walk cross the street, toward the entrance of her building.

"Son of a *bitch,*" she said aloud, dropping her half-eaten Popsicle on the floor. She looked around frantically for a moment and grabbed her wallet and her keys and Hummer's ring and continued to talk to herself: "See you soon my *asshole.*"

Then her buzzer rang. Queenie froze. She looked at the door, then turned and saw the open window and the fire escape. They do it all the time in the movies, she thought. It can't be that dangerous— it's there to save your life for Chrissake.

She pressed TALK on the intercom.

"Yeah?" she said, trying to sound relaxed, and a little hoarse, like she'd just woken up.

"It's Detective Miner, Miss Sells. Please buzz us in," said Detective Miner politely.

"Come on up," she said, pressing DOOR. Sure, she thought, come on up, cuff me, make a clever quip like the *Law & Order* guys. She could practically hear the dad from *Dirty Dancing* saying to her, "No more aces up your sleeve, Queenie—you have the right to remain silent."

Then they'd take her down to the station and put her in the box or the tank or whatever they call the interrogation room, and Olds and Miner and probably another hard-boiled detective (who's a bit of a loose cannon, but he's their best cop, dammit) will grill her for thirty-six hours until she cracks and says she did it. And of course she'll have some hapless defense attorney who'll do his best but he's no match for the DA, and then she'll get nailed, and someone will try to explain to Uncle Si how his little Beauty Queen killed someone, and now she's in stir for life.

Queenie looked toward the open window of the fire escape, and said aloud, "Fuck that."

Then she ran and climbed onto the sill and bent her head down and stepped out the window onto the fire escape. It shook a little, and Queenie thought, Oh, that's just what I fucking need—to fall to my goddamn death as a goddamn fugitive.

She stood up straight, tentatively, and clanked down the slim metal steps to the first-floor landing, holding the pipe cleaner banister tight. She peered down; it was too far to jump. Now she'd have to use the shaky metal ladder. Shit, shit, shit, she thought.

Then she thought about her father in the flowers. It was almost the same drop—about twelve feet. Queenie hadn't been crazy about heights since then. He should've just called a goddamn contractor, she thought.

For about two weeks, there'd been spring rain, and a leak in the roof, and the water dripped right over Queenie's father's favorite spot on the couch. So he would sit with a Scotch and attempt to unwind at ten or eleven in the morning, and the dripping would begin and hit him directly on his left shoulder.

He would try to ignore it at first, too dead-set stubborn to move—he would sit there until he had to drop Queenie off at Uncle Si's and go to work. But after about a week, he gave in a little and placed a bucket on his favorite spot on the couch and moved to the other side, but the experience was simply not the same, so Queenie figured.

And the bucket would fill, and Queenie's father would dump it out, and he and Queenie would watch the slightly browned water spin down the drain.

Once Queenie stuck her hand in the near-full bucket.

"Get outta there," her father said. "That's dirty. It came from the roof."

So finally the rain stopped, but the leak continued, and Queenie's father figured the water soaked through the wooden beams in the ceiling, and he walked around ranting about how he'd have to hire a contractor, and that was just what he needed.

"Bullshit," he said, angry and drunk on a Saturday afternoon, to no one in particular. "I'll fix it my goddamn self."

"What's going on?" said Little Queenie, when she saw him drag the rusty ladder from the garage.

"It's still dripping up there," he said, "And I'm gonna fix it."

And that was the first time Queenie experienced pride. This guy she lived with, who she didn't feel altogether close to in any way, but still, she knew he was her father and her most direct relation (which Queenie's awful grandmother would remind Queenie's father about constantly: "You got to take care of that child better—you're her most di-rect relation."), still and all, he was going to fix the roof, and they wouldn't need the bucket anymore.

Queenie stayed inside, stood by the front window and watched her father squint into the sun and prop the ladder up. His face was contorted, mouth moving, talking to himself, and she watched him climb the ladder unsteadily, holding some small metal tools and a jar of spackle. Up he went—first his head disappeared from her view, then his torso, then the rest.

Queenie watched the ladder tremble. Then she turned away and found something to keep her busy.

I'm always trying to find something to keep her busy, Queenie's father said to people.

Then the thump.

Now Queenie heard three sets of heavy feet coming up the stairs. Looks like it's time to get over all that, she said to herself.

There was a latch—a hook connecting the ladder to the landing, holding it up. Queenie jiggled it a little—it was rusty and hard to move. Fantastic, she thought. I should've known nothing in this fucking building's up to code. She hit it with her fist, kept glancing up at her open window, and the latch slipped a little, so she hit it a little more and finally the whole thing gave and swiveled downward. The ladder shimmied down fast, rattling like crazy and stopped short a few feet off the ground, shaking.

Here we go, she thought and she turned around and gingerly stepped down onto the first rung. The three-dollar shoes weren't making anything easier—she squeezed her toes tight and kept stepping down, gripping the upper rungs with her sweaty hands, trying to move fast but not kill herself. She made it to the bottom three rungs and jumped and landed hard on the concrete. She kicked off the three-dollar shoes and took them in one hand and began to run.

There were hipsters across the street in front of the used clothing store, holding cups of coffee with little cardboard sleeves, staring at her, only barely intrigued. Queenie ran past them and thought angrily, Yeah, sure, take a good long look—take a break from moving into the neighborhood with your berets and your easels and raising my goddamn rent some more. She never liked to think about how the old Polish folks saw her as just another one of the kids, brimming with disrespect and snottiness. Queenie pushed it from her mind.

Get off Bedford, she thought to herself. Bedford's too crowded.

Halfway to Berry, she turned back and saw Miner sticking his head out of her window, looking around. Queenie kept running. Fuck, she thought. You are now evading arrest. Things have officially gotten out of hand.

She took a left on Berry, her mind racing. If I could just get to the subway, she thought, but then her mind flashed on the two cops permanently stationed at the fare booth. On Halloween, Queenie had said to one of them, "Nice costume." He'd told her to move along.

Fuck, why don't cabs come to Brooklyn, she thought angrily. Fucking racists. Fucking Madison Avenue fuckers would rather take drunk businessmen back and forth between Wall Street and Flashdancers than take a nice hardworking girl out of the Burning Grounds at nine-thirty on a Thursday morning. When she's running from the police.

Queenie started to cough, and her breasts hurt. She could not recall when was the last time she had run anywhere. Probably PE in high school, running laps around the track. God, was I in good shape then, she thought. I could smoke half a pack at lunchtime and still run two miles in seventh period.

Then a black sedan passed her at high speed, cruising through a stop sign. Only cops would run a stop sign so effortlessly, she thought. She looked around quickly, searching for some kind of shelter, but there was nowhere to go. No open stores to slip into, and Perry's the burger place was too far down the block. She stood there, frozen, and leaned her head on the brick wall next to her, figuring at any moment they'd look in the rearview and see her.

But the car continued to tear down Berry, not slowing at all. Queenie's face brightened. Who else would have so little regard for human life on the road besides cops? She practically snapped her fingers—a car service!

Yes, yes, now she remembered, the North Grounds car service was two blocks away. She ran, pounding her feet against the concrete, feeling her entire body shake with every step, her chest and head full of bricks.

She saw the yellow awning on the next block, in the distance and ran past the Burning Grounds Ale House and thought, Wow, could I use a pint of Weisse. Lemony wheat beer—perfect for morning, better than OJ. But now was clearly not the time. She kept running and didn't look behind her and thought, The cops only have two cars. Two cars can only do so much, right?

There were three or four black sedans parked on the street outside of the car service office, and Queenie scanned the front seat for drivers but saw none. She ran to the office door and ripped it open and pulled it shut behind her.

She leaned against the door, holding her shoes to her chest, sweating, panting.

There were four guys sitting at a card table, drinking coffee and smoking, three Hispanic fellows and one white guy, and another Hispanic guy behind a counter. They all stared at her.

"I," she said, catching her breath. "I need a car."

Two of the guys at the table looked at each other, and the other two glanced back at the guy behind the counter. The guy behind the counter typed something into his computer and nodded at the Hispanic guy sitting with his back to Queenie. He stamped out his cigarette and stood up.

"Where do you need to go?" he said to her.

"The city," she said. "East Side."

He grabbed a ring of keys off the card table. Queenie dropped her shoes on the floor and stepped into them. Her driver stretched his arms over his head, back and forth, a little shoulder crack. Come on, come on, Queenie thought.

The driver fiddled with his keys and walked outside without looking at her. Queenie followed and kept her head down. He walked around to the driver's side of one of the sedans and pushed the keys around on the ring, trying to find the right one, which seemed to take about twenty-five minutes. Queenie bounced up and down on the balls of her feet.

She walked to the passenger side and tried to open the door, yanking the handle.

"Hey, hold on, don't break the door," he said. He was actually annoyed.

"Sorry."

You'd think, if you were going to have a car service, you could unlock the fucking doors for the patrons, she thought. Of course I wouldn't want to break the door on this lovely vehicle. Whatever funeral parlor you ripped it off from obviously took such good care of it.

He finally slid into the driver's seat, and Queenie watched the metal lock inside pop up, and she tore the door open and got in and slammed the door. The driver looked back and shook his head.

"Sorry," Queenie said sheepishly.

The driver started the car and let it warm up for a second.

"Hey," said Queenie, leaning forward. "I'll give you an extra twenty if we haul ass."

The driver nodded like he heard this all the time. Maybe he did. Then he slipped on huge boxy Terminator sunglasses, and put his hands together for a second, like he was praying. He proceeded to peel out like it was a real getaway, only missing the screech. He sailed down the street so fast Queenie thought the wheels would come off.

Queenie held the strap above the window, and the Burning Grounds sped by outside—Berry to Broadway to the bridge. North Side to South Side. Queenie leaned her head against the glass.

"Hey, are these windows tinted?"

"Yes," the driver said.

He turned on the radio. The Brother Brother Brother song was playing. He tried to sing along with it but kept saying "Mother" and "Brother" at the wrong times. He finally gave up and glanced at Queenie in the rearview mirror.

"Where on the East Side?" he said.

Queenie thought about it. The digital clock on the dash said 10:15. She sure as shit didn't want to be early for Hummer at the Four Seasons; it was a pretty fair bet she'd draw attention to herself in her sweaty tank top and workout pants and flip-flops. She tried to think of what bar was near, but she was at a total loss on the Upper East Side. People don't even drink beer on the Upper East Side, she thought. Except that place, oh goddammit, what was the name? She'd been there with Meade and Tommy Roses and Glueman . . . the toilet was stopped up; Irish guys kept asking her if she had cats. . . . Then she remembered—not the name, but the corner.

"Sixtieth and Third," she said.

The driver nodded. Right before the entrance to the bridge, they hit a detour—all orange mesh and safety cones and big square signs.

"Fuck," said Queenie under her breath. Why is there always construction down here?

"Don't worry," the driver said.

Queenie smiled. She'd never been told that by a driver or a cabbie before, or even an airline pilot. It should be part of the licensing process, really, she thought. Even if it's a lie.

The driver continued to haul ass around the sharp turns and did not traverse the detour passage cautiously, as had been advised by the signs. He cut off a GOYA ("Oh Boya!") truck, and the GOYA driver honked and yelled, "Assfucker!"

Queenie's driver appeared unfazed. I guess if enough people call you an assfucker, it starts to lose its punch, she thought.

They pulled onto the bridge, going a nice even seventy, and Queenie held the leather strap with both hands and gazed out the window, at the city and the water.

Just what exactly was she planning to do? Go on the lam officially? Become a hobo with a busted cigar and ride the rails? Look for the goddamn one-armed man? No, despite scaling the side of her building with aplomb and effectively escaping from the Burning Grounds into Manhattan, Queenie did not think this made her a shoo-in for a successful fugitive. But she couldn't stop just yet.

They crossed the bridge, and Queenie watched the driver in the rearview, with his huge glasses. Queenie pulled out her wallet and leaned forward.

"I'll give you ten bucks for your sunglasses," she said.

The driver raised his eyebrows in mild surprise but all in all, it didn't take him long to think about it. He pulled off the glasses and handed them back to her without turning around. Queenie took them from him, and he kept his hand there, waiting for the bill, and Queenie slid the ten between his fingers, and they clamped shut like a clothespin.

That's cool, Queenie thought of the driver. He's not attached to anything. Keep going, keep moving, don't look back. You should live like this guy, Queenie, she thought. She began to calm down.

She put on the sunglasses and looked at herself in the rearview. They were huge on her, and she had more of a Gloria Steinem slash George Michael aviator thing going instead of a Terminator thing. The rims were greasy.

They finally cruised onto Delancey. Queenie looked out the window and saw a store called Pretty Lady. Even though PRETTY LADY was written in black paint above the entrance, there were burnt-out movie star lightbulbs outlining the letters. Pretty Lady must have been lit up at some point. Was it even open nights, thought Queenie. Did strangers come from miles around to see the lights of the Pretty Lady?

The driver turned up Suffolk and cut off an SUV. The SUV driver honked and flipped off Queenie's driver. Queenie's driver didn't seem to be bothered. Jeez, maybe he's a Buddhist or something, thought Queenie. Lose all desire and gain inner peace and so forth.

They sped down Houston and onto the F.D.R., dodging and constantly changing lanes, Queenie gripping the leather strap but not afraid for her life like she should've been. She looked across the water, which seemed to be moving quickly. It made her feel dizzy, so she turned away and looked at the buildings on the other side. All huge brick apartment buildings, and industrial-looking businesses and hospitals. The streets that far east seemed to be abandoned; Queenie couldn't spot one person.

They took the Sixty-first Street exit, and Queenie looked out the window at the old ladies, thinking that some of the folks up here have lived in their little apartments for a million years. Queenie's driver stopped at a light at Sixty-first and First, and Queenie saw a woman on the corner, holding her hand up to shield her eyes from the sun. She was wearing a blue dress and had saggy little panty hose rings around her ankles.

And then, without really trying to, Queenie thought of her own mortality. Will I ever live as long as that lady, and what will be the point of being alive? she thought. But what is the point of being alive now? Queenie had no answer. Someday, she thought, I will be standing on the street corner waiting for the light to change, and my panty hose knee-hi's will sink to my ankles and I'll have elephant legs. Queenie put her fingers gently on the window, and she felt as if there was nothing between her and the old lady in the blue dress, as if all Queenie had to do was blink her eyes and that would be her.

Queenie had no idea what she would look like at that age. She never knew her mother, and her father didn't live long enough for her to see what he would look like, and Queenie never really looked like Uncle Si, and even so, he'd been an elderly person for as long as she could remember. She stared at the old lady in the blue dress and thought, And then you too, Queenie, you will be tired, tired, tired, and your skin will be as wrinkled as tree bark. And, actually, she told herself, there is nothing separating you from that old lady right now—maybe something, maybe time is all, but that's really nothing when you think about it. After all, thought Queenie, it's just days.

Then the light changed, and the car bounced along, and the old lady in the blue dress was out of sight, and Queenie forgot what she'd been thinking about. Now all she was thinking about was the bar on Sixtieth and Third, and she quietly hoped it was open. Not only because she needed a safe house for a few minutes, but she could also really use a pick-me-up. Maybe they could make her a red eye.

The driver pulled up on the corner, and Queenie peered out the window. The Metro—that was the name, and it was open! Things are finally starting to go my way, she thought.

The driver didn't turn around, just stretched his hand back and opened his fingers in the same clothespin fashion. Queenie pulled out two twenties and stuck them in his hand.

"Thanks," said Queenie.

The driver nodded.

Queenie pulled out another twenty. "You never saw me, okay?" she said. "Or make me a blond or something, yes yes?"

Again the driver was unfazed by her directions. He opened his fingers again, and Queenie slid the twenty into his palm.

"Have a nice day," she said.

Then he finally looked her right in the face and smiled. She smiled back and stepped out of the car. She noticed he continued to smile through the open window, and it made Queenie embarrassed for some reason. Then he pointed at her.

"You have a *great* day," he said.

"Thanks."

Then Queenie's driver sped off and was technically no longer Queenie's driver.

Queenie turned around and briefly glanced at the bar through its front window. It was black and narrow inside. She pushed the glass door open and walked in. It didn't quite smell like a toilet yet, but Queenie knew that would come as the day wore on. There was only one patron, a fairly fat young man sipping a dark mixed drink daintily, pinky up and out. He wore a black T-shirt and black pants and had a huge double chin. It looked like a pillow.

The bartender was an older fellow, with hair so light Queenie couldn't tell if he was still blond or had gone gray. He walked back and forth, carrying boxes, unpacking beers, doing the kinds of things you would do before a bar got full. There was golf on the television with no sound.

Queenie sat down a couple of stools away from the fat man and looked at herself in the mirror behind the bar. She then realized she was still wearing the Terminator glasses. Smooth move, she thought, taking them off. Way to not draw attention to yourself.

The bartender nodded at her while screwing a plastic pour top on a bottle labeled FANCY GIN. What a misleading name, thought Queenie. Though she'd certainly had a few well drinks in her day, she didn't quite get used to the vinegar paint thinner taste of the supercheap alcohol until at least the fourth or fifth.

"What can I get you?" the bartender said.

"Can you make me a red eye?"

He quickly looked beneath the bar.

"I don't have tomato juice right now, but I can set you up with Bloody Mary mix."

"That would be fantastic."

"What kind of beer?"

"Miller Lite, please."

He nodded again and placed a mug on the bar and filled it halfway with Bloody Mary mix. He cracked open a bottle of Lite, and filled the mug the rest of the way. He set the mug and bottle in front of Queenie.

"That's three-fifty," he said.

Queenie paid and was very happy for a few minutes. The red eye was thick and cold with a slight spicy twist from the Bloody Mary mix that Queenie really enjoyed.

"How is it?" asked the fat man.

"Oh, it's just perfect," said Queenie. "It has a slight spicy twist that I really enjoy."

The fat man nodded and looked happy for her. He had a plastic bag sitting on the bar in front of him, and now he removed some sort of round food item covered in tin foil and began to unwrap it.

"What are you drinking?" asked Queenie.

"Jack and Coke," he said.

He has one of those voices fat people commonly have, thought Queenie. It's as if their throats are a little clogged up, or heavily padded. Maybe there's just a lot of mucus, she thought—from all the dairy products perhaps.

And sure enough, inside the tin foil was a thick egg and cheese. The egg was folded over twice or three times like cardboard, spreading wide out past the roll.

The fat man pulled the top off the roll, and the cheese was hardly melted—just a glistening orange square. Then he reached into his bag and came out with a two-cube pack of Hotel Bar butter and a small white plastic knife. Queenie watched intently.

He opened the pack of butter and shook out a cube. Then he peeled the wrapper off, again daintily, using only the tips of his fingers, and sliced two thick slices of the butter as if it were cheese. He proceeded to spread the two slabs of butter on the folded-up egg and placed the top of the roll gently back. Then he turned the roll over and repeated the procedure—two more chunks thick as wet cement on the bottom side. Finally, he folded up his sandwich and leaned the knife on the cube of butter.

He lifted the roll to his mouth and took a bite. Melting liquid butter dripped out of the back of the roll and onto the bar. The fat man wiped it with a napkin. He glanced at Queenie who was staring, horrified, but also a little impressed.

"You know the Sunshine Deli, on First?" he said.

Queenie shook her head.

"They never put on enough butter," he said, kind of quietly, like he was letting her in on the ground floor of a scheme.

Queenie nodded slowly, and then she got a great idea.

"Hey, do you have a cigarette?" she asked the fat man.

He made a poo-poo face and wrinkled his nose.

"I don't smoke," he said. "It's very, *very* bad for you."

Queenie forced a smile and thought, A lot of things are bad for you, Butter Boy.

"Hey, boss," she called to the bartender, who was wiping the taps. "You got any smokes to spare?"

The bartender nodded and pulled a pack of Camels from his pocket. He handed one to Queenie and lit it for her.

"Thanks," she said.

She breathed in. It didn't feel fabulous. The fat man continued to eat his butter sandwich and sip his Jack and Coke.

"What do *you* do for a living?" he said to Queenie.

"I'm currently unemployed," she answered.

"No kidding!" he said, genuinely surprised. "So am I!"

"No kidding," echoed Queenie.

Quite a coincidence, pal, she thought. Here we are at ten in the morning on a weekday, getting drunk—and neither of us have a job!

"Well, you could say I have a night job, informally," he said.

Queenie nodded politely.

"I just came from a long night—that's why I'm here so early," he added, cheery.

She nodded again.

"I mean, most people wouldn't even call it a job," he said.

"Uh-huh," said Queenie.

"Most people don't consider *illegal activity* to be a real job," he said, leaning in, whispering "illegal activity."

"Oh," said Queenie.

She sipped her red eye.

Finally, he started to crack. "You can guess. Go ahead—try to guess what I do," he said coyly.

Queenie looked up at the peeling yellow ceiling and pretended to think.

"Um, do you work in a restaurant?" she asked.

The fat man's face dropped.

"That's not illegal," he said, disappointed.

"It could be," said Queenie mysteriously. "It depends on what they serve at the restaurant."

"No, that's not it," he said impatiently. "Go ahead—guess again."

"Do you beat your wife?" said Queenie.

"I don't have a wife," he said, even more deflated. "And you can't do that for a living."

"That's what you think," Queenie said, winking at him.

"Well, that's not it either," he said, at a loss. "Would you like me to tell you?"

Queenie paused for effect, then said, "Sure."

The fat man leaned over. "I'm a thief," he said, almost giddy.

"Wow," said Queenie. "What kind of things do you steal?"

"Oh, all kinds of things," he said wistfully. "Televisions and computers, mostly."

"Uh-huh," said Queenie. "And how much do you make a year from thieving? You know, roughly."

"Hard to say," said the fat man, putting down the butter sandwich. "Anywhere between sixty and eighty thousand dollars."

"Do you get benefits with that, or what?" said Queenie.

The fat man looked at her like she was just nuts for asking.

"No," he said.

"What if you get sick? Let's say you're in the middle of thieving and you're lifting a home entertainment system with the works—the hi-fi, the Atari 2600, and your back goes out and you get a hernia? You go to the emergency room and what—it's all out of pocket?" Queenie said, shocked.

"Yes," he said. He did not seem to want to answer those kinds of questions about thieving.

Queenie shook her head. "What a fuckin' country, man," she said.

He ignored her.

"It's very detail-oriented work," he said.

"I can imagine," said Queenie. "Do you rob people at gunpoint?"

The thief blanched and started to talk with his mouth full. "God, no, I only take things when people aren't there."

"Doesn't that take all the fun out of it?" said Queenie.

"No, not really," he said. "A woman kissed me though, one time."

"Is that so?" said Queenie.

She sipped her red eye and knew he was just dying to tell her all about it, so she thought she'd let him hang on for a few more seconds.

He couldn't take the pressure; he was bursting at the seams. How bold, thought Queenie. And then she started thinking about the appetizer at the Howard Johnson's in Times Square called "The Bold Ones." It was potato skins and buffalo wings. Queenie never knew what made those items so bold, as opposed to, say, mozzarella sticks and jalapeño poppers, which sounded much bolder to her. Then Queenie became hungry. She poured the rest of the beer into her mug.

The fat man told her, "I'd been watching an apartment in the West Village for quite some time, and I knew the man who lived there left on weekdays around eight and returned at six-thirty. I could tell he had a lot of money because those apartments don't come cheap, and he wore very expensive clothes." He paused and looked at Queenie, waiting for a reaction. Then he held up one finger and continued. "I knew that because they had logos," he said proudly. "You see, the thing people don't really think about is that thieves have to be very observant. You have to notice every little detail because anything can make or break a job." He paused to take a bite of the butter sandwich. He didn't wait to finish chewing to continue his story. "The apartment building was in the process of being painted, and so there were always painters walking around, in and out of the building and on scaffoldings and such.

"And one day, it was a Monday—" He paused. "No, it was a Tuesday, I bought white overalls and a white cap to make it look like I was a painter, and I even bought a roller brush to make it realistic. Because that's what a painter would carry—a roller brush or a can of paint or a ladder of some kind.

"And I just walked right in and no one gave me a second look because I was so convincing. They looked at my clothes and my roller brush and just assumed I was a painter," he said, getting excited. "And I walked up to the third floor—there was an elevator, but there are generally fewer people on stairs, and I was trying not to be seen as much as possible, trying to blend in, you know."

"Like a chameleon," Queenie added.

"Yes, like a chameleon," he said. It threw him off a little,

Queenie interrupting like that, but he quickly recovered. "So I found his apartment and picked the lock open. It was a tough lock, too—some are quite easy, but this one gave me a run for my money. And that's one of my specialties, too—picking locks."

"How were you sure the guy wasn't there? That he wasn't taking a sick day or something?" asked Queenie.

The thief paused and shook his head quickly, a little confused. "Oh, well, I'd been watching from across the street to make sure he had left."

"Were you in a car or were you just standing there?" asked Queenie.

He paused again. "I was sitting on a bench—that's where I always watched the apartment from."

He looked at Queenie tentatively. She smiled and nodded.

"Where was I?" he said.

"One of your specialties is picking locks," said Queenie.

"Right. So it didn't take me long to pick the lock—"

"Even though this was a tough one," Queenie added.

"Right, but I picked it, and I opened the door and closed it behind me quietly—because you don't want to make too much of a ruckus in that type of situation. And right there in front of me was a tall gorgeous woman. She looked like a movie actress, like Ingrid Bergman with raven black hair."

Raven black hair? thought Queenie. He must read a lot of Danielle Steel. Queenie had read a few Danielle Steels in the past, and everyone in the books either had raven black or flaming red or sun-kissed golden blond hair, and everyone, simply everyone had blue or green eyes like the fucking ocean. Christ, Queenie had thought, doesn't anyone have regular brown hair or eyes that don't sparkle all the goddamn time, maybe just on the weekends or something?

"What did you do?" asked Queenie, sounding interested.

The thief smiled. Now she was involved. Now she couldn't wait to hear the end.

"At first, I didn't know what to do. Can you imagine—I'd just broken into an apartment, and here is this beautiful woman!"

"I can't imagine that," said Queenie encouragingly.

"Neither could I! So I said, no—*she* said, 'What are you doing here?' And I thought very quickly, and said, 'I work for the painters. I guess I'm in the wrong apartment,' and she said, 'I guess you are.' But to tell you the truth, she didn't look very disappointed.

"So I turned around to leave, and she put her hand on my shoulder, and said, 'Why don't you stay and have a drink?' "

"Oh, man!" said Queenie. "What did she make you?"

The thief thought for a second. Then he said, "Martinis. She made us martinis in real martini glasses, with olives. And after one, she began to get a little drunk, but I didn't—I can hold my liquor, and she said, 'You're not really a painter, are you?' and I said, 'No, I came here to rob your boyfriend's apartment.' "

"No way!" said Queenie. "Why'd you blow your wad like that?"

The thief widened his eyes and reared back a little like he'd been poked, a bit surprised by Queenie's phrase. Then he continued. "Because somehow I felt I could trust her. We had a connection. I can't really explain it," he said dreamily. "I don't know if you've ever had a connection like that, but it really is something."

Queenie smiled and appeared thoughtful.

"What happened then?" she asked.

"Well, the woman laughed and said that man wasn't her boyfriend—she had just met him and had a one-night stand with him, and she didn't even like him very much!"

"What a break!" said Queenie.

"No kidding. Then she said I could take whatever I wanted because she thought he was such a major jerk."

"God, this just keeps getting better and better!" said Queenie.

"I know. And then she kissed me, right then and there."

"Jeez Louise."

"Believe you me, it was the weirdest experience I ever had robbing a place," he said.

Then they sipped their drinks, both quiet for a moment.

"So what did you end up taking?" asked Queenie suddenly.

"What?"

"What did you take from his apartment?"

"Oh," he said, pausing. "A computer," he said sheepishly.

"That's all?" Queenie scoffed. "I thought it was an all-you-can-eat situation. I would've thought you'd clean him out."

"Well, it turns out he didn't have such nice stuff after all. So I just took the computer. And a Discman," he said quietly.

"Did you get the chick's number or anything?"

"Uh, *no,* " he said, laughing, like it was an absurd thing to ask. "I didn't want to put her in any danger."

"Right," said Queenie. "You wouldn't want the cops after her or anything."

He laughed again, and said, "No *duh.* "

Queenie nodded pensively and said, "No duh, indeed."

The thief ate the other half of his sandwich so fast the butter didn't have time to make a puddle on the bar. It must have really been torture for him to tell that story and not eat the whole thing immediately.

Then he licked and sucked on his fingers like they were oyster shells. It was fairly disgusting.

"Hey, what time is it?" asked Queenie.

The thief glanced at his (probably stolen!) watch.

"It's twenty after eleven."

Queenie drank the rest of her red eye quickly and slid off the stool.

"Nice talking to you," she said to the thief. "Good luck with your career and everything."

"Thank you," he said politely.

Queenie grabbed her Terminator glasses and walked out into the heat of the sun.

She began to walk south on Third, looking around her, looking for familiar faces, looking for cops. Relax, she said to herself, they probably don't have an APB out on you just yet. You're not Patty Hearst or anything.

She crossed over to Lex, and the neighborhood got a little bit swankier, all the companies, taller buildings, businessmen, ladies with shopping bags with names that sounded like various types of pasta, Mexican and Jamaican women pushing white babies in strollers. The streets were starting to get crowded for the lunch rush. The red eye in her belly swished around. On the corner of Fifty-fifth and Lex, she waited for the light to change with a group of people, and she heard this piece of dialogue from a man and a woman standing behind her:

Man: Just shut up, okay? Will you just shut up?
Woman: Sure, I'll shut up. Like I have a problem.
Man: You do have a problem—you're an asshole.

Then the light changed and blared WALK, and Queenie could no longer hear the couple. Jesus, thought Queenie, tough room. She turned her head slightly and saw them—fairly well dressed, young, both smoking. They sped ahead of her when they hit the sidewalk, still together. Seems like a pretty ironclad relationship to me, thought Queenie. She could only hope that one day she would have a deep enough connection with a man so that he could call her an asshole and she wouldn't mind so much.

She turned onto Fifty-second and saw the Four Seasons awning, long and black and thin, with the name lit up in tasteful little letters. Queenie looked up and squinted; she hadn't realized the Four Seasons was on the ground floor of an office building. It seemed a strange location for a restaurant. Queenie walked to the entrance and a man in a suit looked her up and down and held the door open for her. Oh Jesus Christ, she thought. You have got to be kidding me.

She walked into the lobby, which was beige and kind of abrasively lit by bright yellow lights. The floor looked like the floor in a museum—speckled tile, very sixties, she thought. She turned to see a bored-looking woman standing in the coat-check room, who seemed to stare right past Queenie. There were carpets on the walls. Ah, fine art, thought Queenie. She looked at a small low table in the corner with some magazines, and flat leather chairs surrounding it.

There was also a staircase leading up, where Queenie guessed the restaurant was.

A few people stood around in the lobby, men in suits, and women with a lot of gold and silver watches and bracelets. There was one ancient woman who weighed no more than fifty pounds in a fancy green dress with a gold brooch the size of her head. She had no expression, just clung loosely to the arm of a younger man in a suit who chatted it up with other men in suits.

She glanced around but didn't see Hummer, and she looked up at a clock on the wall with thin hands and numbers. It was 11:32. Queenie started up the padded stairs.

The room upstairs was huge and dimly lit, with incredibly high ceilings, all wood walls, and to her right was a four-sided bar with strange gold spikes hanging over it. Maybe if you have a few too many and get out of hand, they drop a spike on you, thought Queenie. But probably not. It was probably more fine art.

There was a dining area behind a long wall of glass with spider crooked lines through it, like it had been cracked. Like someone had taken a spike and gently chiseled all over the whole thing. She headed toward the dining room, walking past the maitre d', who stood at a wooden podium.

"Ah, eh, excuse me," he said to her. "Can I help you, miss?"

He looked like Uncle Pennybags from Monopoly, only a little taller and without a monocle.

"Yeah, I'm meeting a friend here," said Queenie briskly.

Pennybags smiled gently, an I'm-sure-you-must-be-mistaken smile.

"And what is your friend's name?" he said skeptically.

"Hummer Fish."

He looked down at his list and frowned.

"This way, miss," he said, turning toward the dining room.

It was relatively busy, filled with various business types, early-lunchers clinking ice in their glasses. The room smelled like grilled vegetables and garlic and candle wax. Queenie couldn't help looking at the food as Pennybags led her through and around tables—

pretty little salads with soft green leaves and pink baby shrimp.

Queenie saw Hummer at a table in the corner with an older gentleman, who Queenie assumed was his father. Hummer looked better than he had the day before; he was back in his pink dress shirt and slacks, looking red-cheeked and healthy.

When they arrived at the table, Pennybags said, "Your guest, sirs."

Hummer stood up, panicked.

"Queenie," he said.

Pennybags looked relieved that Hummer knew her.

Then Hummer's father stood up as well. Queenie recognized him when she examined his face—a very fit, older man with a ring of gray hair around his head. He wore more or less the same outfit as Hummer, except that his shirt was tinted blue, and he had the same gray eyes as his son—all in all looked exactly like his son, except that his smile was much more genuine.

"Hello," he said congenially.

"Hi," said Queenie.

Pennybags kept standing there, and Mr. Fish turned to him, and said, "Thank you very much, William."

William nodded at Mr. Fish and forced a smile at Queenie and left.

Hummer began to stammer. "You were supposed to wait for me in the lobby," he said, teeth clenched.

"Hummer, don't be rude," said Mr. Fish smoothly. Then he extended his hand to Queenie, and said, "Benjamin-Franklin Fish. Pleasure to meet you."

"Queenie Sells," said Queenie, shaking his hand. He had a businessman handshake, tight and firm. "We've actually met."

"Have we?" said Mr. Fish. Then he gestured to an empty chair. "Please join us."

Queenie sat, then so did Hummer and his father. A waiter appeared, and his apron was straight as an index card.

"Would you like something to drink, ma'am?" the waiter asked.

Queenie glanced at Hummer, who still looked nervous, then at

Mr. Fish, who smiled encouragingly. He had a mimosa in front of him.

"A mimosa?" she said tentatively, pointing at Mr. Fish's glass.

"That's a bellini, ma'am," said the waiter patiently. "Would you like that?" Yes, little girl, it's a Shirley Temple—would you like that?

"Sure."

The waiter disappeared, and Mr. Fish said, "You were saying, Queenie, that you and I have met before?"

"Yes, sir," said Queenie. "I went to the same high school as Hummer."

"Really? I'm sorry I didn't recall. Hummer routinely fills me in on the other Westmoreland alumni here in New York, but I don't think he's told me about you."

What a surprise, thought Queenie. I wonder what else Baby Boy hasn't told you.

Hummer smiled uneasily. Mr. Fish continued to smile as well, and it seemed like he meant it, quite unlike the times she had met him before. She remembered at the graduation tea at the Fish house, how Queenie and the three other scholarship kids (including a black guy!) were watched like hawks in general, by Mrs. Fish and the servants, and Queenie remembered Mr. Fish looking at her out of the corner of his eye, polite robot smile pasted on.

"And at where did you matriculate?" Mr. Fish said.

"Oh, I went to L.U.N.Y. here in the city for a couple of years, but I had to leave for financial reasons," said Queenie, without adding, Also I was drunk all the time and wasn't learning anything.

"You will stay and have lunch with us, won't you?" Mr. Fish said.

"I'm not sure I can do that," said Queenie. "I'm kind of on the run."

"I can certainly understand. I've been in town for almost a week, and I've barely had a chance to breathe. This is the first I've seen of Hummer. Of course it's always a pleasure staying at the Waldorf in the summer," he said cheerily. Then he laughed.

Queenie laughed, too. Ha-ha. Small talk's great! she thought. It's what the world needs more of. Jesus God knows there isn't anything important to talk about. How many times have the Fishes and their friends stood by and made small talk while the Triggers were lying dead in their crappy apartments. All the bodies pile up, and the Fishes make small talk and laugh. Queenie laughed harder and let her head fall back.

"Ha-ha," said Queenie. "Hey, Hummer, the police came to my apartment this morning," she said, still laughing.

Hummer looked green. Mr. Fish was silent.

"I had to take the fire escape," she said, still laughing. "And now they're after me—ha-ha, what do you think of that?"

The waiter arrived and placed a bellini in a long flute glass in front of Queenie.

"Thanks," said Queenie. "Oh, hey, could I get a double Johnny Walker Blue, neat? Blue's the oldest one, right?"

"Yes, ma'am."

"That'll be fine, pal," she said, patting him on the elbow.

She looked over at Mr. Fish, who was not green. He stared expectantly at his son, but he seemed surprisingly calm.

Queenie drank her bellini in one gulp.

"Mmm, peach," she said, holding the flute up. "So like I was saying, Hummer, I don't know what *you* told the police, but I'm going to have to tell them everything I know pretty soon."

Hummer looked down.

"Sorry, Mr. Fish," Queenie said to Mr. Fish. "Sorry to be so tacky, but these issues are pressing in my life right now, and I just have to"—she sighed—"get them off my chest."

"Quite all right," said Mr. Fish, still staring at his son. "Should I leave you two alone?"

"No," said Hummer, pissed, glaring at Queenie with how-dare-you eyes. "He already knows most of it," he said to her bitterly.

"Oh, good," said Queenie, reaching into her pocket. She pulled out the ring and dropped it on Hummer's silver octagonal plate. It produced a gentle clink.

Hummer swiped it up like a hawk.

"Hummer," said Mr. Fish. "You didn't tell me anyone else was involved in this business."

"See, Mr. Fish, I'm not really involved," said Queenie, reaching for the bread basket in the middle of the table. She removed the cloth napkin from the top and grabbed a warm roll. Then she glanced at the small icy butter cubes and thought of the fat thief and decided she didn't want any butter just then. Then she continued. "I've just been working for your son, doing small errands." Then she turned to Hummer. "Was Trigger pregnant, by the way?"

Hummer's eyes widened, his mouth tight. Jeeves returned with Queenie's Scotch.

"Ooo, alcohol," she said. "Thanks." Then she took a large sip and felt like singing. JW Blue, smooth as caramel.

Mr. Fish stared at Hummer and scratched his chin with his finger. "Well, Hummer," he said. "Answer her."

"Yes," Hummer said. "How did you know?"

Queenie swished the scotch around in her glass. "I'm very intuitive," she said. Then she nudged Mr. Fish, and said, "That's something you should know about me."

Mr. Fish didn't respond. Queenie tilted her head back and swallowed the rest of her scotch.

"So, look, Hummer, I just wanted to let you know that I can't keep this whole thing up for much longer. In fact, I may go to the police right now, and I'm not being cagey about anything. Anything they ask me about you, I'm going to tell them."

"They know most of it," said Hummer. "I met with them yesterday, I told you. They fingerprinted me and can't connect me to the scene. I'm . . ." he began, and stopped.

"Off the hook?" said Queenie. "Well, that's just great. Good for you. I'm sure you had a lawyer present and everything." Then she turned to Mr. Fish. "See, I can't afford a lawyer, so one's going to be appointed to me. And because *my* fingerprints are all over Miss Happy's apartment, it's probably going to be an uphill battle."

Queenie glanced at the large clock over the maitre d's podium. A little before twelve.

"Well, gentlemen, if you'll excuse me, I have to figure out what the fuck I'm going to do next. Nice to see you, Mr. Fish." Now Mr. Fish pasted on the old wooden smile—there was the Mr. Fish Queenie knew and loved. "Bye, Hummer. It was really great to run into you. Just don't call me again, ever, and I hope you and Catalina have a lovely life. Remember to be gentle on the wedding night," Queenie said, patting him on the shoulder.

He stared straight ahead like a soldier.

Queenie stood up and turned around and began to walk out the way she came, weaving through tables. The Johnny Blue was having a bit of an effect on her, but at least she wasn't as jumpy as she was before. She almost ran into Jeeves carrying a tray of lobster tails and continued toward the exit. Men in suits and women with hair that didn't move looked up at her disdainfully as she passed, as she grabbed the backs of their chairs for support.

Queenie stumbled down the stairs to the lobby and scanned around for the bathroom. She saw a door marked LADIES' LOUNGE in the corner and headed for it, knocking into a distinguished-looking woman in a tan suit. Very Barbara Walters, thought Queenie. Barbara's mouth opened in utter disgust.

"Sorry, hon," said Queenie, and she punched her in the shoulder lightly.

Queenie stepped into the lounge—the first room had four vanity mirrors with movie star lights around them, and four delicate white chairs.

"Cute," said Queenie aloud. "Like for Smurfs."

She walked into the bathroom, which was all white-and-beige marble, and much softer lit than the lobby. A woman in a black suit sat next to the sinks and smiled at her. Queenie smiled back and slipped into a stall and locked the door.

She sat on the toilet and put her head in her hands. Everything smelled like orchids or lilies, Queenie didn't know which; she just knew it smelled like a funeral. Queenie did her business and came out of the stall and washed her hands at the white marble basin, and the woman in the black suit approached her from the side. Queenie looked at her suspiciously. The woman in the black suit gently placed a towel over Queenie's hands. It was a paper towel, but thicker and softer than any paper towel Queenie had ever used.

"Thank you," said Queenie. Then she saw the tip bowl. There's no way I'm not tipping this nice lady who sits in the pisser all day, thought Queenie.

Queenie placed two dollars in the bowl.

"Thank you," the woman said.

"You're very welcome," said Queenie. "What's it like to work here?"

The woman shrugged as if to say, Could be worse.

Queenie walked out of the bathroom and was approaching the front door when she saw a cop standing right outside the entrance, talking to two young men in suits. She quickly ducked over to one of the flat leather chairs around the coffee table and picked up a *Newsweek* and opened it to cover her face. There's no way he's looking for me, she thought. Right?

Then the cop shook the hands of the men in the suits and ambled across the street to his car. He didn't get inside, just leaned over to talk to his partner in the passenger seat.

Now's your chance, thought Queenie. She put down the magazine and pulled her sunglasses from her pocket. She made a beeline for the door, kept her head down, tried to dodge people walking around her and past her. There was one man in a dark suit who was coming too close, Queenie knew, and she tried to stay out of the way but he clipped her, his shoulder pressing against hers.

"Terribly sorry," he said.

"It's cool," she said, looking up for a second.

It was Rip Torn, the actor!

"Hey, are you Rip Torn, the actor?" she said.

Rip Torn smiled.

"Yes, yes I am," he said.

"I really like you in the pictures," said Queenie.

"Thank you very much," said Rip Torn genuinely.

"You're welcome," said Queenie.

She glanced outside to the cop across the street. He was speaking into a walkie-talkie.

"I have to go now," Queenie said to Rip Torn.

Rip Torn nodded. Of course Rip Torn understood. He's fucking Rip Torn.

Queenie walked away from Rip Torn and slid on her sunglasses, and they blocked out all light immediately. The doorman opened the door for her, and she nodded and hung a sharp left down Fifty-second and didn't look back.

She turned south on Lex and sped up a bit, glancing at the cop as she crossed the street. He was talking to his partner, and it didn't seem like he was in a big hurry. Queenie sighed audibly.

She continued south and felt depressed and tired. It was time to think of what to do next. You can't possibly think of what to do next, Queenie, she thought. Not in this state of mind. You're not thinking straight.

What she needed was another beer.

She found a deli down the street on Lex and walked in and was overwhelmed by how hot it was. No a/c, all still, dead air. She walked to the back and slid open the beer box and let the cold air freeze her skin for a second. Then she freed two tall boys of Bud Light from their plastic ring prison. Really, it's more altruistic than anyone thinks, she thought. I have an extensive rehabilitation plan in mind for these beers, and how many citizens can honestly claim that?

She brought them to the counter, and the nice Korean lady rang them up.

"Seven dollars," she said.

She must be joking, thought Queenie.

"Are you joking?" she said.

The woman shook her head and smiled.

"I hate midtown," Queenie muttered, shelling out the bills.

"Thank you," said the lady, still smiling, taking Queenie's wrinkled money.

The lady slipped the beers into a brown paper bag.

"Could you throw in another bag?" asked Queenie.

The lady stopped smiling. Now Queenie had crossed the line. The lady slid a folded bag into the larger one, but was not happy about it.

"Gee, thanks," said Queenie.

She picked up her bag of beers and left.

She came to the 6 train stop, Fifty-first Street Station, and started down the stairs, thinking, Where are you going now, Queenie? She swiped in with her train card and looked at the downtown side. You could just go back home now, back to the fuzz waiting outside, and you could get carted away in front of the HeySitDown girls. Hey, are you, like, a murderer? No, Queenie would say, I really prefer the term, "Scourge." I would like everyone to refer to me as the Scourge from now on.

A train rattled through on the downtown side. Queenie cracked the first beer and sipped it and thought about Olds. He didn't even get off his stuttering ass to come get me himself, she thought, getting angry. I thought we had a goddamn relationship. No, she thought, not moving, letting the downtown train go. If she was going to turn herself in, she'd go straight to Olds. She didn't have his card with her—where was the precinct again, she thought. Ninety-eighth—maybe.

Then an uptown 6 of the outer space variety pulled in and screeched. The doors opened and some people came out. Queenie stepped in and sat down.

"Fifty-ninth Street is next. Stand clear of the closing doors, please," the robo-host said.

Queenie looked in the window opposite her and stared. She was still wearing the sunglasses but didn't remove them. The train chugged along obediently. She took huge sips of beer and started to cry. Again, it wasn't sobbing, just those nice soap opera tears—silent and beautiful. They fogged up her glasses and slid down her cheeks and dripped into the paper bag on her lap—she was literally crying into her beer. She let her head hang down and cried and cried and cried, all the way to Ninety-sixth Street.

Here's your stop, if you want to go to the precinct, she thought.

And then, maybe because she was scared or sad or confused, she just didn't get off at Ninety-sixth Street. She wanted to go one more stop. She wanted to go to Trigger's place.

There's nothing there, she thought to herself. Yellow caution tape over the door and chalk outlines. There might be no one guarding it anymore, but what will you find, Queenie? What will you find that the police didn't?

How did you get here, she thought, her eyes sliding closed. How did you get here. There must have been a fight. There must've been a blowout. Things were said that can't be taken back. Trigger's a senior in high school and she's always out with her friends, drinking at bars and meeting strange men, sometimes sneaking into Manhattan. She and her sophisticated father eat in separate rooms, and one night she comes home late and drunk, and he's sitting in his big leather chair in the living room, waiting for her.

"Where have you been?" he says.

"Out," she says.

"With whom?"

He says "whom" and things like that.

"The girls," says Trigger. "Janet and Chrissy."

"You're a liar."

He says she's been out with boys again, and she says she was at Janet/Chrissy's watching *Twin Peaks*.

He calls her a slut.

She tells him to fuck himself.

He tells her to get out of his house.

She does. She comes to New York and doesn't even tell her little blond cousin. On the train she decides that's the last time she's going to care about a goddamn thing.

"Excuse me," someone said to Queenie, a shadow above her.

She looked up. It was a cop. He was dark-skinned and stocky and strong, and he had a thin mustache. The name on his pin read, VELEZ. He looked at Queenie with gentle eyes.

She took off her sunglasses and thought, Don't even have the luxury of going to Trig's place first. But look on the bright side,

Queenie. Now you don't have to find the precinct. You've got a personal escort. How nice.

"Hi," she said mournfully.

"Hi," said the cop.

Queenie stood up and held on to the bar for support. The train pulled into 103rd Street.

"Do you mind getting out here, ma'am?" asked the cop politely.

Queenie sighed. "No," she said.

"This is . . . the 103rd Street Station," the robo-host said.

Queenie walked in front of the cop, her head down, her beers at her side. She stepped off the train and slowly trudged toward the exit.

"Um, ma'am," said the cop, behind her.

She turned around, and he was still standing by the train doors and didn't appear to be reaching for his cuffs or anything like that. Instead, he pulled out a long pad and crooked his finger at her. "Could you come here, please?" he said quietly.

Queenie squinted and walked back over to him. The train pulled away, loud for a second. Then it was silent.

"Do you have some identification?" he said.

"Sure," she said trepidatiously. She pulled out her wallet, then her driver's license, and handed it to the cop.

He began to write something down.

"Is the address current?" he said, not looking up.

"Yeah," said Queenie. "I still live there. Even though the license is expired."

"I see that," said the cop.

Queenie tried to peek at what he was writing but really couldn't read upside down. Who trained this guy? she thought. It's me, okay? There's my name right there. I'm a wanted suspect.

He tore a page off the long pad and handed it to her, along with her ID. Queenie stared at the sheet of paper—Ordinance 24-6HB—Open Container.

"I'll need to confiscate your beverage," he said.

Queenie stared at him like he was a space alien.

"Your beer," he said, quieter, pointing to her beer.

"Right," she said, looking down at it.

She handed the bag to him. Then they stood there, looking at each other, Queenie with her mouth open a little and tears still on her face.

"You know," the cop said, leaning in. "Alcohol *is* a depressant."

Queenie was frozen with shock. "Right," she said, shaking herself out of it, smiling like an idiot. "No, you're right. You're totally right."

The cop smiled back. Then he walked toward the exit, dropping the bag of beers in the trash on the way out.

Queenie stood there and laughed for a minute. Suddenly she felt full of energy. She started to walk fast, almost run to the exit, skipping up the stairs two at a time.

She headed east and crossed Third Avenue, where the street was full of children. There wasn't the obligatory busted fire hydrant spouting glorious crystal water in suggestive streams, but there was a green garden hose getting passed around.

There were about ten little kids (four, five, or six years old, Queenie could never be sure), not gross kids who pick their noses and asses and scream all the time—these kids were sweet-faced and giggling and running around in the street, spraying each with the hose. And then one little girl in tiny biker shorts and a T-shirt started peeling off her clothes, laughing like crazy.

You can hardly blame her, thought Queenie. It's not full-throttle summer yet, but it's still pretty warm today.

This little girl was running around naked as she could be, stamping on the black concrete, her feet making little wet slaps. And at first all her little friends stared, gawking, and then, Queenie could hardly believe it, there was a revolt! One by one they took off their tiny tank tops and T-shirts and pink and red shorts, running around like it was the goddamn Garden of Eden.

The adults nearby, on stoops and leaning against cars were silent for a moment, shocked, then a couple shouted in Spanish and English, Put your clothes on! Where are your sabatos? But the rest just laughed, in a weary but amused way; they let their heads drop down or back and laughed and laughed.

Queenie covered her mouth and watched the sweet babies with their smooth bodies and glassy harmless genitalia running and giggling, and again, Queenie began crying without even realizing it. She wiped her eyes with her thumbs, squeegeed out the teary crust from the corners, watching the naked children in the street.

She let her head fall back, let herself look up as her breath got caught in her throat and made her cough a little. And then when she put her head back down, she was somewhat disoriented and out of breath. She forgot where she was, why she was there; she was so out of it, it didn't strike her as strange at first to see such a familiar figure in a bright green New York Jets jacket and a white baseball cap with peach fuzz hair poking out. Queenie stared. It was the Jets fan, from Rey's pictures, walking along Third Avenue, crossing up to 104th, carrying a goddamn bag of groceries.

Queenie stood motionless for a second and could only hear the smacks of the kiddies' feet and their high, floating laughter. She stared at the Jets fan as he walked up the street in an absolute straight line, head down, feet chugging along in small steps like he was on a chain gang.

Then Queenie started to run. She crossed 103rd and trotted up the street after him, slowing as he neared the corner of 104th and Third. He turned right on 104th, and Queenie kept following him, a few feet behind. He continued walking in a straight line, close to the buildings, small steps, denizens parting around him. He's gotta be sweating like a maniac under that jacket, Queenie thought.

Maniac being the key word. Queenie didn't even know what she was going to do, what she was going to say. All right, you fucking fuck, was all she could come up with in her head.

She kept trailing, staring at his back, her heart beating louder and louder. He wore large orthopedic-type shoes, and he continued to inch along. Tiny steps. Head still down. Maybe he's drunk, thought Queenie. She fought the impulse to speed up—if she did, he would see her. Hell, at the rate he was going, she'd pass him in thirty seconds.

He crossed Second Avenue, Queenie right behind, leaving about a yard in between. They were now on Trigger's block. What the hell is this, thought Queenie. They were nearing Trig's building, and Queenie looked around briefly for cops but didn't see any. She saw a minivan that she thought might have been undercover, but then it pulled away playing loud salsa music.

Jets Fan kept looking down, watching his feet inching, putt putt putt, his pasty fat hand clasped tight around the plastic handles of the grocery bag. He began to slow down. Queenie stopped and held her breath; she stood behind a phone pole and watched him, and would have been generally more stealthy about the whole enterprise except that Jets Fan didn't appear to be paying attention to anything except his feet.

She watched his hand reach into his jacket pocket and pull out keys. Then he turned sharply at the entrance of Trigger's building and walked calmly up the steps and stopped to open the door.

Time seemed to slow down. Be rational, thought Queenie, just wait here. Just wait here for a few hours and see when he comes out. She inadvertently and reluctantly thought of Rey. What would Rey do? He'd wait across the street with a Coke. That's what professionals *do*, she thought. That's why he's a professional.

Fuck that, she thought.

She let out a huge exhale and ran the few yards to Trigger's building and stood at the bottom of the steps, and Jets Fan turned around, having just gotten the door open. For a second she examined his face and noticed he looked exactly the same in the pictures—the small eyes behind hugely thick glasses, the bright green jacket zipped up to his neck, up to his chin practically. He was covered with sweat.

Queenie pointed at him but couldn't get any words out. They stood there, silent, not moving, Queenie breathing heavy from the fifteen feet she'd run. Jets Fan's face was white, his mouth open in fear, revealing a few tan-colored teeth.

He turned and ran for it, pushing the door open to get in, Queenie a step behind. He was just inside and pushed the door against her, tried to close it, but she slapped both her hands on the glass and kept it open. There was panic in his eyes, and he looked like a scared gopher or a hedgehog or something, not that Queenie could remember when was the last time she'd seen a gopher or a hedgehog, but still, tiny furry scared animals came to mind, as he frantically pressed against the door, his bag dangling and knocking the glass below.

"Hey," said Queenie.

He let the door go and turned and pushed through the second door in the vestibule. Queenie's hands were sweaty, sliding down the glass as she pushed it open and saw Jets Fan run down the hall, past the stairs, where it was dark.

"Hey!" Queenie yelled, pushing through the second door.

She ran after him, her shoes flopping around like duck feet. She saw the dim light of the hallway bounce off the shiny green jacket, which was all she could see, sinking deeper and deeper into the blackness.

She heard keys jangling, and she was right behind him. He moaned—a low terrified moan like he was Frankenstein, like the Elephant Man, like he was deaf. He slipped into the door marked "2" and tried to shut it fast, but Queenie was right there, and she slammed her hands on the door. It wasn't shut yet; she could still see a sliver of the green.

It made her think of a reading book in the fourth grade. All the kids had the same book, but some had shiny lamé covers and some had regular dull textbook covers, and everyone was clamoring for the shiny books, just out of their minds in only the way you can be in the fourth grade when everything is so fucking important. Goddamn cheap-ass school, thought Queenie, the images of the covers flying through her head. Couldn't afford lousy shiny books for everyone.

Queenie made a quick decision not to think about the shiny vs. dull book controversy just then. Instead, she kept holding the door open with her hands and leaned back just a bit, then she threw all her weight at it, and Jets Fan lost his grip on the other side. Wow, Queenie thought. Turns out the stomach flab is a secret weapon. Ha!

A strong smell of garlic poured out from the apartment as

Queenie pushed inside. Jets Fan tumbled to the ground, and his plastic bag fell; garlic cloves and apples rolled out.

"Nooo," he moaned, sounding like a hurt dog.

There wasn't much light in the room, and it was incredibly stuffy; there was just one thin high window, like a slightly oversize domino, near the ceiling, and Queenie couldn't tell if it was open or closed. Jets Fan lay with his head near a couch and hollered again when Queenie walked and stood over him. She stared down at him like he was a bug.

Her head went nuts—images flew and in and out fast like a speed freak's slide show. First it was just Jets Fan behind her, watching on the street—what street, she didn't know, it wasn't from any of Rey's pictures specifically—all she could make out were his beady eyes swirling around in his head, watching her lecherously. But then she looked down at his hands, big and awkward like paws, and then she saw them around Trigger's slim column of a throat, squeezing, narrowing, until she dropped like a marionette.

He scrambled to his feet like a spider and was breathing heavy and fast, almost hyperventilating, and Queenie grabbed him, her fists gathering up the slippery green material of his jacket.

She pushed him the few feet to the wall. He was bigger than she, at least six foot, and he must have been stronger, too, but he wasn't resisting her at all. He bowed his head and seemed to shrink, his skin bright white and glossy, his eyelashes clear. His mouth was still open, framing a little drool, and his teeth were a mess of gray-and-brown stumps—sugar cubes just dropped in coffee. Fuckin' freak of the week, thought Queenie. He's big enough to crush Trig's head like a walnut.

"Did you do it, you fuck?" shouted Queenie, shaking him. "Did you kill Trigger? Did you?"

"Noooo," he cried, and he crumpled in on himself.

First his arms folded, then all of his bones seemed to turn to mush, and he let everything go limp. He was too heavy for Queenie to hold up, so she let go, and he fell to the ground, his legs loosely crossed, like a five-year-old. He started sobbing.

Queenie looked at her hands shaking.

"Who are you?" she said to him, not recognizing her voice.

Jets Fan choked and cried.

"I'm Mill. I'm Mill," he said in choppy breaths.

Queenie was so sweaty her hair was wet. She ran her hand over her head.

"Why were you following me?" she said, shaking, everything on her shaking.

"You might come back," he said, grabbing his right thumb with his left hand and pulling like it was a carrot in the ground.

"Where?"

"To Tara's."

Queenie shivered hearing Trigger's real name. Queenie imagined she would shiver if she ever heard her own real name, the one she was born with.

"What the fuck do you know about her?" she fired at him.

He kept tugging on his thumb. Sorry Rain Man, she thought. You're barking up the wrong tree for sympathy.

She kicked at the floor near his knee but didn't touch him. He howled as if she had.

"Speak, goddammit!" she shouted.

"Noooo," he moaned.

Queenie's head pounded. She could taste the JW Blue in her throat, in her nose, the red eye, too, a twist of peach from the bellini—it was all ready to come up.

"What?" Queenie said, gnashing her teeth. "Did you wanna fuck her? Is that why you did it?" she said, her mouth dry. "You didn't know what you were doing, right?"

He continued to pull on his thumb and cry. Queenie crouched down and felt her knees crack and grabbed him by the jacket again.

"Right?!" she yelled in his face.

"Nooo," Mill cried. "I made her breakfast."

Queenie didn't know how to respond. Looking at his mushy lion face, she tilted her head to the side like a dog who didn't understand. He was just like a kid—Queenie could actually see little wheels turning in his oversize brain, as he tried to find the right words. It was like Uncle Si, like there was a language barrier, but even beyond that—it was like being dumb drunk all the fucking time, and everyone else in the world was cold sober. It was like trying to think and talk through sheets and sheets of bubble wrap.

"I," he began, and he stopped to gather his bearings and swallow some spit. "I cleaned her up. I cleaned her up."

Queenie let go of him. Her thighs hurt, and she leaned back, suddenly exhausted. She sat on her ass with her legs spread out, toes pointing up. She rubbed her eyes, her heart slowing down, the thump in her head lightening up.

"When did you clean her up?" she asked, quieter.

Mill swallowed. His nose ran clear glossy trails.

Without a word he rolled to his side and pushed himself up with his right arm and leg, his jacket still zipped but riding up above his belly button. He stood up straight and pulled the jacket down, the stretch band around the bottom snapping on his skin.

Queenie stayed put and watched Mill walk to his small kitchen counter and open the cupboard under the sink and pull something out—a long brownish red towel with white edges, then he came back over to Queenie and handed it to her.

It was very heavy and crusty, and Queenie stared at it and realized it wasn't red with white edges; it was white, it had been white and now it was covered with dried blood.

"Holy shit," Queenie gasped, dropping it on the floor. "Is that . . ." she said, pointing. "Is that Trigger's blood?"

"Yes," said Mill. "She had blood coming out of her head on the floor."

Queenie shut her eyes and let her head sink down.

"You thought I hurt her?" she said.

Mill nodded. "Yes. Yes."

"Well, I didn't," said Queenie, pissed off and a little offended, frankly. "I didn't touch the girl," she said, standing up. Except for collapsing on her, she thought to herself, and her eyes fixed on something on the counter next to the sink, something heavy and metal and small.

She walked to the sink. The kitchen setup was the same as Trigger's—sink and oven right next to each other, a slim strip of counter space in between. Queenie leaned down to inspect the small metal object and saw that it was a garlic press. She didn't touch it, just stared at it, at the square of forty or fifty tiny metal pegs, little strands of garlic threaded through.

The press looked old. Queenie remembered Uncle Si having things like that—a kitchen full of heavy inconvenient utensils, enough to make your local Williams-Sonoma representative blanch.

Queenie touched the side of her head; the tiny imprints in the square shape above her ear were softer but still there. She turned around.

"Did you hit me?" she said softly. "With the garlic press?"

"Yes," Mill said, looking down, standing straight, hands at his sides like deadweight. "Sorry."

"You should be," said Queenie. "It really fucking hurt, and I had a concussion and everything."

"Sorry," he said, quieter.

"Yeah, yeah," she said, like she really couldn't be bothered, and she began to pace. "You thought I was going to hurt her, blah-blah-blah."

"I found her," he said again quietly.

"So what?" Queenie said rudely. "Did you just sit there? Did you call anyone?"

"No. No."

"Well, that's great, buddy. God knows if you see a dead person, you shouldn't call anyone. Don't you ever watch TV? Don't you ever watch *Law & Order?*"

"Yes. S. Epatha Merkerson," he recited.

"Goddamn right S. Epatha Merkerson," said Queenie, rubbing her eyes. Then something occurred to her. "How long did you sit there, you know, before you hit me on the head?"

"Two days," said Mill.

"That's a long time," said Queenie.

"They might come back," he said, and for the first time, he

looked directly at her. "They might still come back. But she's dead, though."

Queenie folded her arms and shook her head gently.

"Yeah," she said, sighing. "Yeah, she is."

"If I was there, they might not come back," he said, "No ticky, no shirty, as they say."

Is that what they say, thought Queenie. Then she got it—Chinese laundry. She started to laugh.

"Yes," he said.

Queenie's legs hurt, like she'd been standing for hours. She walked to the couch and sat down, while Mill remained standing. They were both quiet for a minute.

"Do you want a garlic omelette?" Mill asked.

Queenie thought about it.

"Sure," she said.

He bent down and picked up the garlic cloves and the apples and didn't put them back in the plastic bag but held them in his arms like flowers.

He took them to his kitchen area and tried to place them all on the slim counter space, but some rolled into the sink.

"Do you need any help?" said Queenie.

"No," said Mill.

Queenie didn't move and watched him from behind as he peeled clove after clove of garlic and stuffed the little nude pieces into the heavy metal press and squeezed them, his huge hands wrapping around the levers. The garlic made a soft sound being crushed—to Queenie, it sounded like the carding of cotton, which Si did manually at the Lawrence Mill a very long time ago. He'd kept two of the heavy steel brushes and showed her how to brush the raw cotton fibers into smooth gentle strings.

Then Queenie heard a sizzle, and the smell immediately filled the room—garlic in olive oil. Queenie's stomach growled, and she breathed deeply.

Mill took six eggs from the refrigerator and held them all in his large hands. One by one he cracked them over the stove, and Queenie heard them spill into the pan and sizzle louder than the garlic and eventually settle. Even though she couldn't see it, she knew what it looked like—all those lovely little eggs swirling and spinning as Mill beat them with a fork, and then finally they gelled into one soft circle.

"Soup's on," Mill announced casually.

Queenie stood up and walked over and peered into the pan as Mill deftly folded the omelette over into a half-moon. The edges of it were perfectly browned, and Queenie's eyes widened as Mill split the omelette in half with a spatula.

He opened a cupboard above the sink and pulled out two white plates and slid the spatula under one-half of the omelette and shimmied it onto a plate and handed it to Queenie. Steam rose gently to her face.

Then Mill put his half of the omelette on his own plate and stood there, opposite her.

"I eat on the couch," he said, looking up, addressing no one in particular.

"Okay," said Queenie.

He went to the couch, sat down, and began to eat. Queenie followed and sat next to him and cut into her omelette and more steam came up and was hot on the tip of her nose.

She watched Mill, who ate with his head bent down, his knees locked together, the plate resting gently on his thighs. He cut huge pieces of the omelette and wrapped his mouth around them gently, then slid the fork out. It was almost like someone else was feeding him.

Queenie cut a small piece with part of the brown edge hanging off in a webby strip, and she tasted it. It was hot and soft and very garlicky. Some of the garlic was a little crunchy, but Queenie didn't care. She ate the whole thing.

And it was the best omelette in the world.

At five Queenie met Meade at Lisa's on Avenue B. Meade was sitting at the bar, near the front window that opened onto the street.

He didn't see her at first, and Queenie stood in the doorway and watched him sip a pint of dark beer. He kept looking down at his lap and placing his hand over his stomach. Queenie could see him suck his very slight belly in. Good old Meade, she thought.

She sidled up to the bar, and he turned and looked excited at first, but then he remembered he was angry at her, so he turned away quickly, stared at his beer, and made his face flat.

"Hi," he said quietly.

"Hi," said Queenie, sitting next to him.

The bartender was a thin lady who clacked over on pointy shoes and nodded at Queenie.

"Pint of MGD," Queenie said.

The bartender nodded again and grabbed a pint glass.

"What're you drinking?" Queenie asked Meade.

"Guinness."

"Really?" she said, surprised. "That's not on the plan."

Meade shrugged. "Do you really think I need to lose more weight?" he said bitterly.

Queenie's face became hot. "No," she said.

The bartender brought Queenie's beer, and Queenie took a large sip.

"Sorry about yesterday," Queenie said, staring straight ahead.

"Forget it," Meade said, not looking up.

Then he took a sip of his beer and burped a little. Queenie smiled at him. He smiled, but very much against his will.

"I'm sorry, too," he said. Then he turned. "So are you going to jail or what?"

"I don't think so."

Meade held his hands up in frustration. "Well, that's fucking anticlimactic," he said. "My fucking caller ID says Det. D. Olds, and of course I think the worst, that you're in a gutter somewhere, but then when I hear your voice, I'm expecting something good like you need me to bail you out or you need me to sleep with the warden, but all you want is a beer," he said, outraged.

"Sorry," Queenie said, grinning.

"So you're not going to jail?"

"I don't think so. I may have to go to the station tomorrow or Saturday."

"Oh yeah? What for? To split a milk shake?"

"Just to answer some more questions."

"That's just *great,*" said Meade. "I thought they had your 'prints,'" he said, making quote marks.

"They did, but none on the shower curtain. Just on various things around the apartment, but you know, since I just fell on it and never really put my hands on it, they're not so interested anymore."

"So who's this guy who hit you? They got his prints?"

"Oh yeah—everywhere. All over the shower curtain, inside, outside—they lifted a footprint of his shoe from a squeezed-out bottle of lotion on the floor."

"Did they arrest him?"

"Not yet. Not when I left." Queenie thought for a minute. "I kind of felt bad about calling Olds."

"Why?"

"Because I don't think he did it."

"Olds?"

"No—Mill. The guy with the garlic."

"The guy with the prints."

"Right."

"So why were his hands all over the dead girl?"

Queenie sighed. "You know, they were friends. He used to make her omelettes. They used to leave their doors open for each other. So he hasn't seen her for a couple of days and he goes up there with his garlic press, and he finds her dead with a hole in her head and a puddle of blood on the bathroom floor. And he freaks out and wipes up the blood with a towel because he doesn't want her lying in it and he doesn't want to leave her there all naked so he takes down the shower curtain and wraps her up."

Queenie paused. "He thought she was gonna get cold or something," she said quietly. "And he sits there for about two days, crying, not eating, not sleeping, watching her, making sure nothing else bad happens."

"And then you show up," added Meade.

"And then I show up, and he hides in the closet and watches me walk around touching everything, and he thinks I did it."

"So he clocks you."

"He clocks me with the industrial-strength garlic press and bolts."

"Where?"

"Back to his place downstairs. Then I wake up; I call the cops."

"Yeah, yeah, I know this part," said Meade.

"Oh, *I'm* sorry, I didn't mean to bore you," said Queenie, snotty. "Maybe you'd like to *guess* how the rest turns out."

"Come on," said Meade.

"The cops come, question me, and I leave—"

"In a stupor."

"In a stupor, and what I don't know is that Mill follows me."

"All the way home?"

"All the way home. And he waits outside my place, across the street."

"And now the dick's following you too."

"Of course he is—I'm like the fucking Pied Piper of freaks. They both follow me for a while, totally unaware of each other. Mill thinks I'm gonna go back and do something gross to Trigger; the dick thinks I'm humming Hummer, and so Mill peels off when I get on the L to go home that night."

"As does the dick."

"As does the dick," repeated Queenie. "And you know the rest."

Meade nodded and finished his beer, held up a finger to Skinny Minnie.

"But you don't think Mill did it?" he said.

Queenie shook her head. "No, I don't. I think he had a sweet little *Flowers for Algernon* boner for her, but I don't think he killed her."

"Does Olds?"

"I don't fucking know. All I know is Mill's a better lead than me. Now he's their prime."

Meade laughed. "Their *prime?* Ten-four, good buddy, nice fucking lingo."

"Fuck you."

"Time and place, sista," Meade said, and they both laughed. It was an old joke. "And Olds didn't mind you dodging arrest?"

Queenie winced. "Yeah, it appears I overreacted just a little on that. They didn't have enough to arrest me—they were just going to ask me more questions. But all things considered, since I brought them to Mill, I think Olds just chalked it up to bygones."

"I'm sure he said you weren't off the hook yet."

"Oh, yeah. I still shouldn't 'go on vacation all of a sudden.' "

"Like you ever go on vacation."

"I know, right? I haven't been on vacation since I went to Nantucket about twenty years ago."

They paused and sipped their beers. A slow fan turned on the ceiling.

"So if Mill didn't do it, who did?" said Meade.

Queenie shook her head. "They don't know. I don't know. Olds says half the homicides he works on never get solved."

"Half?" Meade said, incredulous. "What the hell do we pay them for?"

Queenie laughed and shrugged. "Who knows?" Then she said, "So what've you been doing?"

"Not much," he said. "I decided I don't like the magazine girl anymore. We got a drink yesterday, and I was talking to her and I looked down and saw her fat shapeless ankles, and I thought, I'm not fucking asking this girl out again."

Queenie laughed again, and they both turned around on their stools, hiking their elbows back on the bar behind them. They watched various denizens pass by.

A thin Hispanic man with tattoos and a muscle tee walked by, talking to his hand in a high voice. It took a second for Queenie to realize he was holding some kind of puppet. Queenie and Meade laughed, largely because it was disturbing for so many different reasons, and they were unsure how to react.

The man must have heard them laugh because he backed up and put on a little show. The puppet was a tiny plastic baby.

"No, no, don't take my bottle," the man made the baby say in a high chirpy voice. "They want my bottle," the man/baby said, referring to Meade and Queenie.

Queenie was paralyzed with laughter and embarrassment. She covered her face with her hands as if that would make her disappear.

"We shouldn't have encouraged him," said Meade.

Then the man/baby moved on, and Meade continued.

"Because, I mean, shit, I think I deserve a girl who's evolved enough to have ankles. At the very least."

Then the man/baby returned for an encore.

"Here we go," said Queenie.

"Don't take my bottle! Don't take my bottle!" cried the man/baby.

"I think it's best if we just turn around," Meade whispered.

And so they did. Queenie felt badly that she and Meade were not a more enthusiastic audience. Oh well, she thought. You can't be everything to everybody.

She heard the man/baby move on, unfazed. He continued to accuse various strangers on the street of wanting his bottle, but it seemed like no one wanted to play along. It's a lonely town, thought Queenie.

Soon Meade and Queenie were almost done with their beers and looked at each other.

"What are you doing now?" said Meade.

Queenie rubbed her eyes and kept them closed. What was Queenie doing now? She didn't feel prepared to answer. She was just so tired, and then, she wasn't conscious of it, she thought she was just blinking, but her eyes slid shut and stayed that way, and her head sank gently. Her fingers slipped down the pint glass, cool on her tips.

And then there was Trigger again, sitting on the edge of the tub, wearing the shower curtain like it was a strapless dress. She was smoking. Her legs were crossed. She was kicking the top one up lightly. She smiled wide the way she did, and blue smoke curled out between her teeth and out of the corners of her mouth. Then the smile disappeared, and she looked cold as hell, and she rolled her eyes up to the ceiling and stuck her tongue out to the side, playing dead.

Then Meade's arms were around Queenie.

"Whoa, Slugger," he said.

"Huh," said Queenie, leaning against him. The pint glass was on its side, beer spilling. Queenie couldn't feel her hands for a second.

Skinny Minnie clacked over and grabbed the glass nonchalantly, wiped the bar down with a rag.

Queenie heaved her arms up on the bar and put her head on them. Meade put his arm around her shoulders.

"You all right?" he said.

"I don't know."

"Maybe you better go home."

Queenie nodded. "Yeah," she said.

"Come on," he said, standing up. "I'll walk you to the train."

"Yeah," said Queenie again.

They stood, Queenie somewhat unsteady, and Meade hooked his arm around her waist firmly. She took a couple of tentative steps and felt like a Franklin Mint doll—all white glass.

"You okay to keep going?" said Meade.

"Yeah."

They came out into the air, into the sun, and Queenie breathed in deep and felt sort of okay. They walked up Avenue B and turned left on Fourteenth, and the street was loud and crowded. Meade went first, and Queenie followed, weaving between people.

On the corner of Avenue A, Meade crossed laterally in front of a young man pushing a stroller.

"Yeah, go on, cut me off, motherfucker," the man said to Meade.

"Sorry, man," said Meade, and he and Queenie kept walking.

"Hey, yo man, *fuck you!*" the man shouted.

Meade turned and called plaintively, "I *said* I was sorry, dog."

The man kept yelling.

"Jesus, what's he want? What the fuck's wrong with people?" Meade said to Queenie.

"I don't know," she said.

The air felt hotter and stuffier the farther they walked down Fourteenth. Queenie's mouth became dry. Then they were at First Avenue.

"Are you okay to get home?" Meade said, standing in front of the subway entrance.

"Yeah, where are you going?"

"I'm gonna go see Baker."

"He's working today?"

"Yeah."

"Would you get me one of those . . ." Queenie paused, trying to remember the name of it. She snapped her fingers twice. "You know, one of those croissants with all the stuff in it?"

"The ham and cheese?"

"Yeah," Queenie said dreamily. "Ham and cheese."

"Sure," said Meade, starting to walk away. "Don't pass out anymore, Queenie," he called. "It's just not professional."

Then he crossed the street and went into his hunch walk, and she watched him for a second until she lost him in the crowd.

She went downstairs into the subway and heard the clanking sounds of the Japanese tambourine players. One of them had a regular tambourine, but the other one had bells on his ankles, and he stomped while he played the guitar. Though the coordination of it was impressive overall, the end product sounded like kids playing on Fisher-Price instruments.

Queenie swiped in and walked down the stairs and past the musicians. There were people everywhere. She leaned against a bare spot of wall; the dirty tiles made it look like a public bathroom, and the air on the platform was stagnant and hot and dry.

Then the subway came, and Queenie filed in, feeling the air-conditioning surround her instantly and almost crying she was so relieved. The train car was fairly full, and Queenie nestled herself between a man who smelled pretty bad and a girl with headphones blasting dance music. Queenie could just barely reach the pole for support and had to cling to it with the tips of her fingers. But no matter, she thought, it's cool in here—I can breathe.

She looked up at the ads as the train started to move. There was one with a photo of a bored-looking woman in a suit, who had a lot more elbow room than Queenie, holding a pole on the subway. The ad read, "Future at a Standstill?" It went on, telling Queenie to call this number and learn to be a technical doodad.

Maybe that's what I should do tomorrow, Queenie thought. She started thinking about unemployment. Even if she learned how to be an IT specialist in nine short weeks, she would still have nine short weeks without anyone paying her anything.

She let her head fall back and thought, Again with the unemployment dance. You had to call between such and such hours, and you could only be eligible for so many consecutive weeks, and sometimes they make you go to an orientation.

If only I could go back to this morning when I was being chased by the police, when everything was so much *easier,* she thought. Ha-ha, Queenie made a funny.

The train stopped at Bedford, and Queenie got off with everyone else. She watched the herd of people move like a wave up the stairs in front of her. Her eyes went to something bright green—it was a woman wearing a green hippy-dippy shawl.

Queenie thought of Mill.

After Olds and his guys fingerprinted Mill with a portable kit, Olds had said to her, "You can l-leave, Miss Sells," and Queenie started to walk out the door and she glanced back at Mill, and he looked at her with his small dice-dot eyes, blinking hard.

No ticky, no shirty, Queenie thought as she came above ground. The sun was still bright and orange and seemed to be nowhere near down. Queenie passed two punk kids sitting outside the pet store.

"Can you spare any *change,* " the girl-punk said aggressively.

Queenie didn't respond and kept walking. Her head felt fuzzy. Since when do I get knocked out from an afternoon beer, she thought. She still felt full from Mill's omelette, and she could still feel the not-quite-cooked garlic on her teeth, but she thought maybe if she ate something else, she'd feel normal.

She looked into Zia Maria's, and it was packed with people, then she looked into one of the hip coffee places where they would also make you a gourmet sandwich the size of your thumb for a mere seven dollars, but she just couldn't face any of them. They were all going to be crowded—lines out the door, no room to move. Why is everyone up your asshole in this town, she thought.

She resolved to order something later—maybe a cheeseburger from the pub or pierogies from the Polish diner where the girls always asked if you wanted bacon on top of that, even if you're ordering the pork loin sandwich. And a pork loin sandwich with bacon didn't sound too terrible to Queenie either, but not just then. All she wanted to do just then was lie down.

She turned her corner, and both of the HeySitDown girls were lingering around the entrance. They wore flower wreaths on their heads.

"Heyyy," they said.

"Hey," said Queenie.

"Hey, did you see that thing on TV last night when they paid that guy to eat a bicycle?" the blond one said.

"No, I didn't," Queenie said, pulling out her keys. "What's with the wreaths?"

"We're going to a solstice party in the park," the brunette said. "Today's the longest day of the year."

"No, shit," said Queenie, pushing the door open. "See ya."

"Byyyye," they said.

Longest day of the year, Queenie thought, opening her mailbox. There was a phone bill and yet another goddamn mailer from Columbia Flowers in Columbia, South Carolina. How in hell did I get on this mailing list, thought Queenie, looking at the photographs of tall slender lilies. Six for only sixteen dollars.

She trudged up the stairs and smelled meaty tomato sauce. Maybe she would get a pizza with a lot of meat on it. Or pasta, or lasagna, she thought, getting excited.

Not yet, girl, not yet, she said to herself. Just lie down for a while. Shut your eyes. Worry about food later. Worry about everything later. Don't think about Trigger or Mill or anyone. Just sleep. Since she'd only had one beer in the last couple of hours, this was going to be a fairly new and rare experience for her—going to sleep relatively sober. Actually going *to* sleep. Preparing for sleep, taking off her bra and shoes. Going to sleep like normal people.

Who cares, thought Queenie, as she fumbled for her apartment door key. Going to sleep is probably overrated; passing out like a corpse is where it's at.

Her key turned free and loose in the lock, in easy circles all the way around. Oh yeah, thought Queenie. The cops busted the lock. The doorknob was loose, and Queenie rattled it and her door opened, and she stepped in and shut it behind her. She looked on the floor and saw the plate for the chain lock, with the chain still attached.

She picked up the pieces and dropped them on her coffee table.

"Real nice," she said.

She dragged a chair from the kitchen and propped it against the door, under the knob.

All of the shades were pulled down about halfway, but it wasn't quite dark, largely because it wasn't quite dark outside. All the windows were open, too, blowing a warm breeze through. Queenie would have preferred a cool breeze, but she couldn't complain.

The red dash on her answering machine was blinking, and she walked over and pressed the button. She stared out the window at the asphalt piles. At least you guys never change, she thought.

There was an unfamiliar voice on her machine: "Miss Sells, this is Officer Bulliard from the Thirty-seventh. Detective Olds wanted me to confirm that you'll be here on Saturday at 2 P.M., and also to let you know that the autopsy of T. Rote revealed that she was not pregnant at the time of her death, nor was there any evidence of a recent pregnancy. Please call if you have any questions."

All very professional, thought Queenie, as she stared out the window. She folded her arms across her chest, strangely chilled. I guess that makes it better, she thought. It should, anyway.

Then she saw the HeySitDown girls walking down the street, alongside the lot with the asphalt piles. They were holding hands with a tall gangly fellow in a pith helmet, all of them giggling.

Maybe they have the right idea, thought Queenie. Maybe I should smoke a lot of pot and watch a lot of TV and go celebrate the solstice. Maybe that's what I'm missing. Maybe if I did that, then I wouldn't think so much about other things, and then other things wouldn't make me so goddamn upset.

She was thinking these thoughts in these exact words, and this time she wasn't even looking at a dead body, and she didn't even think she heard a mouse or a roach or anything moving behind her at all.

Suddenly there were arms around her, an arm in black leather around clamping her arms to her midsection, cutting off her breath in a sharp gasp, and then a hand in a black leather glove over her mouth.

Queenie tried to move her mouth; her lips and teeth were jammed against the tight leather hand. She tried to wiggle but couldn't budge; the man with the leather jacket seemed to lock her body to his. Her eyes darted back and forth; she breathed furiously through her nose and screamed as well as she could, which was really not at all, and tasted the leather on her tongue. It was salty and sour.

Then he spoke.

"Quiet, now," he said softly into her ear. Warm breath, smelled like smoke.

Queenie whined like a puppy, her chest heaving up and down.

"Listen," he said calmly. "I'm going to take my hand off your mouth, but if you make a sound, it will be over for you very quickly."

He slowly removed his hand from Queenie's mouth, and she gasped loudly. Then he held a gun in front of her. It was black and looked like they looked in the movies, for the most part—large and heavy and cold. Queenie was frozen.

"You see that?" the man said. "Nod your head."

Queenie nodded.

"Now we're gonna back up a step," he said in the same calm voice. Slowly, both of them stepped back. He took the gun out of her sight, and she felt it poking into her back—a hard thick quarter.

Queenie had never had a gun pointed at her before. She'd only been mugged once, and it hadn't been very traumatic. She'd been listening to a Walkman (this was years and years ago, when Queenie was new to the city, when she actually purchased music), and she was drunk, and it was about 3 A.M., and a skinny white man in a ratty T-shirt cornered her and had a pocketknife, and said, "Gimme the walkman." Queenie sighed, like it was really all so inconvenient, and she handed it to him, and said, "Can I keep the tape?" He grimaced and nodded begrudgingly, popped open the Walkman and threw the tape to her; and then he ran away.

Now the man in leather said, "I'm going to count to three, and on three, you're gonna kneel down. Nod your head if you understand."

Queenie nodded.

"One," he said, removing his arm from her waist. "Two," he said, placing his hand tight on the arch between her neck and shoulder. "Three," he said, and pushed her down gently to her knees.

Queenie looked around frantically—the phone, Elegant Elks, a pen, pair of sneakers.

"That's good," he said, almost soothing.

"What do you want?" said Queenie.

He didn't answer.

"You can take whatever you want, pal," she said, and she thought to herself, Don't cry, Queenie, don't cry, but she started anyway, in between tight breaths. "I don't have shit, but you can take it. I have, like, two hundred bucks in my wallet—you can have it."

He still didn't speak. He placed one hand on her head, like he was blessing her.

Then she felt the cold nose of the gun pressing into the base of her head, right where the spine ended.

Her brain was on fire, eyes moving from side to side.

"Popsicles," she said, her voice cracking. "The fucking sheets on my bed. You want them? Take them. Mustard. . . . Comet . . . lotion." Tears poured down her face, her hands somehow stuck at her sides; mucus clogged her throat and sinuses.

"It's a fuckin' gold mine around here," she choked out, laughing. He petted her head gently. His hand felt heavy.

"Shh," he said. "I don't want anything you have. Just close your eyes."

Now some part of her said, Grab the base of the phone, reach out and grab it and whip around and try to hit him. Scream, just scream. Flail your arms around—do something, do something, you pussy, why don't you ever do anything, she thought angrily, but she couldn't move.

She pissed her pants without trying to stop it, and it actually felt a little warm and pleasant. She started to laugh, thinking, Thank God I'm dying now because I don't see how I'll be able to live knowing I like to pee on myself.

And what did Queenie think about before she died?

She thought about the Merrimack River on a bright cold April day, walking along the footpath and looking across at the green top of the church. Looking at all the gray water and the white sky with tiny ovals of turquoise—everything was still winter, patches of snow still on the ground, and the branches on all the trees bare with crispy yellow leaves waving and shaking and tumbling down to the water.

God it was so cold in Lowell in April, the white sky against all the faded brick, and she was running now along the Riverwalk path with her sweatshirt zipped up all the way but feeling sniffly because of the wind. Running toward the bridge, getting scratched by the chicken bone branches of the trees, all on her neck and face, and the river was loud and fast, moving like a machine next to her, rushing, flying, and she ran next to it like she was trying to beat it, laughing, her mouth dried by the cold air, almost to the bridge now.

Then a voice from above said, "Drop it right now."

Queenie, a few feet from the bridge looked down at her hands, skin flaking from the cold. She wasn't holding anything; she had nothing to drop.

She opened her eyes, her face wet with tears and sweat and snot. She stared straight ahead.

"You heard me, pal," the voice said again. "Drop your piece."

Then Queenie felt the pressure leave, the gun no longer at her head. And then, next to her, the gun was dropped and landed with a thud, near her left knee.

"Hands on your head," the voice said.

Queenie, like a robot, began to lift her hands up toward her head.

"Not you, Queenie," the voice said gently. A familiar voice, Brooklyn accent. "Stand up, Queenie."

"I can't," she said.

"Sure you can. Hold on to the phone table."

Queenie stretched her arm out and placed her hand on the top of the phone table. She slowly pulled herself up to a standing position and turned around.

It was like she was looking at it through a telescope, like all this action was very far away—Rey frisking the gray-haired man wearing a black leather jacket and gloves and black jeans.

Rey held his gun on the man with the leather jacket as he moved up and down his body, patting his jacket and pants. Queenie stood there, not moving.

"Queenie, honey, could you pick up that gun?" Rey asked politely.

The man with the leather jacket began shifting his shoulders around, readjusting. Rey slapped him on the head.

"Don't move, motherfucker," he said.

Queenie bent down and picked up the gun. It was heavy, and the base was warm. The only time she'd ever held a gun was at the LazerTag-arium. But that was obviously a different ball of wax.

Queenie stared at the man with the leather jacket. He had brown eyes and an almost distinguished face, all smooth regal features, not bad-looking, probably in his midfifties. He appeared to be annoyed, almost rolling his eyes. He looked back at her like, "What's the problem?"

"You okay, Queenie?" said Rey, sticking his gun into Leather Jacket's back.

Queenie nodded. "I pissed my pants," she said.

"Why don't you go change them," Rey said nicely. "I'll be right here with our friend."

Queenie looked down at the gun she was holding.

"Take that with you," Rey said.

Queenie nodded.

She walked to her closet and pulled out the Dickies from yesterday and another pair of underwear, which weren't exactly clean but at least they weren't covered in urine. Then she shuffled like a zombie to the bathroom and closed the door.

She set the gun down on the toilet tank and took off her workout pants and her underwear. Her legs were wet, and she took a towel from the shower rod and turned on the water in the sink and wet the towel, then gently mopped up her thighs and her privates.

Then she slid on the dry underwear and pants and put her hands in the sink and patted her face down with cold water. She looked in the mirror.

Her face was puffy and streaked yellow for some reason—maybe it was the light in the bathroom off the yellow-and-blue tiles. And her face looked so much rounder, like a pie plate with tiny eyes. Her hands were still shaking and didn't look like her hands for some reason. They seemed smaller; the fingers looked thinner.

Queenie turned around quickly and stuck her hand behind the shower curtain. It looked just like Trigger's.

"How . . ." she whispered, "did you get here?"

She must've taken the train. She always loved New York. She'd come a few times a year for special occasions and then with her friends and it was just like in the movies, but that's not the part Trigger liked. It was a real place to her, and not like the people who just get here and are drunk on street corners on the Upper West Side with other people they know from college, or who work with them in publicity. With their arms around each other's necks. New York's so much fun for them; for them it's a colorful backdrop for their adventures. For them it's a lily pad on their neat little pond, just a springboard to whatever, to a two-story house, to peace and quiet, to three beautiful babies, to dinner after dinner after dinner.

No way Trig, that's not what you liked. You liked the hard part—the brick, the street, the squared-out sky above your head. You liked your thick neighbor downstairs and the girls at the Paper Doll and the kids running in the street. You liked that you could talk to a new person every day forever and forever and still not possibly know everyone—and no one would know you. That's what you liked best of all, isn't it, Trig? That's what you thought about while you came here on the train, not anything else, not the little town you came from or the kids you grew up with or your father facedown in the flowers.

Queenie slapped her hands over face and tried to breathe.

Then she clenched her fists and pushed the bathroom door open, and it slammed against the opposite wall. She tore into the other room where Leather Jacket sat in a chair with his hands cuffed behind him, and Rey stood in front of him, still pointing the gun.

Queenie ran for Leather Jacket, clothesline-style, her arms out, her feet landing heavy, ready to scream, ready to land and crash into him and eat him alive, but Rey's arm caught her; he wrapped it around her like a sash and held her in front of him, his head next to hers. Queenie could smell his cologne.

"Whoa," Rey said in her ear. "It's okay, Queenie. He can't hurt you—he's never going to hurt you."

"Who . . . who," Queenie gasped.

"He's a contract man," said Rey.

Queenie's body loosened a little. Rey removed his arm, and she backed up and stood next to him. They stared at Leather Jacket, who appeared nonplussed.

"Who the fuck are you?" Queenie said to him.

"He's not going to tell you," said Rey. "He'll probably talk in a few days. But my guess is he killed Hummer's girl, too, and he was sent here to kill you."

Queenie looked back and forth between them, from Rey to Leather Jacket and back to Rey.

"Why?" she said.

"I don't know, honey," said Rey gently. "You're obviously pretty dangerous to somebody."

Queenie stared at Leather Jacket's eyes. They were dark and blank. It was like they were glass; there wasn't anything behind.

"How much do contract killers cost?" asked Queenie, still staring at Leather Jacket.

"A guy like this?" said Rey. "Anywhere from twenty-five grand to fifty."

"Pricey," said Queenie.

"Oh yeah. Not a poor man's game," said Rey.

That echoed in Queenie's head for a minute: *Not a poor man's game.*

"I have to go," she said suddenly.

"What?" said Rey.

"I have to go," she said, looking on the floor for her shoes.

"We have to call the police," said Rey.

"I can't," said Queenie. "I have to go into the city."

"Would you wait a second?" said Rey, putting his hand on her shoulder. "You might be in danger—let's just call the cops and wait for them and go from there."

Queenie looked up at him. His face was just the slightest bit stressed, eyes squinting a bit, little overbite on the bottom lip—all gentle concern. Queenie smiled at him. She reached out and cupped his face in her hand. He looked surprised, his eyebrows raising gently. Jesus, thought Queenie, his eyes are so fucking blue.

"Rey," she said quietly. "Why are you here?"

Rey shrugged and looked a little sheepish.

"I was worried about you," he said. "I'm sitting at home this afternoon, and I just thought I'd come out to the Burning Grounds for pierogies and stuffed cabbage, and since I'm in the neighborhood, I think maybe I'll stop by Queenie's house and make sure she gets in okay," he said, a little embarrassed. Then he glanced at Leather Jacket, and his face tightened up. "And then Mr. Personality here comes into the building about an hour ago, and I don't like the looks of him, so I sit on the fire escape and wait until you get here, and he makes his move."

Rey smiled shyly. "Lucky for me the ladder on the fire escape was down."

Queenie laughed and felt tears pushing at the edges of her eyes.

"Oh, Rey," she said, like she'd known him for years and years. "It's been such a long day."

"I know, honey," said Rey. "I know."

Then she took her hand away from his face and grabbed her cordless phone and handed it to Rey.

"Hey, do you have a cell?" she said.

"Yeah," he said, and he reached inside his jacket and pulled out a slim blue phone and gave it to her.

Queenie picked up Olds's card from the phone table and gave it to Rey.

"Call him. Tell him to come over. I'm taking this," she said, holding up Rey's cell. "I'll be back soon—I have to go talk to someone."

"Queenie, please—" Rey said. Then he stopped midsentence and just looked at her. There must have been something in her face. "Please be careful."

Queenie smiled and headed for the front door. Before she left, she turned to him, and said, "I'm always careful, Rey."

The Waldorf-Astoria was a beige mammoth of a building on Park Avenue and Forty-eighth; it seemed to take up the whole square block, and maybe it did. Queenie couldn't tell, standing in front of it around eight o'clock, the sun still out, the sky not quite dark but getting there. The doormen opened cab doors and blew whistles, and various well-dressed people milled around.

Queenie pushed in through the gold-plated revolving doors, and they were heavy and slow. She hung her head while she went through; it seemed to take everything out of her. Maybe they made them that way on purpose, she thought.

Instantly there was soft music coming from somewhere, she couldn't tell where—invisible speakers, and cool monitored sweet-smelling air. Queenie took a deep breath and walked up a short flight of green padded stairs, holding the chilly gold banister gently.

She came to a wide hallway, with pointy art deco lamps and dark wooden walls. There were gold-and-wooden cabinets with glass windows, holding headless and legless mannequins wearing fancy dresses. Where are the heads? thought Queenie.

It smelled like rugs smell right after they're vacuumed, and also like a hundred different kinds of Bloomingdale's counter perfumes.

Queenie walked past an oakey bar with waiters in maroon tuxes. She saw a tired rich family—Mom, Dad, Junior, and Princess all in Gucci sportswear with shopping bags at their feet, sitting around the table, silent. Mom with her golden glass of Chardonnay and Dad with a silver martini, chomping olives.

Queenie turned down another hallway with a different carpet— blue kaleidoscopic designs, and she followed the signs to the lobby.

The lobby had ceilings as high as a train station and counters all around, leather couches with men in suits and more bored tourists. Bells and phones ringing, and people moving around, but no one seemed in very much of a hurry, unfolding long subway maps and squinting.

These people were so easy to spot, despite the universal tourist look of cameras and maps and fanny packs, you could see them on the train, trying to maintain normal conversation, but they peer through the windows with a slight look of paranoia; every time the train stops, they strain to see what station they're at, scared to death that they might have done the unthinkable—they might have *gone one stop too far.*

Queenie realized she was being hard on them. She guessed New York was a scary town if you'd never been there and didn't have the dough or desire to take cabs and go to musicals all the time. But ever since she passed out on the A train the first week she got there and didn't wake up until Far Rockaway, she was no longer nervous of where she'd end up if she missed her stop. I mean, hell, she thought, it was the beach. It could be a whole lot worse.

Queenie moved silently through groups of people passing left and right, and no one looked at her in any way; it was like they couldn't see her. It was like she was a ghost. She heard gentle soothing violin music but again, she had no idea where it was coming from.

She walked up to a tan young woman with coifed hair standing behind a registration counter.

"Can I help you?" the woman said earnestly, smiling. She was probably a few years younger than Queenie. Her name tag said, SAMRA.

"Hi, yeah, I'm looking for a guest here—his name is Benjamin-Franklin Fish."

Samra click-clacked on her computer. Queenie watched her eye-lined eyes bat back and forth. Then Samra pursed her lips a bit and glanced at Queenie.

"Mr. Fish is staying in the Towers," she said.

Queenie nodded like she knew what that meant. The Towers, sure, with Rapunzel and Batman.

"I'll need to get your name and ring up to him," Samra said apologetically.

"Oh, sure, that's okay," said Queenie, her mind racing.

Samra blinked at her expectantly and smiled.

"It's Charlotte," Queenie said confidently. "Charlotte Fields."

Samra smiled encouragingly and picked up the phone. She punched in some numbers and waited a moment.

"Hello, Mr. Fish, this is Samra at the front registration desk. You have a visitor here by the name of Miss Charlotte Fields—May I send her up?" Samra said, sweet as sugar. Then she nodded. "Right away, sir. Have a good night."

She hung up and beamed at Queenie.

"It's Suite 2904. Go through the door with the porter right over there," she said, pointing to the corner of the lobby. "You can go right up."

"Thanks so much," said Queenie.

"You're very welcome. Have a great night," said Samra.

"You too," said Queenie, and she turned around and headed for the corner—a glass cube with a porter behind the door.

What a fucking ray of sunshine, thought Queenie.

A black porter in a green soldier-type outfit opened the door for Queenie and smiled genuinely.

"Thanks," said Queenie, walking to the elevators.

She pressed the UP button, and it lit up.

The porter opened the glass door again, and a very athletic blond woman walked in with a little boy and two large FAO Schwarz bags.

"No," the boy said. "That game's got two. Copfight's only got one, so you can't play that one."

"All right," the woman said, not listening.

They stood next to Queenie at the elevator. The woman wore a pressed linen skirt and a silk blouse and tiny pearl earrings. She looked at Queenie briefly, then away. Then she pressed the UP button.

Because I didn't press it good enough, thought Queenie.

The boy kept chattering like a monkey.

"An', an' you can make the cormorant fly or drop a bomb and they make explosions," he said, tugging at Mom's arm, very animated.

The elevator finally opened, and some people stepped out, and the blond woman stood right in their faces, making sure she got in before Queenie.

The blond woman set her bags down with a sigh and dabbed her eyes with a tissue. She pressed "25" and looked at Queenie.

Queenie smiled and leaned forward and cavalierly tapped "29," and she looked back at the blond woman, who seemed markedly disappointed that Queenie was getting out on a higher floor.

The little boy continued to squawk.

"You can take the arms off too an' they'll have no arms. Wanta see that? Do you wanta see that?"

"Maybe later, Gilbert," the blond woman said, obviously exhausted.

The elevator shot up, and Queenie looked around. The walls were all polished wood, delicate moldings on every side. It looked the wood of a humidor. Which would make us the cigars, thought Queenie, glancing at the blond woman. Me, you, and Gilbert, she thought—all of us cigars kept wonderfully moist and fresh.

They reached the twenty-fifth floor with a very soft landing, and the doors opened, and Gilbert bolted, dragging the blond woman by the sleeve behind him. The blond woman picked up her bags and sighed again like they were so impossibly heavy, like they were full of phone books.

Then the doors closed and opened again in about a second. Queenie stepped out.

The doors closed behind her, and she was alone.

There was a sign—SUITES 2900–2910, with an arrow, and Queenie followed it down the hall. The carpet was lighter up here; everything was. Floral pink and blue carpet with ornate ivory doors and silver door handles and tiny mail slots.

At the end of the hall was a small room to the side with a marble floor, and a tiny placard on the wall in front: SUITES 2904–2905. Queenie stepped onto the marble and stood in front of the door marked 2904. A sign saying, PRIVACY PLEASE hung on the long silver handle.

Queenie knocked. There was a pause, and then the peephole became dark. She stood, her feet firm, staring straight ahead.

The door opened.

Mr. Fish stood in front of her, wearing the same slacks and starched blue shirt he had on at the Four Seasons. He smiled and looked mildly amused.

"You're not Charlotte," he said.

"No, I'm not," Queenie said.

They stood, staring at each other, not moving.

Then he said, "Won't you come in, Queenie?" and he stood aside.

"Thanks, Ben," she said, walking past him.

The room was dimly lit by a lamp in the corner, and everything looked so smooth—tables, chairs, all light-colored furniture, with pink-and-white thick-striped wallpaper. The windows looked out onto Park Avenue and beyond. Queenie could see clear across Central Park; the trees looked like broccoli.

"Please," he said, still smiling. "It's Frank."

"Sorry," said Queenie. "Frank."

To her left, French doors opened into a bedroom where everything was baby blue—the wallpaper, the carpet, the bedspread. An open briefcase lay on the bedside table.

"Nice place you have here," said Queenie.

"Isn't it?" said Mr. Fish, crossing in front of her to a small refrigerator. "I always request an 04 or 05 suite anywhere above the Twenty-fifth floor. The view is spectacular," he said, waving his hand toward the window. "Would you like something to drink, Queenie?"

"No thanks."

"Would you like to sit down?" he said, gesturing to a peach-colored couch with a high back.

"No thanks."

"You won't mind if I sit, will you?" he said.

"Not at all."

"Wonderful," said Mr. Fish.

He sat on the couch and crossed his legs casually.

"Now, Queenie," he said calmly. "What can I do for you?"

Queenie inhaled deeply. For a moment she didn't know where to begin. For a second there, she was genuinely a little nervous. What can Mr. Fish do for me? she thought. Well, really, what *hasn't* Mr. Fish done for me, she thought, and that made her laugh a little. So she started to speak.

"You know, Frank, I don't quite know what you can do for me at this point, because I really feel like you've done enough."

Mr. Fish raised an eyebrow.

"I'm afraid I don't know what you mean," he said.

"I think you do."

He smiled. "And what is it that you imagine I've done?"

Queenie smiled and shook her head gently. She started to speak in a calm, even voice, like the man who'd come to kill her.

"For starters, I think Hummer came to you a couple of weeks ago in tears and told you he knocked up some stripper, and she said she wanted to keep the baby and screw up his wedded bliss to the cookie heiress," she said in one breath.

Mr. Fish still appeared fairly blithe about the whole thing, still kept the one eyebrow raised.

So Queenie kept going.

"And you, being the good father that you are, you tracked Trigger down and unbeknownst to our boy, you set up a meeting with her at the Dark Horse last Friday, and you tried to convince her to have an abortion."

Queenie paused and stared at him—still the genuine amused smile. She began to speed up.

"She refused, she said you couldn't ask her to do that, and she stormed off. At which point, Frank, you went to Plan B, and you hired Mr. Personality to kill her and get it over and done with so you can stand up as the Proud Papa on little Hummy's wedding day knowing you cleaned his mess all up."

Queenie wasn't looking at him anymore. It felt to her like she wasn't even talking, like someone else was pulling a dolly string in her back and making her mouth just run off. She didn't even realize she was smiling.

"Then, what you didn't know was that your darling son hired me to find her."

Queenie slapped her face in mock surprise.

"Who knew he would actually miss the whore?" Queenie started laughing. "And I did find her, Frank, oh boy did I—all nice and chilly like you wanted with a free gift-wrap job by her neighbor, which you didn't even pay for.

"And, of course I blow the lid off her and Hummer, so the police get up his ass, and now he's being questioned, and we can't have that, can we, but you think, That's okay, we'll get him a Johnnie Cochran to beat the band, and it will all go away 'cause there's really nothing to link Hummer or you, Frank, for that matter, to the crime scene.

"But then you meet me today at lunch, and I know things—I know Hummer gave Trig a ring, I know he was more attached to her than he let on, I know Hummer knew Trig had other johns but more important, I know Trig was pregnant—and all of these give Hummer pretty solid motives for killing her.

"And then you go to Plan C. Or maybe it's Plan B, part 2. You send Mr. Personality to take care of me the same way he did Trig. Shot to the back of the head—two unrelated tragedies."

Queenie took a breath and shrugged.

"I mean, a coupla lowlifes like me and Trig—who's gonna miss us, right?"

They were both silent. Mr. Fish sat in the same position, still casual, still like a gentleman. He ran his palm over the bald part of his head.

"I see," he said quietly, still smiling, all teeth. "And why exactly did I have Miss Happy killed in the first place?"

Queenie folded her arms. "I'm a little fuzzy on that myself. All I can think is you didn't want your baby boy to have the headache—family scandal and all that," Queenie said, and she laughed.

"Trust me, Frank," she said. "It seems to me like you overreacted a little bit, but then again, I'm not fucking insane," she said, and her smile disappeared.

Mr. Fish stood and slowly walked to the small brown refrigerator.

"Are you certain I can't interest you in a drink?" he said, opening the door.

"Yes, I'm certain," said Queenie.

Mr. Fish pulled out a small Bombay Sapphire and a yellow-labeled tonic water. He shut the door and took a tumbler from a small silver tray.

"Where are your people from, Queenie?" he said, not turning around.

"Lowell," said Queenie.

"No, no," he said, chuckling gently. "Originally."

"Somewhere in Ireland."

Mr. Fish dropped ice cubes in his glass, and they clanked around.

"You know that the Irish were treated just like Coloreds once, don't you?" he said, pouring the entire bottle of gin into the glass.

"Yes," said Queenie. "My uncle remembers."

He poured a splash of tonic and took a sip, still facing the window.

"I'd like to tell you something about my family," he said.

Now he turned around to face her, his gaze intent.

Queenie didn't respond and kept her arms folded, staring back at him.

"My family has been in this country since it started," he said gravely. "There was a Fish on the *Mayflower*, and a Fish settled Jamestown. A Fish man was one of the original founders of the city of Boston, and it was he who whispered in Samuel Adams's ear and recommended dumping all that tea into the harbor."

Mr. Fish paused to sip his drink and continued calmly.

"It was my ancestor who first called Boston by its original name— Trimountain. Do you know why it was called that, Queenie?"

"Because of the three hills, next to the Charles," recited Queenie.

Mr. Fish smiled. "That's very good," he said gently. Then he continued: "Fish men helped found Harvard, Dartmouth, and Princeton. They have been senators and congressmen, and attorney generals. They have been investment bankers and entrepreneurs, oil and shipping magnates."

He suddenly appeared wistful.

"Every single male Fish has attended the Ivy League, and every one founds at least one company before the age of thirty. And every one marries a girl whose family history is as venerable as, if not more so than, ours."

Mr. Fish cocked his head to one side, and his face remained still.

"And every one only has children born of those two lines." He smiled. "Every man has whores," he said, in the same tone. "But no one in our family *ever* leaves a trail. We've all learned that much from Thomas Jefferson."

He took another sip of his drink and ran his tongue over his teeth. Then he added, "Miss Happy was part Puerto Rican, too. Not that it matters, of course."

Queenie shook her head in disbelief.

"All you are is a redneck with a Rolex," she gasped.

Mr. Fish continued to smile.

"Perhaps," he said. Then he exhaled loudly, and said, "So, I don't suppose you have any real evidence to support your theories."

Queenie looked down and felt all the skin on her body get very hot. She pulled Rey's cell phone out of her pocket.

"No, not really, but it's a pretty funny story anyway, and I'm sure my detective friends won't mind hearing it," she said, her voice growing hoarse.

Mr. Fish took a step toward her. The smile disappeared; his mouth became tight.

"And how do you know I won't kill you right now, Miss Sells?" he said softly.

She could smell his breath—mouthwash and gin. She stared at the soft lines in his large forehead, creased but still relaxed. He was not at all alarmed, still holding his drink like he was at a cocktail party.

Queenie's face broke into a slow wide smile. She took another step toward him, and they were face-to-face. She could smell his aftershave and the hotel soap on his skin.

"You never had dirty hands in your whole life," she whispered. "And I have *never* been less afraid of anyone than I am of you right now."

Then she stepped back, and Mr. Fish didn't move from his spot, but his shoulders seemed to go lax.

Queenie headed for the door.

"Oh, you know what else, Frank?" she said, turning around. "Trig wasn't even pregnant. So it looks like you didn't have to go through all this trouble anyhow."

Queenie felt triumphant saying it, but immediately felt sick to her stomach, felt sweat pouring down her forehead while Mr. Fish smiled politely.

"Oh well," he said, cheery. "My mistake."

Queenie backed up to the door and opened it. Mr. Fish continued to smile and raised his glass to her in a toast.

She ran.

Down the hall to the elevators, pressed the button, her hands shaking. She dialed her phone number while she waited.

"Queenie?" Rey answered.

"Rey," Queenie said, closing her eyes. "Is Olds there?"

"Yeah, do you need him?"

"No—just tell him to send some people to the Waldorf-Astoria on Park, Suite 2904. The guy who took out the hits is there."

"You got it. You okay, Queenie?"

"Yeah," she said, as the elevator doors opened. "I just need some air. Tell Olds I'll be out front."

"All right. I'll call you in a few minutes," said Rey.

"Okay."

Queenie stepped into the elevator and pressed L and the doors closed, and she leaned against the back wall and put her face in her hands. She couldn't cry. She couldn't even breathe. She opened her mouth and tried to gulp up air, but could only get very little streams, like she was breathing through straws.

The doors opened at the lobby, and Queenie bolted out, past the porter and the glass door and through the lobby, past a thousand people and glass cabinets and cigar smoke and hairspray until she got to the gold revolving doors and finally outside, into the air.

The sky was dark blue; finally, finally it was nighttime. Queenie leaned over and propped her hands on her knees like she'd just run a sprint. But her knees felt too weak, so she got down, down on her knees, fell on them harder than she'd meant to and heard them crack against the pavement. She put her hands over her face and breathed, felt the sweat on her forehead glaze over.

"Um, ma'am?"

She looked up at a doorman in a green blazer.

"Do you need a taxi?" he said.

"No thanks," she said, not moving.

She closed her eyes and took deep breaths and stayed on her knees, heard faint sirens, and said, "My ride's on the way."

Friday

Now it was really starting to heat up. Queenie read over a man's shoulder on the train: Ninety degrees with rising humidity. She sighed. It's almost July, she thought. What do you expect.

The train was moving slowly—chugging along like a little kid was pulling it on a string. They finally made it to the First Avenue Station, and Queenie said good-bye to the sweet air-conditioning and stepped off and held her breath. She was instantly overwhelmed with the heat of the station, and it made her feel like a baked potato wrapped in foil. She walked upstairs, into the sun and the thick air and headed down First, feeling blasts of air-conditioning as she passed shops and restaurants and the doors swung open.

There was a man with a gash in his head stumbling around St. Mark's Place. He had a bottle of beer in a brown paper bag and was smiling a lot.

"It's a happy fuckin' day!" he shouted. "These are happy fuckin' people!"

See, Queenie, she said to herself. Why can't you be more like this guy? Things get him down, sure, but look at what a great attitude he has.

The streets were beginning to fill. It was close to five. People were clamoring to get out of town. Everyone who doesn't live here busts their ass to get here, she thought, then they spend all their time trying to get away for the weekend. The weekends here are the best part, she thought.

Queenie stood on the corner of Houston and First Avenue, where there appeared to be no traffic laws whatsoever. It was chaos—horns honking and buses making U-turns, the street black and blurry from the heat. There were many pedestrians waiting to cross, looking from left to right, staring at all the many traffic lights for some kind of signal, trying to read them like Rorschach tests.

All of the cars became gridlocked—all of them frozen in centipede lines up and down Houston. Even though DON'T WALK had stopped blinking, Queenie, along with the other pedestrians, stepped into the street and started weaving and passing through the cars, their hips and hands brushing against the hot bumpers and hoods. The cars continued to honk, but not at her or the other pedestrians specifically, she didn't think, and she didn't mind anyway. Honking in this town is practically free speech, she thought. The ACLU should really get on that.

She reached the other side of Houston, and the crowd dispersed every which way. She walked to Orchard and peeked into the Pomme Frites shop on the way, with its huge cone of plaster fries hanging over the entrance. I could really use some pomme frites, she thought, but then decided against it. Beer first, then food.

When she saw the sign for Wintertown, something came over her. She sped up, started to trot, then run; she couldn't get there fast enough, feet flopping all the way, and she finally came to the door and pushed it open and felt the cool air inside.

"Hey, now," said Stanley. "Where's the fire at?"

Queenie laughed. "I dunno."

Meade turned to her from behind the bar and nodded as he filled a glass with Coca-Cola, then set it in front of Rey. Rey smiled. Then Felix, sitting next to Rey, turned.

"Hello, Miss Queenie," said Felix. "How are you today?"

"I'm okay, Felix, how about yourself?" said Queenie, sitting down next to Rey.

"I'm exhausted. I hate this weather. It makes me feel like a Bangkok whore."

Rey put his head down, laughing silently.

"I *always* feel like a Bangkok whore," said Queenie.

Meade placed a pint of beer in front of her and folded his arms.

"Tough week?" he said.

"No way," said Queenie. "It was a breeze."

She sipped her beer, and it was light and ambery, with a little bitter aftertaste.

Someone at the other end of the bar shouted, "Bartender!"

Meade closed his eyes in frustration and breathed deeply. Then he yelled, "Customer!"

Queenie and Rey laughed. Meade walked to the other end, and Felix stared out the window.

"How are you?" said Rey gently.

"I'm fine," she said, staring at her beer. She couldn't look him in the eyes just yet.

Rey nodded and sipped his Coke.

"How was it when you left?" he said.

"All fine," she said, shrugging. "Mill's still being questioned, but Olds said they were gonna let him go this afternoon."

"What about Fish and the hitman?" asked Rey.

Queenie smirked. "They're in custody. Of course there were already about ten lawyers there when I left."

"And . . . the body?" Rey said tentatively. "Where is she going to go?"

Queenie felt itchy suddenly. She scratched at the back of her neck, and said, "They found—Olds and his guys found the next of kin. It's her mother. In Phoenix, Arizona."

Palm trees, right? thought Queenie. They have palm trees there, and cactuses, and deserts and flash floods. That was all Queenie knew about Arizona. And that it was hot as hell but it was a "dry heat," whatever that meant. And *Alice,* the TV show, took place there. She had to admit, she felt good that Trig was going home to a mother. Queenie like to think about her: Trig's mother, maybe a sassy redhead type like the gal on *Alice.* Queenie shook her head. Hell, she said to herself, maybe not. Maybe Trig's mom isn't sassy at all, maybe she's not fragile and dramatic and sickly either—maybe she's the plainest Jane you ever met, who knows.

"Phoenix, Arizona," repeated Rey quietly. "Do they need you again?"

"Probably—what about you?"

Rey nodded. "I'll get called for the grand jury in a few weeks. You know you'll be too, right?"

Queenie sighed. "Olds already lectured me on all the various steps and statements." She rolled her eyes and tried to look tough, as if to say, Being a witness is such a hassle.

Rey put his hand on her chin and turned her face to his.

"I've done it before," he said softly. "It's not so bad."

Queenie's stomach jumped.

Then Felix shouted, "Meade! Meade!"

Meade came back to their end.

"Please, sir, can I have some more," said Felix, holding up his martini glass with both hands. "Just not *quite* so dirty this time, okay?"

"You hear that, everyone?" said Meade grandly. "Felix doesn't want it so dirty this time."

They all laughed. Meade grabbed the Tanqueray and poured a large dose into a silver martini bullet.

Queenie sipped her beer. "What the hell is this anyway," she said, lifting the glass.

"It's new," said Meade. "It's from a small company upstate—actually a spin-off from another microbrewery."

"What's the name?" said Queenie.

Meade looked at her sideways, coyly. "You don't believe me?" he said.

Queenie laughed. "No, I don't. I won't believe you until you tell me who made this beer."

Meade pulled a pen from his pocket and stuck it in his mouth like it was a pipe. He grinned but didn't answer her.

"Who, goddammit?" said Queenie.

Then Meade said slowly, "Top. Men."

Queenie laughed like crazy. She felt tears come to her eyes and put her head down on the bar.

She loved the new beer. She loved Felix. She loved Meade. She loved Rey. She loved everything just then.

DATE DUE	ON LINE 10/04
OCT 2 7 2004	
FEB 2 2 2005	
MAY 3 1 2005	
JUL 0 1 2005	
C	PF